From *Happy Returns*

The Citroën swung into the parking-space beside the café, which stood back from the road with small blue-painted tables and chairs set out in front. There was a waiter pottering about with a duster; when he saw the car come in and draw to a rather abrupt stop he left off dusting and stared at it in plain disbelief. The Latimers got out, leaving the monkey, Ulysses, in the car; it was only when the waiter did not even move his eyes as they passed that they realized what they were doing.

"Charles! We are not materialized—we shall frighten the man into a fit—what shall we do?"

"Come behind him, here. No one else about? No—now then!"

A table behind the waiter was occupied by two tall gentlemen patiently waiting to be served, but the waiter did not move, one would say he was turned to stone. Charles threw his hat upon an empty chair and smoothed back the lank, dark hair which had blown about his ears. His dark eyes were full of laughter and his wide mouth curled up at the corners.

"It seems we are not to be served today, Cousin," he said.

The waiter spun round at the sound of his voice.

"Messieurs! How did—where did you come from?"

"From the car, naturally," said James. "Where else?"

"The one with the monkey in it?"

"Monkey?" said Charles in a puzzled voice, and James backed him up. "What monkey?"

"That one," said the waiter, turning, "in that— It has gone."

"Are you assured that it was ever there?" asked James.

"But, naturally! I was standing here looking at it!"

"We saw you standing there," said Charles, "engaged in thought. Yes, sir, deep thought. We opined that maybe it was your hour for your private orisons and we were reluctant to break in. Yes, sir, that is how it was."

"But now that you tell us you were thinking about monkeys it would seem that that cannot be," said James.

"I was not thinking about monkeys," said the waiter. "That is I was watching one. It sat in that car."

"And you did not think about it at all," said Charles. "Very sensible of you. Yes, sir, very."

"It drove the car in," said the waiter obstinately.

Books by Manning Coles

Ghost books
Brief Candles, 1954
Happy Returns (English title: *A Family Matter*), 1955
The Far Traveller (Non-series),1956
Come and Go, 1958

The Tommy Hambledon spy novels
Drink to Yesterday, 1940
A Toast to Tomorrow (English title: *Pray Silence*), 1940
They Tell No Tales ,1941
Without Lawful Authority, 1943
Green Hazard, 1945
The Fifth Man, 1946
Let the Tiger Die, 1947
With Intent to Decieve (English title: *A Brother for Hugh*), 1947
Among Those Absent, 1948
Diamonds to Amsterdam, 1949
Not Negotiable, 1949
Dangerous by Nature, 1950
Now or Never, 1951
Alias Uncle Hugo (Reprint: *Operation Manhunt*), 1952
Night Train to Paris, 1952
A Knife for the Juggler (Reprint: *The Vengeance Man*), 1953
All that Glitters (English title: *Not for Export*;
Reprint: *The Mystery of the Stolen Plans*), 1954
The Man in the Green Hat, 1955
Basle Express, 1956
Birdwatcher's Quarry (English title: *The Three Beans*), 1956
Death of an Ambassador, 1957
No Entry, 1958
Concrete Crime (English title: *Crime in Concrete*), 1960
Search for a Sultan, 1961
The House at Pluck's Gutter, 1963

Non-Series
This Fortress, 1942
Duty Free, 1959

Short Stories
Nothing to Declare, 1960

Young Adult
Great Caesar's Ghost (English title: *The Emperor's Bracelet*), 1943

Happy Returns

by Manning Coles

The Rue Morgue Press
Boulder, Colorado

To
Christopher Columbus
without whose
Courage, Enterprise, and Perseverance
the authors of this book
would be so very much poorer.

Contents

The family of
LATIMER

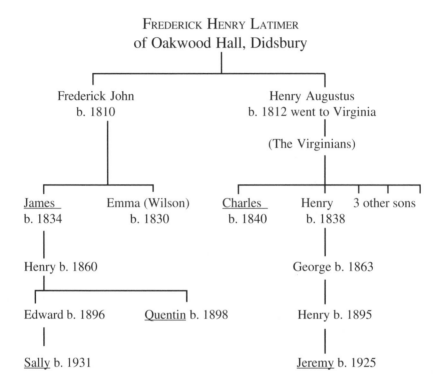

FREDERICK HENRY LATIMER
of Oakwood Hall, Didsbury

Frederick John
b. 1810

Henry Augustus
b. 1812 went to Virginia

(The Virginians)

James
b. 1834

Emma (Wilson)
b. 1830

Charles
b. 1840

Henry
b. 1838

3 other sons

Henry b. 1860

George b. 1863

Edward b. 1896

Quentin b. 1898

Henry b. 1895

Sally b. 1931

Jeremy b. 1925

Cast

Jeremy and Sally Latimer
James and Charles Latimer

At St. Denis-sur-Aisne, France

Police Sergeant Jules Boulestier
Police Constable Vautout
Bertrand Dugrand, felon
Paul-Marie Gascogne, felon
Aristide Vigneron, shopkeeper
André, garage proprietor
George Fowler, courier of a touring coach

At Besançon, France

Rene Frachot
Delors
Thevenet
(Three Friends)
Pierre Champeaux, reporter
Ernie, the Educated Elephant

At Andermatt, Switzerland

Henry Mortimer, in limbo
Joshua Perkins, not a nice man

At Menaggio, Italy

Quentin Latimer, a bachelor at risk
Buscari, manager of the Hotel of the Patient Fisherman
Poppy Thompson, a widow (and the risk)
Dr. Williams, poltergeist hunter
Orsino Monteverde, a hotel thief
The Conte and the Contessa, whose marriage has lost its excitement
Other guests, waiters, police, etc.

And, of course
Ulysses, a monkey

About Manning Coles

MANNING COLES was the pseudonym of two Hampshire neighbors who collaborated on a long series of entertaining spy novels featuring Thomas Elphinstone Hambledon, a modern-language instructor turned British secret agent. Most of Hambledon's exploits were aimed against the Germans and took place from World War I through the Cold War, although his best adventures occurred during World War II, especially when Tommy found himself, for one reason or another, working undercover in Berlin.

Some of those exploits were based on the real-life experiences of the male half of the writing team, Cyril Henry Coles (1899-1965), who lied about his age and enlisted under an assumed name in a Hampshire regiment during World War I while still a teenager. He eventually became the youngest officer in British intelligence, often working behind German lines. After the war, Coles first apprenticed at John I. Thorncroft shipbuilders of Southhampton and then emigrated to Australia where he worked on the railway, as a garage manager, and as a columnist for a Melbourne newspaper before returning to England in 1928.

The following year his future collaborator, Adelaide Frances Oke Manning (1891-1959), rented a flat from Coles' father in East Meon, Hampshire, and the two became neighbors and friends. Educated at the High School for Girls in Turnbridge Wells, Kent, Manning, who was eight years Coles' senior, worked in a munitions factory and later at the War Office during World War I. In 1939 she published a solo novel, *Half-Valdez*, that failed to sell. Shortly after this disappointing introduction to the literary world, Coles and Manning hit upon an idea for a spy novel while having tea and began a collaboration that would last until Manning died in 1958. Coles continued the Hambledon series for an additional three books before he died in 1965.

Critic Antony Boucher aptly described the Hambledon books as being filled with "good-humored implausibility." That same good humor—and a good deal more implausibility—is to be found in the collaborators' four ghost books, which began with *Brief Candles* in 1954 and included two other books featuring the ghostly Latimers, *Happy Returns* in 1955 (published in England as *A Family Matter*) and *Come and Go* in 1958. A fourth ghost book, *The Far Traveller*, which features a displaced, displeased and deceased German nobleman who finds a movie company employing people of the most common sort invading his castle, appeared in 1956. Appearing in the U.S. under the Coles byline, they were published in England under yet another pseudonym, Francis Gaite. Boucher described this new venture "as felicitously foolish as a collaboration of (P.G.) Wodehouse and Thorne Smith."

For more information on the authors see Tom & Enid's Schantz' introduction to The Rue Morgue Press edition of *Brief Candles*.

Chapter I
Floral Tribute

ST. DENIS-SUR-AISNE, like most towns, has a cemetery. French cemeteries are, for the most part, made to one pattern; a square or oblong enclosure surrounded by a high brick wall pierced by one wide iron gate flanked by a wayside calvary. There will be a small mortuary chapel with a thin, sharp spire. The grass grows long over the close-packed graves but at least it conceals the round glass cases containing wax flowers. Marble angels, broken pillars, and black crosses bearing small framed photographs of the dear departed are all about one on every hand.

The iron gate creaked open and three people came out; the Curé of the parish in his long black soutane, a young man with that expression upon his face of mingled solemnity and impatience characteristic of men visiting burial grounds, and an extremely pretty girl with fair hair. While the Curé was closing the gate, the two young people looked back through the bars at an oblong space where the grass had been cut short. A wreath of real flowers, fresh and sweet, lay upon it; English roses for an Englishman and American Beauty roses for an American. The gray granite cross showed the names of James and Charles Latimer, who both died upon September 1,1870.

"I wish they could come back again," said the girl, speaking in English. "Don't you, Jeremy? I'm sure they would help us with this trouble over Quentin."

"Why, yes," said Jeremy. "I'm sure that they would deal very capably with this affair and I'd be glad to have them handle it. But, Sally, I think we owe them plenty already."

"Oh yes," she said eagerly, "of course we do. My brother particularly—"

The Curé turned away from the gate and came smiling towards them.

"You are satisfied?" he asked in French. "We keep well the graves of your distinguished ancestors? They will be more at peace there than lying like dead dogs in a hole at the edge of a field. Yes, truly. That is a most beautiful memorial which you have caused to be set over them. Speaking of animals, there was also the little creature who was their faithful companion. Here."

"The monkey," murmured Jeremy as they followed the Curé to the point outside the wall nearest to the Latimer grave inside. "You should have brought a wreath of nuts along too, Sally."

9

"Here," repeated the Curé, stopping at a small rock which had been partly sunk into the ground. One face of it had been smoothed off sufficiently to carry one word cut deep into the stone, the name Ulysses.

"A year ago today," said the Curé, "we laid these men to rest. May they have rest eternal."

Sally clasped her hands, Jeremy shuffled his feet in an embarrassed manner, and they all turned away to stroll together towards a Rolls which was drawn in to the side of the road.

"You are, then, leaving us at once?" said the Curé. "You are not staying here tonight?"

"We have to go to Italy," said Jeremy. "I have a cousin who lives at Menaggio and we are going to pay him a little visit."

"But we shall come again someday," said Sally, shaking hands with the Curé. "Thank you very much indeed for all you have done for us."

"We are indeed grateful," said Jeremy. "Until next time, then."

"Good-bye" said the Curé. "May the good God be with you wherever you go, my daughter, my son."

He turned on his heel with a smile and a gesture and walked away with long strides, the skirts of his soutane flapping about his legs. A few minutes later the Rolls, with Sally and Jeremy Latimer, purred away in the opposite direction. They were husband and wife and distant cousins as well; he an American descended from a Latimer who had immigrated to Virginia in 1835 and she a daughter of the English branch of the same family.

At about ten o'clock that night there were two more figures standing on the clipped grass before the granite cross, two tall men in clothes of outdated fashion. Their coats were short and wide, their trousers narrow and so long that they were strapped under the men's boots. One man was a little taller than the other and looked more so because he was long-legged and thin; the other, rather stouter, was the elder of the two though they were both in their thirties.

"I take it very kindly indeed," said the elder, "of our young relatives to remember us like this. How say you, Charles?"

"Not only to remember us," said Charles, "but also to come all this way to visit us. Yes, sir, I will maintain that that was a very kind and courteous act."

"Such beautiful flowers, too. A most elegant floral tribute."

Charles agreed and went down upon one knee to examine the wreath more closely. He picked out an exquisite pink American Beauty and put it carefully in his buttonhole. His cousin, who had been fingering the incised lettering upon the granite cross, turned and suddenly noticed this.

"Cousin Charles, what do you do! To take from a memorial wreath for your—"

Charles broke into a laugh. "Dear Cousin James, since it is our own, why not?"

"By Jove," said James Latimer, "you are in the right, Charles. I had not considered the matter. I will follow your good example." He also selected a rose and drew the stem through his lapel. "Now, what next? To the hotel to reclaim our baggage? I assume the landlord has kept it safe."

"Surely, since no doubt he expects us to return. But not, I think, in these clothes, Cousin. The man might wonder where we had been in the interval, and that would never do."

"Most undesirable," agreed James. "That shop which keeps everything, near the bank in the main street, I wonder if it is still there?"

"Let us go and see," said Charles Latimer, turning towards the gate. "Why not, since it is only a year since we saw it last?"

"A whole year? I can scarce believe it to be so long—"

"The Curé said so, if you remember."

"That is so, Charles. Let us go. In any case, I weary of these ill-informed emblems of mortality."

They left the place and walked past the railway station into the main street of the little town.

"Should we, perhaps, take pains to avoid being seen, Charles? Our present dress may cause remark."

"You are in the right, James. But let us just walk along as we are for the present; we can step aside into some shadowy corner if anyone should come. It is very pleasant to feel like this again." He executed a few dancing steps. "In any case, if there should be anyone abroad at this late hour, it will only be the gendarme."

"We will keep a lookout for the gendarme. There he is, walking along in the shadow of the houses." James indicated a dim figure slipping furtively from one doorway to another.

"That is no gendarme," said Charles, taking his cousin's arm. "The police do not slink like tomcats on the prowl, they march slowly but steadily forward, upheld by the dignity of their office." He began to laugh quietly. "I think, James, that our friend in the shadow is as anxious to avoid the police as we, and with better reason. I think, James, that on our first night out we may see some sport."

"Do you tell me that that is a burglar?"

"S-sh! Here comes the gendarme, look, from under the trees in the *place*. Now—"

"The man has vanished!" said James. "As well as we could do it ourselves! Do you think—"

"There is a narrow entry there if I remember right. He has gone to earth, Cousin, behind somebody's dustbins. Now, the policeman will soon see us.

Shall we also look for a dustbin or shall we—"

"I never cared greatly for the close proximity of garbage receptacles," said James primly, and Charles laughed again. The next moment the place where the two men had been standing together was empty, there was not even a shadow to show where they had been.

The patrolling gendarme came slowly on, shining his light into dark door-ways, trying doors to see if they were locked, and glancing at ground-floor windows to see if they were closed. As he came by he shivered suddenly and looked over his shoulder for no particular reason; he was a young man with a thin, eager face and the whites of his eyes showed as he looked about. Charles thought him a nervous and sensitive type and James agreed with him. "Probably percipient," he concluded. "We must beware of that man."

When the gendarme had passed by, there appeared in the dark entry the slinking form of the man whom they had first seen. He put his head out cautiously, looked about him, and saw nothing although the Latimers were almost within his reach. He came out and went on his way with greater confidence since the policeman had gone by; he carried a small suitcase in his hand.

The man went on down the street past the Hôtel du Commerce, still lighted and open for the arrival of the late train from Paris, past the Bank of France on a street corner, past the school, and past André's garage until he came to a house larger than the rest and a little back from the pavement, with a forecourt enclosed by iron railings and a gate standing open. The man turned in at the gate but made no approach to the front door; instead, he crept across the fore-court and very quietly along the side of the house to a small window at the back, the only one unbarred upon the ground floor; perhaps it was thought to be too small to be vulnerable. He stopped, peered keenly about him, and listened intently while all the time the Latimers, unheard and unseen, trod closely upon his heels and stopped, when he stopped, within a yard of him.

Reassured, he attempted the window with implements taken from his pockets, a rubber sucker to attach to the glass and a glass cutter to engrave a circle round it. A quick thump with a gloved hand and the circle of glass came out to leave a hole large enough for him to put in his hand and undo the latch. The window opened quietly and the man, small of stature, slim and agile, proceeded to climb in.

The Latimers consulted together.

"We should go at once, Charles, and summon the police."

"There may be ladies in that house, James, perhaps unprotected. There was one lighted window only, at the front."

"You are in the right, there is no time to be lost."

"In with you, James. Oh, James! Am I not clever? I said at sight that he was a burglar!"

"You should join the police, Charles."

The small man moved quietly on through the darkened house until he came to the lighted room at the front. Here he set down his suitcase in the passage and listened intently. The door of this room was shut but not locked; the intruder laid his hand cautiously upon the handle and turned it suddenly. The next moment he was inside the room, with his back to the door, a gun in his hand, and a singularly unpleasant smile showing a row of discolored teeth.

"Good evening, Bertrand Dugrand," he said. "I am indeed happy to find you here. I have searched for you long enough. Your hands flat upon your table, please."

The man addressed as Dugrand was sitting in a revolving chair at a writing table, a large, stout man with a round, enormous, pallid face. He continued to sit there, not moving, with his fat hands upon the table before him. One would almost have taken him for a wax figure, so utterly motionless he was, except for his eyes, which, sunken to mere slits between rolls of fat, were yet furiously alive.

"I seem to have struck you dumb," continued his visitor. "Surely it cannot be that you have forgotten my name? No, I cannot believe that."

The large face did not so much move as dislimn and resettle, as scum does when the bubbles begin to rise. A crooked slit appeared, dropped half a dozen words, and vanished again.

"Gascogne. I thought you were dead."

"I do not believe that. Pepé the Rat told you that I am still alive after I break out of jail, so you leave Paris. Yes? Perhaps you were wise. He told me that you had gone but he did not know where. I said it was of no consequence, that I would look for you until I find you. Eh? It took me two years, but here we are."

His eyes slid quickly round the room. The writing table with the fat man behind it was backed against the wall to Gascogne's left; opposite him was the curtained window; there were a couple of easy chairs of dimensions to suit their owner; and finally, away on the right, a large safe with its door half open.

"I think we will make certain we are not interrupted," said Gascogne. He backed against the door of the room, which opened inwards, pushed it shut with his shoulder and, putting his left hand behind him, turned the key which was in the lock. "That is better. Two old friends alone again after all the long years of parting, that is pleasant, is it not? Is that where you keep my money for me, in that safe?" He sidled round the room until he could glance in at the safe door. "You were always so neat and tidy, Bertrand Dugrand, were you not?"

He pushed the safe door wide open with the hand which did not hold a gun, keeping a continuous watch upon Dugrand behind his table and casting only momentary glances inside the safe. The remark about neatness was justified; the shelves of the safe were tidily stacked with bundles and bundles of French currency notes sorted out into their different denominations. Gascogne purred approval.

"One would say a bank," he said. "Even quite a large bank such as that of Nogent-St. Maury, which was rifled by two robbers seven years ago. A famous bank robbery, was it not? They only caught one of the robbers, if you remember, a poor muttonhead called Gascogne who tripped over something, they thought, and knocked himself out. The police picked him up but they never found the other one, did they? Nor any of the money. No." He laughed unpleasantly.

Dugrand rumbled into speech with preliminary noises like a clock preparing itself to strike.

"One could not," he remarked, "be expected to carry an unconscious man up a ladder, across two roofs, and over a high wall."

"But how did the other become unconscious? That is a point which has always intrigued me."

"You fell," said Dugrand firmly. "The pipe to which you were clinging broke and precipitated you into a stone-flagged court."

"On the head?"

"On the head, certainly."

"Strange," snarled Gascogne. "On the back of the head, as you say. It is odd that an active man whose handhold gives way should fall on the back of his head. You lie, Pig-fat. You struck me down from behind."

"No," said Dugrand.

"It does not matter to me now. It is going to matter to you in a moment." Gascogne gave another of his quick glances at the safe. "It seems that you have it all in notes; how wise you are. None of it identifiable. One must always say for you that you had plenty of sense. Quite impossible, too, to trace, so that even if one went quite mad and tried to turn honest one could not find the original owners. Only me, Pig-fat, only me. No doubt I should thank you, my old friend, for keeping so much for me; some men, in your place, would have spent it all. Eh?"

"Not at all," rumbled Dugrand, "not at all. There it is, we will share it. Enough—just enough—for the simple needs of my few declining years and the rest is yours." He leaned heavily upon his outstretched hands and made as though he were about to rise. "Let us share it out like good comrades—"

"That for a good comrade," said Gascogne, and shot him through the head.

The great bulk did not so much drop as settle into a shapeless heap and the head sank forward. The fat hands stiffened and clawed for a moment at the table top and that was all. Gascogne watched the body until the last spasmodic movement ceased and then nodded to himself.

"That is half your debt paid, my good comrade," he said aloud. "I will now proceed to collect the other half." He turned to the safe and began taking out the bundles of notes, glancing rapidly through them and tossing them into the seat of one of Dugrand's comfortable armchairs.

"I must get my suitcase," said Gascogne. "I may as well pack as I go." He straightened up, turned towards the door, and stopped.

"The key was in the lock," he said in a surprised voice. "I turned it myself and left it there. I thought so. I must have pulled it out and pocketed it." He began to feel through his pockets. "I can't remember doing so, I must have been excited. My nerves are not what they—I haven't got it. Where the devil is that key? On the floor—I should have heard it drop by the door. It must be on the carpet."

He went down on his knees to feel about for the key; the carpet was thick, uneven of surface, and heavily patterned in dark colors; it would be quite easy for a key to lie upon it and yet not readily be seen. "Must have caught it with my cuff," he muttered, crawling backwards and sweeping his hands over the carpet, "and jerked it out." He backed towards the safe, of which the open door swung slowly towards him for no ascertainable reason; the next moment it nudged him behind and he spun round.

"Ah—the door. That is all. I thought for a moment—"

Somebody laughed softly and the sound appeared to come from behind the writing table. Gascogne was instantly upon his feet, his mouth open and his eyes staring, but the body of Dugrand had not moved and the bullet wound in the center of his forehead was reassuringly evident.

"Somebody," gasped Gascogne, "it was somebody passing in the road who laughed. I am certainly suffering from nerves. After this I shall retire. But where the devil is that key? I suppose I did lock the door?"

He tried the handle but the door was certainly locked. He shook it, but nothing happened. Gascogne pulled himself together and addressed himself in tones of firm reproof.

"This is an idiocy, Paul-Marie Gascogne. Because you are in a room with a dead man and a small key is temporarily mislaid, is that any reason for behaving like a six-year-old child? Command yourself at once and let there be no more of this nonsense."

There was a noise behind him, a rustling noise as of soft things falling. He spun round in time to see a small cascade of garments falling from a point in the air some four feet from the floor. They appeared from nowhere and fell upon the carpet; what horrified Gascogne more than anything else about this unnatural sight was that they were his own things which were falling, his shirts, his socks, his spare collars; in a word, the contents of his suitcase. There followed a bump and he saw his suitcase upon the corner of Dugrand's table, empty and with the lid thrown back.

He staggered, clutched at a chair, and leaned heavily upon it with his eyes closed so tightly that bright wheels rotated before his sight.

"It is the fever," he said loudly. "That is all it is, the fever. I had it in Mogador. As for my suitcase, I brought it in here with me. I remember now."

He opened his eyes again and saw, without believing, the packets of notes upon the chair rather mistily disappearing, only to reappear tidily packed into his suitcase. When all those upon the chair had been moved, those which had remained in the safe followed until there were none left and the suitcase was full. The lid was shut down—it was not very clear how that happened, but there it was with the lid shut—and the spring locks clicked home.

There was a brief silence which seemed to Gascogne to be full of meaning, though what the meaning was he could not tell. He shook off a certain leaden lethargy which hung about his limbs like fetters and sprang forward to seize upon his treasure.

"Mine," he cried, "all that is mine—"

But he could not reach far enough; his hands beat the air and his suitcase was no longer in sight.

"Villain," said a deep voice, speaking French with a strong English accent, "in your predicament it will serve your turn better to consider your sins and repent."

Another voice chimed in, a lighter voice with an unfamiliar drawl.

"I would say that that is right good counsel," it said. "Besides, consider, fellow. Why distress yourself about the money? You will have no need of it where you are going."

"We will leave you now," said the other voice. "At least, you are not without company, are you?"

"If not very enlivening company, you have none but yourself to blame, have you?"

"Let me out," yelled Gascogne, hurling himself against the door, "let me out, let me out—"

"Someone will come to let you out," said the first voice, growing thinner and fainter. "Wait, wait—"

"Wait, wait. Someone will—"

The voices and the room, indeed, the whole house, sank into silence broken at intervals only by thumps on the door and hoarse cries of "Let me out!"

Chapter II
The Cat

SERGEANT Jules Boulestier, in charge of the subdivision of police at St. Denis-sur-Aisne, sat in his little office at the police station with his feet in the fender before a small fire, for September evenings are apt to be chilly in northern France. He had a glass of wine at his elbow; he sipped it occasionally as he sat there thinking how pleasant it was to be a Sergeant at last after so many years as Constable, so that one could with a clear conscience sit by the fire with a glass of wine on a chilly night while a younger man was out patrolling the streets and waiting for the last train in from Paris. Trying doors, examining window fastenings—

There was no particular reason why Boulestier should not simply go to bed. Young Vautout was a perfectly good officer; careful, dutiful, and conscientious to a fault, he could perfectly well be trusted to complete his patrol, sign off, lock up, and go to bed without supervision. It was just that after all these years in a subordinate rank it was very nice to be a law to one's self even if it consisted only in staying on duty longer than one need. Besides, it impressed one's wife.

Boulestier's head nodded, a coal fell from the grate and disturbed him, then he nodded again. He was at that stage of sleepiness when thin, distant voices utter disconnected sentences within the mind; high, tinny voices speaking most urgently words which, if one can manage to grasp them, mean nothing at all or nothing comprehensible, like half a telephone conversation imperfectly apprehended. Boulestier was familiar with this manifestation of fatigue, it amused him rather than otherwise.

Tonight, as he nodded, the distant voice dropped into his mind a name which, for once, did mean something. "The Nogent-St. Maury bank robbery," it said.

Boulestier's mind reached out and caught it. That was a famous bank robbery where two men had broken into a bank, murdered a porter and the chief cashier, and got away with a really large sum. Thousands. At least, wasn't one caught? Yes, surely, he thought, waking to rather fuller consciousness. He remembered the "Wanted for Robbery and Murder" notices which hung about for years, and that was only for one man. They must have caught the other. Years ago, that was.

He emptied his glass and settled down again. Vautout would be in soon and they could all go to bed. Nogent-St. Maury.

His eyes closed and the next moment the voices were at it again, rather less high and tinny than usual, more human. Another name came up, and another. Bertrand Dugrand—ah! On the notices—Bertrand Dugrand and—and—Gascogne. Paul-Marie Gascogne. Odd, very odd. What had started him off on that tack tonight? He had never had anything to do with that case, it was miles away, down near Dijon. Dijon, where the bears came from. No, that wasn't Dijon, that was Berne. The bears—

The whispering started again, more continuous, more insistent. Twenty-six, Rue Mezières; 26 Rue Mezières. That was in St. Denis-sur-Aisne, here, just up the street. That nice house standing back where the fat man lived who never came out or saw anybody.

"They are there," urged the whispering voice. "Dugrand and Gascogne, both there. Gascogne has murdered Dugrand; go and get him. What glory for you to get the Nogent-St. Maury robbers! What honor! They will make you Inspector!"

Boulestier did not stir a finger but his mind was eagerly listening. A very vivid dream, this.

"Gascogne is armed, but have no fear. He will have no power to hurt you. The front door is unfastened, the front door unfastened. Gascogne is locked in with the dead man in the lighted room and here—is—the—key."

There was a metallic tinkle on the floor; Sergeant Boulestier woke up with a start and instantly looked round the room. There was no one there; the window was closed, the door was closed, and there was nowhere for anyone to hide. Boulestier stooped quickly to look under the table and found, as he did so, a key beside his feet.

When Constable Vautout came in a few minutes later he found his Sergeant examining carefully something small which he held under the light. At sight of Vautout he dropped the object in his pocket.

Vautout made his report. "All quiet, *mon Sergent,* and a fine night. The Paris train is in. Not many passengers."

Boulestier, who appeared to be absorbed in thought, merely grunted, and Vautout waited.

"Somehow," he said after a pause, "I don't like our village street tonight, *mon Sergent.* I don't know what it is, but there's a sort of funny feeling in the air tonight."

Boulestier turned his slow gaze upon his Constable and said: "You think so, do you? Curious."

"Sort of shivery," said Vautout apologetically. "I do not suppose that it is anything. I have, perhaps, a chill."

There was another brief pause, during which it occurred to Vautout that his superior did not seem to be thinking so much as listening for something.

Whatever it was, Vautout heard nothing and presently Boulestier made up his mind.

"Come with me," he said. "Perhaps, if we look in the right place, we may find your chill. Have you got your handcuffs?"

Vautout burst out laughing. "Handcuffs to catch a chill?" But Boulestier rounded on him sharply.

"I said: 'Have you your handcuffs?' Well, have you?"

"Yes, *mon Sergent,*" said Vautout, goggle-eyed.

"It is well," said Boulestier. He took his hat from its peg, put it on, and left the police station at the slow regulation stride, with Vautout half a pace behind. They walked up the road until they reached the house with the forecourt and the number 26 in the fanlight above the door. Boulestier walked into the forecourt and stopped again to listen; this time both he and Vautout head something. A thumping noise and a muffled voice shouting. There was one window lighted upon the ground floor.

"Ah," said Boulestier in a satisfied voice. "Vautout, with me."

Vautout drew his truncheon, Boulestier walked up the three shallow steps to the front door and turned the handle, the door opened and they entered the hall. The cries were clearer now. They came from a door on the right, that of the lighted room. The door was being hammered inside and a voice cried: "Let me out!"

Boulestier strode towards this door and Vautout could almost have sworn that he inserted a key, but that, of course, was absurd. The key must have been in the lock. Boulestier bellowed "Stand back!" and flung the door open.

Inside, in a state of extreme agitation, was a small, slim man with a gun in his hand. As soon as he saw the police sergeant in the doorway he leveled the pistol at him, but before he could fire, some sort of nervous seizure jerked his arm and the bullet went into the lintel of the door over the Sergeant's head. One would have said that something or somebody had struck his arm up. Boulestier, completely unruffled, took the gun from the man's hand.

"Paul-Marie Gascogne," he said, "I arrest you for the murder of Bertrand Dugrand." He stepped aside to admit his Constable. "Vautout, effect the arrest."

Vautout, completely speechless, automatically obeyed and Gascogne was handcuffed and firmly held. Boulestier looked majestically round the room.

"That," he said, indicating the dead man behind the table, "is Dugrand. The prisoner is Gascogne, as I said. They are the men who carried out the great bank robbery at Nogent-St. Maury seven years ago."

Gascogne made a dive for the door but Vautout stopped him.

"I don't want to escape," babbled Gascogne, "I just want to get out of here. Let me get out."

"You'll be in a cell in ten minutes," promised Vautout.

"Yes, let's go—"

Boulestier walked across and looked into the empty safe.

"What was in here?" he asked.

"Money," wailed Gascogne, "my money. It's been stolen. I've been robbed."

"Robbed?" said Boulestier. "By whom?"

"I don't know—it just vanished——I've been robbed."

"Tchah!" said Boulestier.

Gascogne had picked up his things from the floor in the course of a fresh hunt for the key and thrown them on a chair. Boulestier did not examine them, as he naturally assumed them to belong to Dugrand.

"Vautout," said the Sergeant, "remove the prisoner to the cells."

"Sir," said the Constable, and had no difficulty in obeying because the prisoner led the way at a smart trot. When he had been searched, entered up, and compulsorily retired for the night, Vautout returned to the office and looked with unmistakable awe at his Sergeant.

"Sir! May I say—"

"What?"

"The way you just stood there when that fellow pointed his gun at you and didn't even duck! It was magnificent, it was breathtaking, it was—"

"In the police force, Vautout, one learns to disregard the weaknesses of the flesh. That is how one becomes Sergeant."

"Yes, *mon Sergent*. But—"

"No buts. You will resume your patrol. I consider it advisable tonight."

Vautout saluted and turned obediently towards the door. In the doorway he swung round and the question burst from him.

"How the devil did you know they were there, eh?"

"Information received," said Boulestier dreamily, "information received. Go, my boy. Resume your patrol."

Vautout went. Boulestier settled down at his table and drew his telephone towards him. He had a report to make.

Ten minutes later Vautout was back.

"Mon Sergent, there is now something else!"

"Well?" said Boulestier, looking at him over the tops of his steel-rimmed spectacles.

"In the emporium of Aristide Vigneron one rings the cash registers."

"Monsieur Vigneron is no doubt checking some error in the accounts."

"In the dark, *mon Sergent?"*

Boulestier thought this over.

"You tried the doors," he said.

"But, naturally. They are all correctly fastened."

"You were mistaken in what you heard."

"With respect, no. Definitely not. I was passing upon my patrol and I heard the little bell plainly. I stopped to listen and it rang again several times."

"It is conceivable," said Boulestier, heaving himself to his feet and once more reaching for his hat, "that some robber has made an entry earlier and fastened the door by which he entered. Or even concealed himself upon the premises before they closed. Come."

They went along the street a good deal more quickly than on their previous errand. Then, Boulestier had been hesitant to act on the strength of a half-waking dream even when it was supported by the quite inexplicable arrival of a key. The affair had turned out well indeed, but it still had certain peculiar aspects which would have to be avoided in his detailed report. This business of someone in Vigneron's shop was much more normal.

The shop was the biggest in St. Denis and was, in fact, a department store upon a small scale. It had five plate-glass windows in a row and the main entrance was within an arcade leading back from the pavement; there was also a smaller entrance at either end of the long frontage. They were all securely fastened, and the shop was in complete darkness throughout its length and utterly quiet.

"Maintain," said Boulestier to Vautout, "an unwinking watch while I inform the proprietor."

Vigneron lived in rooms over the shop and access to them was provided by an inconspicuous door and a steep flight of stairs. Boulestier laid a substantial forefinger upon the button of the electric bell and kept it there; a minute later a window was thrown up above and Vigneron's head appeared.

"What is it?"

"The police, on a matter of some importance, regretting to disturb Monsieur Vigneron, must yet request the favor of a short private interview."

"Ciel! What can it be?"

"Descend," urged Boulestier, "without undue delay, I beg."

The window closed firmly, a light went on in the bedroom, and a few minutes later the door opened to show Monsieur Vigneron in a long overcoat, a warm scarf round his neck, and gray woolen gloves.

"My Constable, passing here on patrol, heard your cash registers ring. He reported it and I considered it my duty to investigate."

"My dear, good Boulestier. No intruder will profit from my cash registers. I empty them myself nightly, when the shop closes."

"I know that," said Boulestier, "you know it, and I have little doubt that half St. Denis knows it too, but would a burglar know it? It is true," he added, having an incurably honest mind, "that all your doors are securely fastened, but perhaps the marauder might have hid."

"I don't believe it," said Vigneron doubtfully, "but perhaps we'd better have a look. Call your man in, too. Oh, it's Vautout. Good evening, Vautout."

Do you ever suffer from singing noises in the ears?"

"No, monsieur," said Vautout, and described what he had heard.

"Come in through my private door," said Vigneron, switching on lights. "Mind you, I don't believe it, but if you police have your doubts you are, of course, perfectly justified in proclaiming them. I'll just make sure of the doors first and see if the bolts have been tampered with."

He pattered off down the long vistas between counters and the two policemen stared rather vacantly about them. The shop looked oddly spacious with no shoppers thronging the counters and no assistants snatching things off shelves, but there was no doubt there were plenty of hiding places and Boulestier said so. Vigneron came back into sight, dodging across from counter to counter.

"I have eight cash registers for the five departments," he said, "two in each except the Gentlemen's Tailoring and the Furniture and Carpets. I am looking at all of them and every one is rung down empty as I left it, so far."

"The one I heard," said Vautout, "would be more about down there." He pointed away to his right and Vigneron trotted across towards it.

"Not only are the cash registers untouched," he said, "but the goods do not appear to—"

His voice stopped abruptly and complete silence followed. The police looked at each other and went to join the proprietor, who was regarding one of his machines which was anything but empty. The row of figures across the top signaled a last payment of 750 francs, and the panel showing the total announced, in cheerful red figures, that it had received no less than 32,650 francs in all.

"It would appear," said Vigneron, "that I owe you an apology, Vautout. You did hear a cash register ring." He pressed a button marked "Change" and pulled the drawer open; inside was an untidy pile of currency notes not sorted into values but in one heap in the largest compartment.

"I do not understand at all," said Vautout. "Thieves take money out, they do not put it in."

The proprietor snatched the money from the till and began furiously to count it. He had spent years of his life counting money, the notes flew through his fingers.

"That is correct," he said when he had finished. "Thirty-two thousand six hundred and fifty."

"Would these little things," said Boulestier, "Possibly offer a clue?" He pointed to a number of small price tickets upon the counter close at hand, and Vigneron, pocketing the money, picked them up.

"Two suits. Two hats. Two vests and pairs of underpants. Two shirts with attached collars. Studs and links from the inexpensive haberdashery. Two pairs socks—shoes—two ties—" Vigneron jotted down the figures, added them up, and announced the total as before. He then took off his spectacles and wiped his forehead with his handkerchief.

"Gentlemen," he began, "I was not hitherto aware that I kept a self-service store such as one hears of in the United States of America, but one—"

He was interrupted by a sneeze, a soft and gentlemanly sneeze but perfectly distinct. It came from somewhere in the department and all three men with one accord rushed towards it. It was Vautout who, catching a glimpse of something moving behind a showcase, dashed round it and nearly fell over the cat, a magnificent striped tabby with a tall and stately tail.

"The cat!" said Vigneron with a cackle of relieved laughter. "Of course, it was he who sneezed! *Mon Tigre! Mon beau trésor! Qu'est-ce qu'tu fais, hein?* He keeps watch in here for the mice."

"Of course," said Boulestier, "that explains it."

Vautout, who liked cats, made to apologize to Tiger, but the cat avoided him. Tiger walked delicately along the carpet of one of the main corridors, passaging from side to side and occasionally going through the motions of rubbing his head against someone's legs as though he were accompanying a friend.

"Cats," said Vigneron, watching uneasily, "often appear to me to be, as it were, acting out some sort of play for their own amusement."

"There are many curious stories," agreed Boulestier, "told about cats."

Tiger passed out of sight, the three men looked at each other and smiled apologetically as people do who have nearly made fools of themselves.

"Well now," said Vigneron, "I think—" and at that moment the cash-register bell rang, the drawer clattered out, there was a pause, and it was slammed shut again. It was the same which had contained money before and was not in view from where they stood. They hurried together towards it but there was no one there, only the cat, who came running and leaping to the main door. One would have said that he expected the door to open, he stopped abruptly and stood staring at it.

Vigneron noticed none of this; he went to his till, which now registered 375 francs. With an unsteady hand he pulled the drawer open; inside it were four hundred-franc notes slowly opening up as notes do which have been hastily folded. In the till with the money were two little tickets.

"Two handkerchiefs," he said. "Two handkerchiefs," and leaned heavily upon his hands.

"Granted that it was the cat which sneezed," said Boulestier, speaking even more slowly than usual, "and also that it is an animal of the most unexampled intelligence, I yet find it hard to believe that it would provide itself with a handkerchief."

"I might even swallow that with an effort," said Vigneron, "since animals are markedly imitative, but to believe that the cat would pay for it—"

"Even granting all that," said Vautout in a high, shaking voice, "where did the cat get the money? Eh? Tell me that, if you please. Unless Monsieur Vigneron pays his cat a salary for mousing—"

"Vautout," said Boulestier.

"Sir."

"Resume your patrol. When it is completed, you may go off duty."

Vautout saluted smartly and shot out of the place as though the devil were after him.

"Sergeant Boulestier."

"Yes, Monsieur Vigneron?"

"Come up to my flat for a few minutes. I think we can discuss this odd affair better over a small glass of cognac. Just one moment while I put the lights out and lock this door behind me, so. Yes. Allow me to lead the way, the stairs are steep. . . Pray take a seat, Sergeant. A little cognac to settle the stomach is good before retiring."

"Thank you," said Boulestier. *"Santé!"*

"Santé!"

They drank ceremonially.

"When I was last in Paris," said Vigneron, throwing himself back in his chair, "I was taken by some friends to see an exhibition of prestidigitation."

"Pardon?"

"Conjuring. The things which were done! My dear Boulestier, one would have said black magic."

"I have seen some card tricks—"

"Upon a scale," pursued Vigneron, "which one would have thought quite beyond human capabilities. The little display which was put on in my shop tonight, for our sole benefit, was as nothing in comparison. Nothing at all! Let me refill your ridiculously small glass."

"It is, then, your opinion that we were privileged to observe a talented exhibition of high-class trickery?"

"Undoubtedly. My dear Boulestier, what other explanation can you suggest?"

Boulestier thought it over, added to it a voice talking in his ears and a key falling beside his feet, and decided not to argue. After all, what reasonable explanation had he?

"I have no doubt whatever but that you are perfectly right," he said.

"Besides! There was nothing taken that was not paid for. There was no theft. I picture to myself a couple of strolling performers reaching the town after closing-time and in need of a change of raiment. They are young, light-hearted, happy. They do not call me up to spoil my evening leisure. No, they perform one of their acts and, having honestly paid for everything they took, they walk out and leave me with a little puzzle to amuse me. I picture them, standing back under the trees in the place outside, laughing themselves into stitches at our puzzled faces. I also laugh, ha ha-ha-ha ha!" Vigneron rolled in his chair.

"But," said Boulestier, who had never found it easy to deceive himself, "how did they work the cash register when there was no one near it?"

"All done with wires," said Vigneron. "Wires and magnets. Magnificent! I should like to stand them a drink."

"They may still be outside, under the trees," said Boulestier with a faint spice of malice, "if you were just to run outside and look—"

"Er—no," said Vigneron, ceasing to be amused. "I—it is getting late—I am not properly dressed. It is cold, too. A little more cognac?"

"Thank you, no," said the Sergeant, rising heavily to his feet. "It is getting late, I must go. You agree with me then, monsieur, that there is no case here? Nothing to report?"

"Nothing whatever. No crime has been committed. In fact, on the contrary, I owe them twenty-five francs."

"Give it to the cat," said Sergeant Boulestier.

Chapter III
Though Foreign

THE PROPRIETOR of the Hôtel du Commerce at St. Denis-sur-Aisne was in the act of shutting up for the night when he heard footsteps stop outside, the door opened, and two tall men came in, smiling.

"Good evening, landlord. You remember us?"

The landlord's face lit up. "But perfectly. The Messieurs Latimer who were here a year ago. But this is charming, I am delighted to see you here again. Be pleased to come in, there is still a fire in the lounge. Have you dined, gentlemen?"

"Thank you," said the older of the two, "we shall not require dinner, I think, eh, Charles?"

"No indeed," said the tall, thin one, "but I think a little glass of something would be pleasant before we retire. How say you, James?"

"You will join us in a glass, landlord."

"With the greatest pleasure in the world, messieurs. When you were here before you found my cognac to your taste, or is there—"

"Cognac will serve admirably," said James Latimer. "Can you accommodate us with a room for the night? I hope that you may do so, I have the most pleasant memories of previous visits to this house."

The landlord said that he would be most happy to do so, they could even have the same room which they had occupied before if it would please them. "I have also your luggage, gentlemen, the two suitcases you left. We have taken the utmost care of them, expecting from day to day that you would return for them."

"Thank you, thank you indeed," said James. "We had not the slightest misgivings about leaving them here, we were assured that they would be completely safe in your charge."

"We regretted having to leave you rather abruptly," said Charles. "We had an urgent appointment."

"We understood, of course," said the landlord, "that your journey must indeed have been both sudden and urgent. The messieurs have traveled far since they were last under my roof?"

"Not to say far," said Charles offhandedly. "I would say circuitous, rather. Yes, sir, circuitous is the word I would choose."

The landlord was far too polite to ask more; he refilled their glasses and changed the subject.

"The lady and gentleman, the young Monsieur and Madame Latimer, your relations, were here to lunch today, as no doubt you already know," he said. "I was very busy at lunch, it is our market day today, I did not have an opportunity of speaking to them at any length. I hope that they are well."

"We missed them," said James. "We were, to speak truth, not up in time to see them here but we hope to overtake them upon their journey."

"We have a regrettable habit of being the late Latimers," laughed Charles.

"Whereas the young folk, they are the early Latimers, *hein?* When one is young," said the landlord, "the happy days cannot begin too soon."

"This one," said James, looking at the clock, "looks like ending rather late, and no doubt you have had a long day. If we might have our valises sent up to our room, landlord?"

"At once, gentlemen, at once."

When the landlord had seen the Latimer cousins comfortably bestowed, he hurried to find his wife, who was doing final tidyings in the kitchen.

"My dear! Imagine to yourself who have just come in! The two Messieurs Latimer who disappeared so suddenly from the house a year ago! They have claimed their luggage. I have put them in the same room, No. 5."

Madame turned slowly. "They have come back? You say that they have come back?"

"Certainly, why not? Just as pleasant and friendly as ever. I always supposed that they would return to reclaim their baggage."

Madame, who was counting spoons, forgot the number and had to start again.

"The two young married ones, their relations, were in to lunch today," went on her husband, busily winding up the clock.

"I know," said Madame. "I saw the young lady for a few moments. She told me that they had come to see the memorial cross that has been set over the grave of their forebears, and to lay a wreath. A most beautiful wreath, she showed it to me. Pink and white roses."

"The English are fond of flowers, as is well known. These two tonight had the most exquisite roses in their buttonholes."

"Tell me," said Madame, shutting the spoon drawer and leaning her hands on the table, "did they explain how they managed to slip out from here that morning without anyone seeing them go?"

"No, of course not. Why should they? They walked out when no one was looking, that is all. The tall one—the American—did say that they were sorry to have left so abruptly, they had an important appointment. They left the money for their room."

"Yes, they did. Yes."

"You let your imagination run away with you. It was all that macabre excitement about the skeletons being found the same morning that these two disappeared which caused foolish stories to be put about. The young Madame Latimer was a little hysterical and all you women have to huddle together and talk about ghosts—"

"There were ghosts!" said his wife angrily. "My cousin Alphonse Dieudonné saw them, also the police—"

"Oh, very well—"

"If there were not, how did they know where to dig?"

"Have it according to your own wishes," said the landlord in a resigned voice. "Let us go up, it is getting late."

"Have you locked the back door?" she said.

The following morning was bright and sunny; the Latimer cousins obviously enjoyed their breakfast of scalding hot coffee, fresh rolls and butter, and went for a stroll round the village. They looked in at Vigneron's windows until, with a twittering cry of joy, Tiger the cat rushed out to welcome them and revolved about them, purring loudly.

"I find it strange," said James, "the affection which cats of all varieties display towards us. When I was mortal I was not so profoundly interested in cats. I am not now, for that matter." The cat sprang at his arm and thence to his shoulder. "These transports are, frankly, unwelcome. I hope I would never wilfully maltreat any animal, but—get down! It has knocked my hat awry."

"Let me help you, Cousin," for James was finding it difficult to dislodge Tiger, triumphant upon the nape of his neck. Charles lifted the cat away and it clung to his coat for a moment, only to utter a cry of terror and rush away out of sight.

"Ulysses to the rescue," laughed Charles. "You should be obliged to him, Cousin James."

"I am, in truth," said James handsomely, "though I must admit that it never occurred to me before that a tame monkey could serve any useful purpose."

They wandered on, having a word with André at the garage on their way. André remembered them from their previous visits and greeted them warmly. "The so beautiful car belonging to your relatives," he said, "it was in the village yesterday, I saw it myself. You are all here together?"

"No, we missed them," said James. "They did but pass through. We shall, I hope, see them within the space of a few days."

"Convey to them, I beg," said André, "the most distinguished expression of my profound respect."

"I will not fail of it," said James.

"Will you not send your love to the car also?" asked Charles.

"That great automobile takes my heart with it wherever it goes," said André with an exaggerated gesture. "The messieurs have, no doubt, heard of the excitement we had here last night?"

"Dear me," said James, all polite attention. "What was that?"

"I heard the bootboys at the hotel telling the chambermaid something about a murder," said Charles, "but I did not understand where it was. Surely you do not have murders in St. Denis?"

"Monsieur, not as a rule, but there was one last night. In a house just below me here, No. 26. Even so, they were not St. Denisois who did it, no. Bank robbers from Marseilles. It appears that they were disputing over the division of the loot." He told them, at some length, the little he knew about the affair.

"Let us walk on, Cousin," said Charles, "and view the scene of the crime."

"By all means," said James. "There are always valuable moral lessons to be learned from contemplation of the details of human turpitude. Good day to you, *Monsieur le garagiste.*"

"Good day, André," said Charles.

"Au revoir, messieurs," said André politely. He leaned one shoulder against the doorpost, lit a cigarette, and watched the cousins walking away down the street.

"One would say a survival," he remarked half aloud.

When the cousins reached No. 26 they stopped at the gateway and looked across the forecourt at the house. The wrought-iron gate upon the pavement was closed and locked for the first time for many years but the front door stood ajar and there were men moving about inside. In the forecourt there stood a handbarrow such as builders use to transport their ladders.

A small boy arrived suddenly from nowhere in particular, pointed a grubby finger at the barrow, and said: "They brought the coffin on that. I saw it, I did."

"Run away, little boy, run away," said James paternally. "Such things are not nice for little boys to talk about." The child stared blankly and James put his hand in his pocket for a small coin. "There, take that and go and buy yourself some lollipops. Run along."

The child fled, meeting a group of young contemporaries on the way. They exchanged a few whispered words and then the small boy ran on while the other six dashed up to the gate and swirled round the Latimers.

"Cousin," said Charles, "I cannot think that that action of yours, though kind, was well advised. These—"

"Monsieur! Monsieur! See that room there to the right? The floor is all swimming in blood!"

"And the man all shot to pieces—"

"That is very naughty," said James severely. "You are not speaking the truth. Run away and play."

"The road sweeper told my maman—"

"I think, Cousin James, we had best move on," said Charles, but at that moment the front door opened wide, Boulestier appeared upon the threshold, and the children squeaked like mice and scampered away.

Boulestier moved with dignity down the three shallow steps and across the forecourt; he unlocked the gate and came face to face with the Latimers. He had seen them before but only indistinctly, by moonlight; he did not recognize them at all but he did, of course, know them to be strangers. He looked at them and James spoke to him.

"Have I the pleasure of addressing Sergeant Boulestier?"

"That is, indeed, my name."

"Then it is the name of a conscientious and intrepid servant of the public," said James warmly. "Sir, your undaunted courage—"

"Monsieur makes a little mistake," said Boulestier. "I have the honor to be the servant, not of the public, but of France." He straightened up and his impersonal gaze passed far beyond them into the blue distance.

"I beg your pardon," said James, seriously deflated. "I did not mean—I only meant—"

"We wished merely," said Charles, coming to the rescue, "to congratulate you upon your gallant capture of a dangerous armed criminal."

Boulestier bowed.

"I thank the messieurs," he said, suddenly becoming human. "It is true that I am a Sergeant now, but even so I am not above appreciating the good opinion of persons of culture and high standing such as I perceive the messieurs to be. Though foreign," he added as an afterthought.

"Let me prophesy," said Charles, leaning negligently upon James' shoulder. "It is that one fine day soon you will open a letter telling you that you are now an Inspector."

"Monsieur amuses himself," said the Sergeant modestly, but there was a gleam in his eye.

"You wait," said Charles. "You will find that I am a good prophet. Though foreign," he added carefully.

They parted with mutual courtesies.

Chapter IV
The Citroën

THE COUSINS strolled on towards the end of the village and paused, looking down the long, straight road which was bordered on either side with poplar trees swaying in the gentle wind and turning out the silver undersides of their leaves to the autumn sun.

"The road to Paris," said James, "it does not change, Charles, does it? It looked like that when the Prussians clattered along it after Sedan, except that no doubt those trees have been renewed since then, perhaps more than once."

"I daresay that you are in the right, James. Tell me, why do the French grow so many poplar trees?"

"That is not within my knowledge, or is it that they are particularly suitable for the manufacture of charcoal?"

"Or possibly, Cousin, there is something in the French character which is just naturally attracted by poplars?"

"That observation borders, I believe, upon metaphysics," said James. "An interesting study, I doubt not, but one for which I could never discover any aptitude. Charles, we must shortly go after Sally and Jeremy, must we not?"

"Certainly," said Charles with great cheerfulness. "Our young relatives are already upon their way, and I opine that we should lose no time in following after them. They are delightful companions; we may rely upon passing some pleasant days in their society, as we did before. Besides, it is necessary for our health not to lose touch with them."

"There is no immediate urgency," said James, turning to stroll back through the village. "As no doubt you are aware, our dear young people were in a highly emotional state when they came to present us with that exquisite floral tribute, with the result that we have a considerable amount of power, as it were, in store. For it is with us as with the ingenious and surprising Leyden jar, which, having been exposed to the operation of the influence machine, stores up within itself a reserve of voltaic power which may be drawn upon until it is exhausted, when a fresh application of the influence machine is necessary."

"Yes," said Charles, "yes. I remember—"

"But at the moment our cells are well charged, to pursue the analogy. It is only to avoid too great exertion and, particularly, any emotional strain, and we shall do very well for several days or even, with extra care, a week."

"You always explain things so clearly, Cousin James. But the point I—"

"I remember giving a simple lecture upon elementary electricity at the Mechanics Institute at home before you came from America, I believe. It was heard with the deepest attention," said James complacently.

"I do not doubt of it. No, sir, I opine that your lecture was received with the greatest gratification, your English mechanics are intelligent men. But the point I had in mind was this. We know that our young friends will be in Menaggio, but do we know where? It may be a large place, Cousin."

"Good lack! I did not anticipate any difficulty, for surely they will stay at the best hotel in the town. We have only to enquire which is the best hotel and there we shall assuredly find them. Our good Jeremy would never take our sweet Sally to any inferior quarters."

"But they might be staying with friends. Or, more likely, at Cousin Quentin's house, and we do not know its direction."

James thought this over for a moment.

"Charles, you are in the right, we should depart without delay. We shall, of course, find them but it might take time. We go by train, naturally; we can make enquiries at the station about the time of running."

"You will think me quite mad," said Charles Latimer a little hesitantly, "but need we travel by train? We have plenty of money; should we not buy an automobile vehicle and drive ourselves to the romantic shores of Lake Como?"

"But—"

"Consider, James. We are both habituated to driving vehicles upon the roads under all conditions of weather—and of roads, by Jove! It is true that carriages were drawn by horses in our day, but is there so much difference? One observes the rules of the road, one drives with care and consideration for other road users, one obeys the orders of the police—in short, one behaves oneself. Nothing in it, Cousin, as our good Jeremy would say."

"But how to control a vehicle at seventy miles an hour—"

"We need not drive at seventy miles an hour, James. There is no law to compel that."

"Jeremy did."

"Yes, but we should not purchase such a vehicle as Jeremy's; there are smaller ones obtainable, much smaller. Consider, Cousin, in our day it took a first-rate whip to drive a four-in-hand, but women and even children drove pony carts."

"True," said James thoughtfully, "very true. But one must know how to work and govern these mechanisms."

"It cannot be so difficult or so many people would not be able to do it.

We will take lessons from the good André. Look at the people who do drive; will you maintain that we are more stupid than any of these? Look at that old man driving that—that tumbril; his beard sweeps the wheel he holds, but does that discourage him? No, sir. He drives like Jehu the son of Nimshi. And here"—Charles seized his cousin by the arm and turned him to face an open Ford truck coming up from behind loaded with vegetables—"look what sort of driver is directing that! A nun, heaven's my witness! Coifed and veiled, a nun!"

The nun drove rapidly past them, her black draperies flapping in the wind and the cabbages behind her leaping in their string bags at every bounce.

"I am coming to your way of thinking, Charles. If such as these can drive these inventions, surely we can."

"There's my gallant cousin. Look, we are now opposite to André's warehouse, if that is the right word? Should it be store?"

"It does not signify," said James, "Since we have only to cross the road and go in."

When the two tall men entered the garage, André abandoned the tire which he was repairing and came forward, wiping his hands on a piece of rag.

"Can I serve the gentlemen in any way?"

"Tell me," said James, looking round the garage, "do you in fact sell motor vehicles as well as—er—attend to whatever needs to be done?"

"But, certainly, monsieur. Secondhand cars as a rule, but if a new one is desired I do my best to get what is wanted."

"I think a good secondhand one, warranted sound—eh, Charles?"

"Provided that it is not too ancient," said Charles, "I believe that a secondhand vehicle will suit us very well. Yes, sir."

"But we want a good goer," said James. "None of your spavined hacks. So to speak," he added hastily, seeing André's expression.

"Certainly not, monsieur. A car of the utmost reliability. I have here a Renault, 1934 it is true, but it has been carefully maintained—"

The cousins walked round the van upon which André was working and were faced with a seven-seater limousine in a particularly dark shade of black which loomed over them like a threat.

"But it is a chariot of the largest size!" said James. "An enormous berlin, upon my honor!"

"More after the manner of a hearse," said Charles. "It needs but the tall black feathers tied with crape and the top-hatted mutes walking two by two—"

André broke into a laugh. "It is just, what you say. To offer such a catafalque to two gentlemen so very far from dead, it is unpardonable. But she is, indeed, a most comfortable car to drive in. With your chauffeur sitting in front and the glass partition drawn up, you are as private as—"

"As the grave," said Charles, pulling down the corners of his long mouth.

"Monsieur will not forgive me—"

"We do not wish for anything so large," said James. "A small and seemly curricle or tilbury, a—a—" he gestured with his hands—"a vehicle for two only."

"There are very small automobiles," said Charles. "We ourselves have seen them upon the streets in Paris, but I can't vision us coiling our long legs into one of those."

"Monsieur means the Rovin."

"Possibly. Have you not something a little more capacious than they but yet smaller than your hearse?"

"I have, but she is rather shabby. She needs a coat of paint but there has been wanting the time to let me do it," said André, dodging round the Renault. "I fear the gentlemen, when they see her, will say they would not accept her as a gift. She goes very well, though; the engine has had a complete overhaul." He added details until his hearers' blank faces warned him to stop. "The gentlemen are not mechanical? Why should they be? There are always garages." He opened the door of a lockup at the back and showed them a "cloverleaf" Citroën which had once been painted gray but had now weathered rather pleasantly, like good stonework.

"She has four good tires but the spare is a—"

"This is more like it," said James. "Something after this fashion was what I had in mind. How fast will this one go?"

André said, in effect, that she would do about forty-five miles an hour under favorable conditions, by which he meant a gentle downslope and a following wind, for though a thoroughly nice man and a good Christian he was yet a garage proprietor. "Her brakes," he added, "are in excellent order, I have adjusted them myself."

"It is, perhaps," said Charles, "indelicate to ask her age?"

"I forget for the moment," said André, "but it is on her registration papers. I will find them."

"If we agree to purchase," said James, "will you teach us to direct and control it?"

"A pleasure," said André rashly. "The gentlemen have driven before?"

"Dear me, yes," said James. "My father taught me when I was young and I have taken pleasure in driving myself ever since. It irks me inexpressibly to be driven by a servant."

"Any man," agreed André, "who is in the habit of driving himself dislikes being driven by another. It is natural. It is axiomatic."

"Though I could never claim to be as good as my father," pursued James. "He was a celebrated whip in his day. You remember, Charles?"

"Whip?" said André staring. "Whip? What is it used for, this whip?" He thought that James, being English, had used the wrong French word.

"I think," began Charles, but James swept over him.

"Whip. A term used in England for one adept at driving horses."

"Horses," said André thoughtfully. "Horses. I see." The Citroën had been standing for some time; he seized a dustpan and brush and began energetically to remove the accumulated dust. He opened the doors and stooped to sweep the floor; even James thought that the back of his neck was unusually red.

"I think," said Charles again, "that André here wonders what experience we have had with automobiles."

"Oh, indeed. Yes, very probably," said James. "He did not say so, did he? It is my fault, I should have guessed. No, we have never driven one of these inventions though we have traveled many miles in our cousin's vehicle, the one you so much admire."

"No doubt even that much experience will be a help," said André, finishing off with a flicking duster. "Now if the gentlemen will come and look at these controls—"

He delivered a short and simple lecture upon the uses of the clutch, the accelerator, and the brake, and found rather to his surprise that James grasped the principle of the gearbox more readily than did Charles.

"I am, in private life, a mill owner," explained James. "I have had to understand mechanical matters. My cousin's interests have been different."

But when it came to driving upon the road—a quiet, unfrequented road to which André took them—the advantage was with the more adaptable Charles. James had a painful tendency to set the car in the right direction and then expect it to behave intelligently. It would seem that André had dust in his eyes; more than once he rubbed them impatiently.

"The trouble with these inventions," complained James, when for the sixth time André had prevented a swerve towards the ditch, "is that they have no sense."

André rubbed his eyes again.

"Do not tell me, I beg," said Charles, "how these things work in their insides. I am not interested in mechanical intestines, no, sir. Tell me what to do, how to do it, and why, and I will do my best to copy you. Sir, I allow I am a child in these matters and I intend to remain one. I only want to drive."

Half an hour later Charles was changing gear noiselessly almost every time and steering a steady course at gradually increasing speeds.

"Monsieur has hands," said the delighted André, "one of these days we shall be cheering him to victory in one of the big international contests."

"This art should be within our powers," said James plaintively, "if nuns can do it. You may find it hard to believe if you did not see it yourself, André, but I saw a nun driving a motor dray only this morning—a nun!"

André laughed. "Filled with vegetables—an old Ford? Monsieur, before the Sister Marie Céleste entered religion, she drove a Lancia in the Monte Carlo Rally three years running, and gained awards, also!"

"A Lancia," said Charles, slowing for a sharp bend, "that is another variety of automobile? Different from this?"

"Oh, monsieur!" Words failing André, he kissed the tips of his fingers and blew the result at an imaginary Lancia. "But, superb!" Then, because although a garage proprietor he was yet a good Christian, he added: "This car will do well enough for the gentlemen to practice on; then, when they are expert, they can buy a Lancia, a Healey, a Chrysler, a Rolls. Come back," he added, "in a year's time and show me what you have then and I will boast to all my neighbors that it was I, André, who taught you to drive."

"What happens," asked James anxiously, "if at any time the air should escape from these tires?"

They bought the Citroën for twenty-seven thousand francs, that being the first figure which André put forward. He was so horrified when they did not attempt to haggle that he put a better cover on the spare wheel and refused to charge for the driving lesson.

"A pleasure, messieurs, and one I shall always remember. Let monsieur," to James, "remember that a car has to be steered *all* the time, and," to Charles, "that it is necessary to draw on the hand brake when standing still, and all will go well. You are staying here, yes, and taking little jaunts into the country?"

"We are driving down to Italy," said Charles, "tomorrow. We shall see you before we go."

"Italy?" said André in a weak voice.

"Certainly," said James. "We anticipate overtaking our cousins at or near upon Lake Como. It is true that they have the faster car but, as in the fable of the tortoise and the hare, we may surprise them in the end. Perseverance is all."

André leaned against the doorpost again to watch them walk away down the street.

"Italy," he murmured, and lit a cigarette. "Decidedly, a survival," he added.

The chemist, who was also the local optician, crossed the road to the café opposite for a cup of coffee; André considered for a moment and then followed him across.

"Tell me," said the *garagiste,* after the usual preliminary courtesies, "is it true that by looking closely at people's eyes you can tell if there is anything wrong with them?"

"There are also certain tests," said the chemist. "Are your eyes, then, troubling you?"

"Not until this morning." André covered first one eye and then the other to look first across the street and then at a newspaper lying upon the table.

"They seem to be in perfect order, but this morning they played me tricks."

"What sort of tricks? Seeing double? Floating spots?"

"I was teaching two Englishmen to drive in my old Citroën. Occasionally they would swerve, as beginners will, particularly one of them, and every time he did this it seemed to me that his hands upon the wheel became transparent."

"Transparent? You mean when he held them up you could see the light through them?"

"No. I mean that when he kept them down I could see the wheel through them."

"Nonsense," said the chemist. "Nonsense."

"Not nonsense at all," protested André. "Am I of those who imagine fairy tales?"

"Not hitherto, so far as I know. But men develop unexpected powers as the years pass—"

"I am not yet in my dotage," said André angrily.

"No, no. I beg of you not to take offense at a harmless jest. Do you know what I think? I think that you have a small disturbance of the liver, which, as all the world knows, affects the eyes directly. A small temporary interference with the mechanism of focusing both eyes alike. Come across to my shop and I will find you a little something which will abolish transparencies."

"Thank you, I will. I do not doubt that you are right."

"Did you say that they were driving that old Citroën? Then what else did you expect? If I drove that thing I should not merely become a little transparent, I should fade away altogether."

"They have bought it," said André.

"Bought it? What for?"

"To drive to Italy."

"They say the English are a great nation," said the chemist. "It must be true, after all."

Chapter V
Crash

DIRECTLY after breakfast on the following morning James and Charles Latimer started for Italy.

They loaded their two suitcases into the boot of the Citroën and drove off, with James at the wheel; the landlord bade them an affectionate farewell and showered them with good wishes; Sergeant Boulestier, standing at the bank corner, saluted as they passed, and André, on the lookout for them at the garage, waved encouragingly as they went by. He stood on the pavement watching till they were out of sight and then walked determinedly along to the church. Here he entered, bought two of the largest candles which St. Denis had to offer, and reverently placed and lit them. The Curé came in just as he was doing this.

"In gratitude, my son, for some successful endeavor?"

"Appealing, Father, for special intervention on behalf of two friends of mine in imminent danger."

The Latimer cousins drove on. James covered more than a mile before he felt confident enough to change into top gear; at the end of five miles he began to flag.

"Shall I take your place for a little?" asked Charles.

"If you will. Now, to stop this vehicle one puts out the clutch—so—disengages the gear-—so—and applies the brake. Thus." The car stopped, James drew a long breath, and took his hat off to wipe his forehead. "Upon my honor, Charles, I have done nothing so exhausting since I spent a whole day getting in the hay on our home paddock once when we were shorthanded."

"If this is going to tire us out," said Charles rather anxiously, "the results may be serious."

"I know, I know. But when the novelty is worn off the task may prove to be lighter than it seems at first. Do you change seats with me, we shall see how you fare."

James settled into the passenger's seat and prepared to enjoy himself as his cousin took over the driving.

"How pleasant this is," he said, "to travel quietly along in our own vehicle with the fresh winds of heaven all about us and the sunshine lighting the way. Credit me, Charles, I like better a car which has no roof nor walls than one which is, in effect, a room upon wheels. How say you?"

"Fine," said Charles jerkily, for his mind was absorbed in what he was doing, "fine on a day like this one. But what if it rains?"

"Suitable clothing," began James, but Charles stopped him.

"Forgive me, Cousin, there is here a horse-drawn wagon which I must overtake when there is opportunity. It requires judgement."

"I am thoughtless," said James instantly, and relapsed into silence.

A few miles farther down the road Charles was driving more confidently, which was as well since there seemed to be something a little queer about the traffic coming towards them. There was a long string of vehicles moving very slowly upon the edge of the road and the motor traffic overtaking it was dodging in and out.

"What in the world is this?" asked Charles, and slowed down, thereby seriously embarrassing a Swedish Line coach which was just behind him.

"Painted coaches," said James, peering round the windscreen. "I have it, they are fair vehicles on the move, swings and merry-go-rounds and gypsy caravans."

"Those in front are no caravans," said Charles, who had sight like a hawk even through a blemished windscreen. "No, sir, they are not. Gentlemen, hush! They are elephants."

"It is a circus! When I was a lad my father took me to a circus, I remember. There was a pig-faced woman and a calf with two heads and a—"

The Swedish coach saw its chance and swept past them, followed by a string of traffic which had been held up behind, and Charles was driven almost on the grass verge. By the time this excitement was over the circus was upon them, the elephants moving statelily along and occasionally snatching a branch from the wayside trees. Behind them came cages of lions and tigers, camels walking two by two as in Noah's day, caravans, cookhouses, gayly painted machinery, and more cages. James was keenly interested but Charles had his hands too full to look at the procession.

As they passed the last cage of all there was a triumphant cry of "Eek! Eek!" and a small Capuchin monkey scrambled into Charles' lap and put his tiny paws upon the wheel. The monkey, dressed in a little red jacket and a tiny round cap to match, bounced up and down, showing every sign of extreme delight.

Charles was so startled that he inadvertently turned the wheel and the car swung out into the road almost into the path of an oncoming Salmson driven at high speed by a young man with patent-leather hair and a tartan shirt *pour le sport* open at the neck. A collision seemed unavoidable, but at the last second the Citroën pulled over and the cars missed each other by, one would say, the thickness of the coat of paint the Citroën had not received. Perhaps André's large candles were pulling their weight; St. Denis was also a traveler. But the escape was so narrow that the cousins' defense mechanism came automatically into action and what the Salmson driver saw quite plainly was a battered 1926 Citroën completely empty except for a small monkey at the wheel.

The Salmson swerved across the road, bounced off the edge of the grass, and scrambled back to its own side just in time to avoid an oncoming lorry, whose driver leaned from his cab to pass a string of the most unkind remarks. Most of them were quite untrue, for the Salmson driver was not only a young man of unblemished ancestry but remarkably temperate in his habits. He did not reply; from his abstracted gaze one would have said that he had not heard. He drove on, slowly and thoughtfully; when he overtook the circus and noticed that the last vehicle was a cage containing monkeys, he became more thoughtful than before.

"That monkey of yours," said the disembodied voice of James Latimer, "will cause a serious accident one of these days, depend upon it. It is true that we have only to dematerialize and nothing can harm us, but this vehicle is solid enough and we might have seriously injured that poor young man."

"Cousin," said Charles' voice, "I will allow that that was a damned near thing, as Wellington said of Waterloo. Yes, sir. Nor can I charge my memory with having turned the wheel the wrong way, but doubtless I did. Let us pull up at some convenient café and have a glass of something. Gentlemen, hush! I am shaken still."

"To me also," said James, "a mild restorative would not come amiss. There is a roadside café here."

The Citroën swung into the parking-space beside the café, which stood back from the road with small blue-painted tables and chairs set out in front. There was a waiter pottering about with a duster; when he saw the car come in and draw to a rather abrupt stop he left off dusting and stared at it in plain disbelief. The Latimers got out, leaving the monkey, Ulysses, in the car; it was only when the waiter did not even move his eyes as they passed that they realized what they were doing.

"Charles! We are not materialized—we shall frighten the man into a fit—what shall we do?"

"Come behind him, here. No one else about? No—now then!"

A table behind the waiter was occupied by two tall gentlemen patiently waiting to be served, but the waiter did not move, one would say he was turned to stone. Charles threw his hat upon an empty chair and smoothed back the lank, dark hair which had blown about his ears. His dark eyes were full of laughter and his wide mouth curled up at the corners.

"It seems we are not to be served today, Cousin," he said.

The waiter spun round at the sound of his voice.

"Messieurs! How did—where did you come from?"

"From the car, naturally," said James. "Where else?"

"The one with the monkey in it?"

"Monkey?" said Charles in a puzzled voice, and James backed him up. "What monkey?"

"That one," said the waiter, turning, "in that— It has gone."

"Are you assured that it was ever there?" asked James.

"But, naturally! I was standing here looking at it!"

"We saw you standing there," said Charles, "engaged in thought. Yes, sir, deep thought. We opined that maybe it was your hour for your private orisons and we were reluctant to break in. Yes, sir, that is how it was."

"But now that you tell us you were thinking about monkeys it would seem that that cannot be," said James.

"I was not thinking about monkeys," said the waiter. "That is I was watching one. It sat in that car."

"And you did not think about it at all," said Charles. "Very sensible of you. Yes, sir, very."

"It drove the car in," said the waiter obstinately.

"Nonsense, my good man, nonsense," said James firmly. "We drove the car in; that is this gentleman did."

"I cannot believe that you mistook us for monkeys—" began Charles.

"One monkey."

"Not even one each?"

"*Merde!*" cried the waiter, and tore his hair.

"Come, my man," said James, "this fantasy is unworthy of a respectable person such as you appear, upon cursory examination, to be. If you are ill, pray retire and apply such remedial measures as occur to you; if not, we came in here to be served with drink. Have you perhaps a passable cognac?"

"Yes, monsieur," said the waiter with an obvious effort. "Certainly, monsieur."

He turned rather unsteadily and threaded his way between the tables to the café, which had a door in the middle and a window upon either side standing wide open, for the day was hot and sunny. As the waiter entered the door there was a crash inside as of a bottle falling to the floor and a wail of: "That monkey again!" The next moment Ulysses came flying out of the top half of the open window and vanished in midflight through the air.

"Charles, you must control that animal of yours. That poor man will go demented."

"Oh no," said Charles, "but he might leave this place. The proprietor will do better without him, the man is a thief. Could you not smell it?"

"Of course, you are in the right, Charles. It is so long since we have met it that I had forgotten. Well, is he bringing our cognac?"

He did not; the proprietor did so himself. He apologized for a few minutes' delay, saying that his waiter had just left him.

"So suddenly?" said James. "He seemed to be well established in his employment here when we came in."

"So suddenly," agreed the proprietor, "that he went straight out by the back way and across the fields; if the messieurs will but glance round the corner of the house they will see him running."

James sat still but Charles got up to look.

"It is quite true, Cousin. A little black figure running madly across a green field with his coattails flapping. He looks like a startled cockroach. Well, well."

"I am sorry," said James, "if you are put to inconvenience by the loss of your servitor."

"I thank monsieur, but I am not sorry. He was under notice, he was light-fingered. I say nothing about an occasional glass of wine, one expects that, one overlooks it, but when it comes to money, that is a serious matter."

"We thought him dishonest," nodded James, "we could smell—"

But Charles was seized with a fit of coughing and the rest of the sentence was lost.

"We thought that he had a hangdog look," said Charles when he had controlled his glottis, "but what decided him to leave so abruptly?"

"He said something about a monkey," said the proprietor, shrugging his shoulders.

"A traveling circus has just passed by," said Charles. "We met it upon the road."

"And there were caged monkeys in the last vehicle," said James. "It may be that he has an abhorrence of them."

"He can, then, take it elsewhere," said the proprietor. *"Je m'en fiche."*

The Latimers went on their way, taking it in turns to drive. It proved to be difficult for James to adapt himself to speeds so much in excess of those to which he had been accustomed; he found the Citroën much more controllable in second gear. Towards the end of one of his spells at the wheel Charles remarked that it was much warmer in the car than one would expect an open car to be and also that there was an odd smell coming from it somewhere.

"If we were within some house," he said, "I should opine that some disaster was taking place in the kitchen. Yes, sir, I should surmise that the cook was negligent."

"Some defect in the provision for cooling the engine" said James. "Let us make a stop and look into the matter."

When they stopped it could be seen that steam was issuing from the radiator cap; when the engine was switched off, a hissing noise made itself heard.

"The water is boiling," said James.

"From your tone of disapproval, Cousin, I gather that it should not."

"Certainly it should not. Also"—he opened the hood—"from the heat of the engine casing I deduce that much of the water has boiled away."

"It is evident when you speak of such matters that you are of the nation which produced Robert Fulton and Isambard Kingdom Brunel," said Charles gracefully. "What now, Cousin, what now?"

"More water must be added. It is poured in at this vent," said James, laying his hand upon the radiator cap and immediately snatching it off again. "We must wait until the mechanism cools and then drive on to the next village there and ask for water. Some farmer with a pump in his yard will doubtless have the civility to let us draw some."

A quarter of an hour later Charles, standing up in the car, announced that there was a farmyard with a pump in it on the right, between those two gateposts. James stopped the car, engaged the lowest gear, drove carefully and accurately into the yard, and drew up beside the pump.

The farmer came out of one of the sheds to meet them. James explained that they were running short of water and that it would be an act of great kindness if the farmer would let him have some more, and also lend him a can with which to pour it in. The farmer said that certainly Monsieur could have as much water as he needed, and, of course, a can. As he spoke he also laid his hand upon the radiator cap and snatched it off again even more quickly than James had done.

"But," he said, "it is imperatively necessary that Monsieur allow his engine to cool first. It is nearly red-hot. To apply cold water to that hot metal, it is to ask for a cracked cylinder block."

"Due to the unequal expansion of metals," agreed James.

"I myself have a car exactly like this," said the farmer. "Monsieur is satisfied with her performance?"

"The vehicle serves well enough," said James carelessly. "No man would call it a smart turnout but I understand that it has been for some years on the road."

"Twenty-eight years," said the farmer. "Made in 1926."

"Indeed," said James. "I was not aware of the date of manufacture. But it has been my experience to find that machinery, carefully handled and maintained, will go on working for many a long year. I have a stationary steam engine over seventy years old."

"The only trouble," said the farmer, leaning against the front mudguard to fill his pipe, "is the difficulty that there is now in getting spare parts. I myself broke a half-shaft ten days ago and I have not yet got a replacement."

James had not the faintest idea what a half-shaft was but saw no need to admit it.

"I wonder whether it is yet cool enough," he said. "We want to get on."

The farmer applied a match to the tobacco in his pipe and asked if the gentlemen were going far.

"Only to Italy."

"What? In that car which I now see before me?"

"Certainly," said James coldly.

The farmer appeared to struggle with his emotions for a moment and then said that he would go and fetch a can. When the radiator had been refilled, the Latimers expressed their thanks in graceful phrases and prepared to go on.

"Will you drive now, Charles, for a time?"

"Certainly, James. With pleasure."

The farmyard was below the level of the road; there was a short but steep little rise to the entrance gates, whose solid square pillars and flanking walls prevented any view of the oncoming traffic. Charles, who had learned from André how not to stall an engine, took the slope at a gallant rush, which, before he could act, carried him out upon the road. There was a flash of gray and silver, a yell of terror in several voices, and a perfectly appalling crash. A thirty-two-seater touring-coach driven at high speed scooped up the little Citroën with its enormous front bumpers and hurled it away. It turned an end-for-end somersault, rolled right over, and came to rest on its side in the ditch surrounded by numerous fragments torn from it in the collision.

Chapter VI
Spare Parts

THE COACH, with squealing brakes, slid to a stop thirty yards down the road; the driver and the courier leapt white-faced from it and rushed back to the scene of the accident, the driver as he ran unbuttoning his white coat to be ready to throw it over any pitiful human relics which might be shockingly displayed to public view. Behind them coach windows were being wound down and heads were being protruded, for the gift of being able not to look at a road accident is given only to few. The farmer, who was inside his house putting away the water can, also heard it and ran out, almost afraid to look round the gatepost for fear of what he should see.

The two tall gentlemen who had just been talking to him were standing in front of the wreckage looking ruefully at it. They were perfectly clean and tidy, they were not disheveled, even the creases down their trousers were not bent, and their hats were still upon their heads. As the farmer approached from one side and the courier and his driver from the other, the taller of the two men edged round the wrecked car, took hold of the lid of the boot, and pulled it to open it. It did not open, it came right off in his hands together with part of the back, to which it had been hinged, and a piece of side panel behind the door. Charles Latimer gathered up his awkward armful and tossed it lightly into the ditch before handing James' suitcase to him and pulling out his own.

When the courier and driver arrived, panting more with agitation than haste, James left off flicking dust from his luggage with a perfectly clean handkerchief and turned an apologetic face towards them.

"Gentlemen, how I am to apologize I cannot conceive. If I have damaged your so beautiful coach"—he was speaking French—"you must permit me to make myself responsible for any reparations which may be necessary."

"Gentlemen," began the courier in English, for he recognized their accents.

"Entirely my fault," interposed Charles, "I was driving. I am ashamed of myself, yes, sir. Covered with confusion is what I am. Sir, I should be degraded from the rank of driver to pushing a handbarrow loaded with scrap iron with the brake permanently in operation. Sir, in future I will propel along the highway nothing more lethal than a wheelbarrow, for I am a menace to public safety."

"I thought you were killed," said the courier. "You have frightened a year off my life. I was sure you were both dead."

"Dear me," said Charles, "do we look it?"

"Anything but," said the courier. "Hang it, you're not even dusty. How the devil did you escape?"

"We sprang clear," explained Charles, "at the very last moment; my cousin and I, sir, can move quickly when need be. At the moment of impact we leapt to our feet; the car, as it were, leapt with us, and as it rolled we kept our feet. With some difficulty, I admit, but we succeeded. Sir, have you never seen a man keep his footing upon a rolling barrel? Yes, sir, that was how we did it. Cousin, you will bear me out."

"Certainly," said James. "By all means. To adapt Addison a little: 'We, unconcerned, would bear the mighty crack And stand secure amidst a falling world.' But let us clear up as we go, the first thing to do is to dispose of this wreckage. How say you, Cousin?"

"Surely," agreed Charles, "surely. I calculate that that automobile's earthly race is run. Yes, sir." He reverently removed his hat. *"Requiescat in pace."*

"But not there, at the side of the road," objected James. "Such remnants are unsightly." He changed into French and addressed the farmer. "My good man, will you be so kind as to have that debris removed and cast upon some midden? Perhaps your men could drag it away."

"But willingly, monsieur."

"And here is somewhat for your trouble," said James, giving him two thousand francs.

"A thousand thanks, monsieur," said the farmer, and was about to hurry away before these amiable idiots changed their minds when Charles stopped him.

"Tell me one thing," he said in a low tone.

"Yes, monsieur?"

"Is there a half-shaft in that wreckage?"

"Probably bent, monsieur, probably bent. Excuse me, we will get this moved out of sight before the police come along asking questions." The farmer hurried away, humming a tune as he went, for to him that melancholy heap of oddments was not melancholy at all, it was a bountiful store of spare parts for his own similar Citroën.

Charles hurried after James Latimer, walking towards the coach with the courier and the driver, who was carrying the suitcases. James was asking anxiously whether the coach had sustained any damage, "for my mind will not be at ease while there is any doubt in the matter."

There was a small group of people, principally men, who had got out of the coach; the rest, principally ladies, were looking out of the windows. The Latimer hats came off, naturally, to be held in the hand while they passed, murmuring apologies, through the group in the road. James, with a businessman's obsession with a business matter, pressed on to the front of the coach, but Charles gave himself time to look up at the windows as he went by and his long mouth twitched at the corners. A friendly interest, evidently. Very friendly. He joined the group inspecting the front bumper.

"It is nothing," said Michel, stroking with his broad fingers a shallow dent in the chromium plating. "The bumper took it all. There is, perhaps, a small scratch or two"—he shrugged his heavy shoulders—"what matter? There will be more before the end of the journey."

"I take Michel's word, always," said the courier. "If he says a thing is so, it is so."

"Then all is well," said James, much relieved, "and we can dismiss this matter from our minds. Now we have only to walk on to that village which I see ahead of us and enquire whether we can hire a car to take us to Rheims. We purpose to take luncheon there."

"Gentlemen," said the courier, "would it suit your convenience to travel to Rheims in my coach? Two of my passengers were recalled to London this morning so we have two vacant seats. Would you care to occupy them?"

"Sir, you are prodigious civil," said James. "How say you, Cousin, shall we take this offer?"

"There are ladies, I see, of the party," said Charles. "Should not enquiry be made whether our company will be acceptable to them?"

"Sir," said the courier, "you are"—he nearly said "prodigious civil" but managed to hold it back—"you are extraordinarily polite, but yes, I will ask them." He climbed into the coach and addressed the company.

"Ladies and gentlemen. You all saw that horrid crash just now which, I frankly admit, frightened me into fits. How those two gentlemen escaped injury I can't think. Evidently the age of miracles is not dead. Not only were they unhurt but they made not the slightest fuss about it. They merely told the farmer to remove the debris as you or I might tell a waiter to clear the table, and just walked quietly away; I don't mind telling you it left me speechless. Well, it now appears that they, like us, want to lunch at Rheims, so I suggested that they should come on with us since we have two spare seats. However, they insisted that your consent—particularly the ladies' consent—should be asked first. What do you say, shall they come with us?"

There were cries of assent all over the coach, one man adding: "Particularly as we smashed them up."

"No fault of ours," said the courier quickly. "Yes, thank you, I'll go and tell them."

Michel put the Latimer suitcases in the luggage compartment in the side of the coach while the courier introduced the Latimers themselves to the party.

"Mr. Latimer, who comes from near Manchester, and his cousin, Major Latimer, an American from Virginia."

"Ladies and gentlemen," said James, "to admit us to your company after our quite unpardonable behavior is an example of benevolence which it would be hard indeed to parallel." He bowed to right and left and sat down in the vacant seat which was in the front of the coach, just behind the courier's.

"Ladies," said Charles with his brilliant smile, "your unmerited kindness—gentlemen, your courtesy—we are most deeply indebted—"

Michel let the clutch in, the coach moved off a little suddenly, Charles nearly lost his balance, and everybody laughed.

"I sit down," he added hastily, "before I act the buffoon again." There was enough noise to make it possible for the Latimers to speak together in quiet tones without being overheard.

"Upon my soul, Charles, never have I had to act so quickly! Even as I dematerialized I felt the car turning beneath me."

"And I, James, and I. I will maintain in any company that that metamorphosis certainly had to be sudden. Turning back, also, Cousin. It made me deuced giddy for the moment."

"We were warned, if you remember," said James rather anxiously, "to take that operation as slowly as possible."

"But if one is in an accident—"

"I think we had no business to be in that accident."

"True," said Charles, "very true. I think that the only person to whom I have not yet apologized is you. Cousin James, I am a blunderheaded, addle-pated incompetent. I thought I could drive—"

"Charles, do stop. I did not purpose to reproach you, I only meant that we were ill-advised to buy that invention. It was plain from the outset that it was too exhausting for us and we ought not to have pursued the matter. See now how things are set forth for us; you are permitted to wreck the vehicle without injury to any and immediately two places are provided to convey us upon the right road. It is as clear as noonday, if one has but the eyes to see."

"You are in the right, James, as always. Yes, and you might add that even by the accident we were permitted to do good. The farmer and his spare parts, Cousin, for his car which was like ours."

"Oh, indeed," said James slowly, "was that what he had in mind? I did not grasp the gist of his remarks." James broke off and began to laugh. "To think, Cousin, only to think that I actually paid him to take the rubbish away! It seems that I am not so good a businessman as I was when I was mortal."

"He was plainly surprised. But not so much, Cousin, as I guess he would have been if he had rushed to the spot and not found us at all. He would have been flabbergasted."

"We were permitted to repair our errors," said James placidly. "It is all arranged." He folded his hands together across his stomach and looked happily out of the windows. "There before us lies the city of Rheims, if I mistake not."

The courier turned in his seat.

"I wonder, gentlemen," he said, "whether you would care to join our party for lunch? Unless, of course, you have other plans in Rheims? There are two lunches ordered which will not be eaten unless you come to our rescue. It is a decent place and serves a good meal."

"Why, Mr. Fowler, that is most handsome of you," said James. "Speaking for myself, I am delighted to accept. How say you, Cousin?"

"Surely," said Charles, "surely."

When the coach pulled up in the cathedral square at Rheims, the Latimers leapt out first and stood in the road, hat in hand, helping the ladies down the steep steps with polite murmurs of: "Pray, ma'am, allow me. Permit me, ma'am, to help you. Ma'am, my arm, I beg you. Ma'am, these steps are monstrous irksome for ladies." There was a good deal of chattering inside the coach when it stopped but the Latimer politeness had the odd effect of producing total silence as the ladies of the party alighted. They murmured their thanks as they passed the doorway and after that fell silent until they were within the restaurant and out of earshot.

"My dear! What marvelous manners! Where do they come from?"

"Out of a book by Thackeray. *Esmond,* possibly."

"Never read it. But really! I hardly knew what to say."

"A person hardly knows how to take it, does one? I mean all that bowing and scraping—"

"You should have seen my husband's face! He was looking out of the coach window."

"Life," said the elderly lady who had referred to Thackeray, "would be a great deal pleasanter than it is today if one encountered such fine manners more often."

"Oh well. I expect you're right."

Charles and James turned from the coach door; James strolled a few steps towards the restaurant but Charles stood looking across the square.

"What is it, Cousin Charles?"

"That café over there is the one where we had coffee with Jeremy and Sally that day he drove us to Paris."

"Were you wishing they were here now? Why, so do I. We must consult upon means of making the journey to Italy. I think that to travel by railroad would be the quickest," said James. "We must enquire about the routes."

"I think the proprietor of this hotel will have a railway timetable," said

Charles eagerly. "Cousin, I spent some time looking at one in our hotel in Paris last year and I will maintain that the author has a prodigious store of miscellaneous information, yes, sir. Why, Cousin, there are even trains going to Russia."

"Indeed! I do not suppose that they would take one much beyond the frontier, if at all."

Chapter VII
Thirty-two Passports

LUNCH WAS TAKEN so rapidly that the Latimers, who liked having time to enjoy their food, were thoroughly left behind; when most of the party had left the table and trooped dutifully out to visit the Cathedral and buy picture post-cards, the cousins still sat at table leisurely finishing with biscuits and cheese and sipping their wine. The courier came over to them and sat down in a vacant chair, bringing with him as usual the despatch case from which he was never parted for a moment.

"You are not patronizing the champagne, then?"

"Why, no," said James. "It may well be, sir, that we are old-fashioned, but we consider champagne a wine to be drunk at late dinner, not at luncheon."

Charles agreed. "To me," he said, "there is something faintly raffish in the idea of drinking champagne by daylight. Not that I would decry a little reasonable raffishness at the right time and place, but not with ladies present."

"My cousin is in the right," said James. "I think that it was seeing your ladies drinking it which mildly surprised us, though even the faintest shadow of an aspersion was far from our minds. Mr. Fowler, will you not drink with us? Pray, Charles, call to that waiter."

Charles did so, and asked at the same time for a railway timetable, which, when brought, proved to be only a local one.

"This does not go far enough," he complained. "Sir, for the compiler of this little book the world stops at Paris."

"That is of not the slightest use," said James severely, "to persons desiring to go to Italy. Waiter, have you no more extensive information available?"

The waiter said that he was sorry, but that little booklet was the only one they had. The courier said that if the Latimers wanted to go by train to Italy they would probably do best to go to Paris and start again from there.

"I am assured that you are in the right," said James. "In any case, Mr. Fowler, we are deeply obliged to you for helping us so far upon our road."

Charles picked up the timetable again and began looking up the trains to Paris while Fowler said that, on the contrary, he was very glad to have had them. "Our two passengers, who were wired for to return to England this morning, have left me with two seats vacant."

"May we know, Mr. Fowler, where you are going?" asked Charles.

"To Italy, Major Latimer, to Italy. May I ask where you are bound for in Italy?"

"Menaggio, on Lake Como."

"We are going to Milan," said Fowler slowly, "by Lugano."

"If I remember my geography," said James, "the Lake of Lugano is reasonably adjacent to Lake Como."

"One takes a bus, Mr. Latimer, from the town of Lugano across to Menaggio on Lake Como. You would, in fact, do the same thing whether you traveled by train or coach, as there is no railway running to Menaggio. But please do not misunderstand me, I am not trying to suggest how you should go. If you go from here to Paris and on from there by train you will arrive twenty-four hours earlier because you will travel through the night, which we do not."

"You stay the night at different places en route, no doubt."

"At Besançon tonight and at Andermatt tomorrow night," said Fowler.

James leaned back in his chair and finished the last of his glass of wine.

"Well, Cousin Charles? How say you? Shall we rush to our destination by train, or shall we appeal to Mr. Fowler to let us journey with him?"

"I believe, Cousin, that we should do better to travel with Mr. Fowler if he will take pity upon such waifs and strays as we. Yes, and for this reason. Our young people are going by road and we do not know how long they will spend upon the journey; it would be foolish to arrive before they do when we might take matters more leisurely and see the country as we go."

"Well, Mr. Fowler, will you take us on?"

"Delighted," said Fowler.

"I do trust," said Charles, gazing idly across the room, "that we shall give you no cause to regret your kindness."

"Of course not," said Fowler cheerfully. "Why should you? Excuse me, I will go and tell Michel he need not take your luggage out." He went, the despatch case under his arm, but Charles still looked across the deserted restaurant, for he had seen a banana unaccountably disappear from a dish on the sideboard, and now, from behind the short curtains at the window, there hung down, faintly twitching, a long prehensile tail.

Fowler went out and found Michel just returning from refilling the fuel tanks.

"Those two we picked up are coming on with us," said the courier, "as far as Lugano. Nice people, if a little unusual."

Michel nodded. "They will be all right, I think. Very correct. But only they shall not drive my coach."

They left Rheims punctually on time and made a fast run down the long, straight main roads of France; stopping only for a short tea break at Chaumont, they ran into the old town of Besançon a few minutes after seven. Dinner was not to be served until eight to give the party time to take a quick look round the town.

"I shall want you away early tomorrow morning," said Fowler just before they reached the town. "I think you would all enjoy a little spare time in Berne, which is a charming and picturesque place, and we must not fail to go and pay our respects to the bears. So an early start, if you can forgive me. Half past eight, in fact. Yes, I know, but once you're up one time is much like another only there's more of it, if you see what I mean."

They were set down at the door of the hotel and there followed the usual scramble to get the luggage out and allot the rooms; Charles and James Latimer had a double room on the second floor. They inspected the room and strolled down again. By this time the courier was sitting in the café belonging to the hotel, drinking a cup of coffee and relaxing for the first time in the day. James greeted him.

"Rest after labor, Mr. Fowler?"

"This is the happiest moment of a courier's day," said Fowler, "when he has brought his party safely to their intended destination at the appointed time and finds the hotel still there in working order, the right number of the right sort of rooms correctly reserved, and his party reasonably contented."

"You still cling to your portfolio of office," said Charles, pointing to the despatch case upon an adjacent chair. The courier patted it affectionately and took it upon his knee.

"Major Latimer, if I lost that I might as well go and jump in the Doubs. That's the river here, as no doubt you know. This case holds all the documents for the tour, the papers for the frontiers, the bookings at the hotels, the details about the intermediate stops, and all that sort of thing. At the moment it holds your passports, also; I will give them out again when we are all assembled at dinner."

"It looks to me an excellent piece of leatherwork," said James politely.

"It's a cheap one; I bought it in Paris when I was there lately. I expect there are thousands like it but it serves my turn very well. It will not look so smart at the end of the season."

"Let us stroll about, Cousin, for a little if you agree. I, believe this to be an interesting old town, Mr. Fowler?"

"Certainly. One moment," hunting in his case, "I believe I have a small booklet here, with a map. How things do hide themselves." At this point a stout, elderly businessman of Besançon bustled into the café, which was filling up, glanced at the clock, sat down in the chair next to Fowler's, ordered a glass of wine and began to sip it, looking up at the clock from time to time. He also, like most businessmen, carried a despatch case, which he put down on the floor beside his chair.

"Got it!" cried Fowler, and produced a bright orange booklet, the Plan-Guide Blay, of Besançon. "Would you care to borrow this? There's a Roman archway you ought to see and some of the buildings are very fine."

"I thank you, sir," said James, "you are most kind. We will return this without fail. Let us visit this Roman gateway, Charles, before the light is too far gone. I see that they call it *La Porte Noire;* that is interesting, for the Roman gateway at Trier is called the *Porta Nigra.* I never saw it, but I have read of it many times."

"While we are perambulating the streets," said Charles, "we might keep our weather eye lifting for Sally and Jeremy, do not you agree?"

"Why, certainly, Charles, and it would be delightful to meet them here, but have you any reason to suppose them to be in Besançon tonight?"

"Only that they, as we, are traveling by road from St. Denis-sur-Aisne to Menaggio. I have no knowledge of what route they have chosen, but I suppose that it is not impossible we might encounter them en route."

They went out into the street in the fading daylight while the courier sat back and relaxed again; the businessman next him, who seemed to be worried about something, continued to sip his wine and watch the clock. Fowler turned his chair to look idly out of the window and the despatch case rolled silently over to come to rest against the leg of the businessman's chair. A thin, dark man with a long nose, his hat over his eyes, and too much padding in the shoulders of his coat leaned over the bar and read a newspaper while the hands of the clock went faithfully round the dial.

Presently the businessman finished his wine, got up from his seat, and went out of the café without a look behind. A moment later the tall man at the bar straightened himself and said that he thought he would go and sit down for a little. He picked up his glass, limped across the room, for he was a little lame, and sat down in the chair which the worried businessman had just vacated.

A few minutes later James and Charles came up the street on their way from the Roman *Porte Noire* to the Eglise Notre-Dame. Just before they reached the café of their hotel, the tall, long-nosed man came out of it and turned up the street ahead of them. He had a despatch case under his arm.

" 'There is also,' " read James from his little book " 'the *Palais de Justice,* built by the architect Hugues Sambin, a pupil of Michael Angelo. It contains the—' "

But Charles interrupted him. "Look, James, quickly, ahead of us there, that tall man who limps. Is he not carrying Mr. Fowler's despatch case?"

"By Jove, you are in the right! What do we do—will you keep the rogue in sight while I go back and inform—"

"I think, Cousin, that we can very well deal with this deplorable affair ourselves. Yes, sir, for it may be that Mr. Fowler has not yet discovered his loss and we may save him some agitation. Cousin James, if we cannot turn the tables upon this knave without enlisting mortal aid we are more of dizzards than I take us to be. Let us draw up upon him."

But there was a crowd of people waiting to go into a cinema and they lost sight of their quarry; when they in their turn had passed the crowd they could not see him. There was a side turning there as well as a number of doorways, any one of which he might have entered.

"Now," said James, checking, "where is your lame man gone?"

Exactly upon the corner there was a recessed entrance to a bank; upon the wide step of this a blind man was sitting on a little stool with his cap upon the ground before him for alms.

"Excuse me, messieurs—"

"What is it?" asked James, hunting in his pockets for a coin.

"If the messieurs were seeking a lame man, he turned this corner and went on down the street, I heard him."

"Thank you indeed," said James, and the cousins hurried on down the side turning.

"There he is," said Charles, "behind that cart. Not too fast, we do not want to alarm him."

"Not yet," said James grimly.

The lame man went for some distance down the street and then turned in at the entrance to a fourth-rate hotel, of the kind that advertises *"Chambres pour voyageurs."* He stopped for a moment in the entrance to speak to the concierge, who sat in a little cubbyhole at the foot of the stairs knitting, always knitting. She pointed up the stairs with one of her needles and he went up as directed.

The next moment the concierge thought that she heard steps in the doorway but no one came in. She rose from her chair to peer round the corner but there was no one there.

The lame man went up to the second floor and knocked on the door facing him; it was opened, he went in to find two men waiting for him, and the door was locked again.

"Well, boys," he said cheerfully, "I've got it," and smacked the despatch case heartily. "It appears to me to be well lined."

"He did as he was told, then?" said one of the others. "No trouble? No signals to anyone? No police about?"

The newcomer laughed. "Would you make trouble if you were a fraudulent army contractor and there was one who could prove it? It is he in whom the police would fix their claws, if all were known." He sat down in a chair at the end of a table. The others also sat down and one of them poured him a glass of wine from a bottle on the table.

"Brown-paper boots," said the wine pourer angrily. "He has earned his punishment, and more. He should be sent to the guillotine."

"I also," said the third man, "have served in the Army. He ought to be shot."

"It may be," said the lame man, "that this little lesson will make him honest in future. Who knows?" One of the catches on the despatch case was giving a little trouble; he put it down on his knees to deal more efficiently with it. "Come on, thou!"

The catch obeyed, the despatch case opened and displayed its contents, the lame man looked incredulously at it and then stared blankly across the room.

"What—" began the others, and rose to their feet since they could not see the case from where they sat.

"I have—" croaked the lame man. "It is the wrong case—what have I done—"

He turned an unwholesome greenish white and fell back in his chair while the despatch case slipped from his fingers and slid to the floor, under the table, with a thud.

One of his friends picked up the glass of wine which had just been poured and threw it in the man's face to revive him.

"You would have done better," said the other, "to have poured it down his throat. His heart, it will kill him some fine day."

"Pour him out some more, then, while I pick up the c—" His voice stopped abruptly.

"What's the matter?" asked the other, a glass in one hand and a bottle in the other. "Why do you not, then, pick it up?"

"It is not there," said his companion in a strangled whisper. "I heard it fall and it is not here. *Dieu-de-Dieu-de-Dieu—*"

"You are an idiot," said the other, banging the bottle and the glass down upon the table, "it must be there, I also heard it fall." He stooped to look under the table and then dropped on his knees, absurdly searching the floor with his hands.

"It is not, then, five francs which we have lost," said his friend angrily. He sprang to his feet and tried the door but it was still locked and the window was shut and latched. "Here, you!" to the lame man. "Wake up. Wake up! What have you done with it?"

The lame man stirred and rubbed his face with his hands. "What—"

"It's gone!"

"Gone! It is impossible that—"

"And I'm going too," said the third man, struggling into his raincoat. "I'm off! This trip was unlucky from the start, I heard thunder on the left as we were starting and that concierge here looked hard at me this afternoon, she remembered me, I know she did, I'm getting out of this place—"

In the meantime the courier found himself nodding over his coffee, for it had been a long day and the crash of the Latimers' car had shaken him more than he would admit even to himself. He picked up the despatch case from the floor beside him and trailed off rather wearily to his bedroom. There were all those reports to get out; he would have half an hour on those and then perhaps his dinner would revive him.

Though this despatch case was in all respects like his own, there was something faintly different in the feel of it. One of the catches on his own case had a habit of sticking, but this one flew back at a touch. He opened it and looked inside; instead of passports and his traveling papers it contained only money. A great deal of money, which looked even more than it was, for it consisted of wads of used notes of small denominations such as even the most cautious criminal would have no hesitation in passing.

Fowler looked at this much as a teetotaller might regard a hippogriff on the washstand; not only did he not believe it, he felt he did not deserve it. After a moment he put the case gingerly down on the bed, got out his sponge, and bathed his face in cold water. Whatever happens, a courier never loses his head. He flung the window wide open, dried his face, and returned to his problem.

It was still there, unaltered.

It was plainly no matter of robbery, for the contents of this case were worth more than his own a thousand times over, but it is an occasion like this which brings home to a man the truism that money is not everything. When he thought of thirty-two missing British passports he broke into a violent perspiration and his hands trembled.

He got up from his chair, straightened his knees with an effort, and went out of the room, locking the door behind him and holding the key firmly in his hand. The hotel proprietor was a sensible fellow and a good friend; Fowler felt that he must confide in somebody or burst into low but penetrating howls. He went down in the lift and was lucky enough to find the proprietor alone in his room.

At this point the Latimer cousins returned unseen of any even in the streets through which they passed. They saw, in the entrance hall of the hotel, the courier, with a face like death, seeking his friend the proprietor.

The Latimers went up to their bedroom and Charles said: "He has missed it, Cousin. Black despair, James, sat upon his shoulders."

"He looked to be monstrous discomposed. I wish we could have anticipated this but it could not be helped. Never mind, we will alleviate his misery.

He is downstairs now but he had not the portfolio with him; no doubt be has left it in his room. You know which room he has?"

"At the end of the corridor above, I heard him say so. We merely change them over. How say you?"

"Assuredly, for neither the man who paid out the money nor those who received it are such as it is desirable to reimburse. Well, shall we go?"

"Take heart," said the proprietor, applying consolation. "It must be a case of simple exchange in error, and when the owner of this despatch case finds that he has lost a large sum of money and gained in exchange but thirty-two British passports only, he will rush to the police. Let us, therefore, also rush to the police and all will yet be well. Courage, my friend."

They went up together to the courier's room; there was a despatch case lying, as Fowler had left it, on the bed. He tilted it to slide out the contents for the proprietor's inspection and immediately there was a cascade upon the coverlet of British passports, nearly all shiny new ones. They were followed by the tour documents and the official cash.

Fowler turned perfectly white and sat down on the chair with an audible bump.

"I am going mad," he said, "I must be."

"No, no," said the proprietor stoutly. "No such thing."

"But the door was locked just now. You saw me open it."

"Of course you did. Listen, my friend. You were overtired, that is all. I thought, when you came in, how tired you looked, and there was also that accident this morning. Calm yourself, monsieur, I beg. It was a momentary waking dream, that is all. I beg of you, do not agitate yourself. What you need is a little glass of good brandy"—the proprietor rang the bell—"and then you will go into bed. Yes, yes, I will stay with you till you do it. Then I send you up a little supper on a tray and you take aspirins, two or three, and sleep all night." He interrupted himself to give an order when a knock came at the door, and then went on. "Tomorrow you forget all this. Look, now I unpack your pajamas; let me help you with your coat. Tranquillize the mind, my good friend, tranquillize the mind. Now, here is your brandy, drink it quickly though, indeed, it deserves more respect, but in that manner it will take more effect. There, like that. Good. Now, into bed—"

"You are extraordinarily kind," said Fowler, with the sheet up to his chin. "About that despatch case—"

"I take it downstairs. I go straight down in the lift and, not stopping to speak to anyone, not though he were the President of France, I walk straight to my room and lock this up in my safe. That is a promise."

Chapter VIII
The Man in the Long Coat

THE LATIMERS were in their bedroom with the door locked, counting the money in the second despatch case. There were two million francs—two thousand pounds sterling at about a thousand to the pound—they counted it out and looked at it with considerable amusement.

"This," said James Latimer, "is a prodigious large sum of money. We have no use for it, Charles, have we?"

"No, sir, we have enough. Cousin, when we have dined—for I confess my stomach is aggrieved—let us play the good Haroun Al Raschid. Let us go about the town and benefit the poor and needy. Let us stuff money into the hospital letter box till it will hold no more, let us buy food for the hungry and even"—he laughed—"a little drink for the thirsty. Let us—"

"The poor blind man," said James, "without whose help we should have lost our man—"

"Certainly—"

"I believe there are boxes at the doors of the churches appealing for restoration funds."

"I have no doubt but that there are virtuous young women only debarred from marriage for want of a dowry. The French are regrettably practical in these matters, Cousin."

James regarded him a little nervously.

"I foresee a certain possible embarrassment in store for a man going about a town in the late evening enquiring for virtuous young woman of—"

Charles' shout of laughter stopped him.

"Dear James, if it were not for you I should be in perpetual hot water, though indeed I did not purpose to seek them out myself. Some reputable body such as the Town Council was what I had in mind. However, doubtless you are in the right, the subject could be plaguey equivocal. We will avoid the ladies, James."

They stuffed the pockets of their raincoats with notes, not thinking it wise to use the despatch case which was so like Fowler's. James picked it up.

"What shall we do with this?"

"Let us take it out under our coats and rid ourselves of it by some convenient means. Someone's dustbin, or we can let the River Doubs receive it."

After supper they strolled along the street and found the blind man still sitting in the doorway of the bank.

"You did us a good turn, friend," said James, "when you directed us how to find the man with the limp. Tell me now, what would you do if you had money?"

The blind man laughed. "That depends, monsieur, does it not, upon how much money! For a certain amount I would buy myself an extra good dinner with, perhaps, a bottle of wine. For a little more I could buy myself a warm overcoat for the winter, and so it goes. If the messieurs were thinking of giving me a small sum in return for a small service I shall be grateful, but I am not greedy, messieurs, believe you me."

"Suppose," said Charles, "that the sum were, say, one million five hundred thousand francs, what would you do?"

"The messieurs are pleased to make fun of me," gasped the blind man.

"Never mind," said Charles, "tell us what you would do."

"Monsieur, I am of Paris. I was born in Montparnasse, in the Rue Delambre. I grew up there. I went to school, I did well, messieurs, for all that I sit here a helpless heap of rags upon a doorstep. I worked hard and became a chemist. After some years I obtained a post here, in Besançon, intending to save money and go back to Montparnasse when I retired, for it was never in my mind, messieurs, to see Paris no more. Then there was an accident with some acid and I lost my sight, and all my savings went little by little, and so you see me here. As to what I should do if I had such a sum as you mentioned, I would go back there where I belong and find a little room somewhere— perhaps even in the Rue Delambre, where I was born—and some woman to come in to cook and clean. There"— he drew a long breath—"I would stroll along on sunny afternoons and sit outside the Dôme with a little glass of wine, making it last a long time, messieurs. I would sit there and people would soon know me and come to talk to me, for we are friendly folk in my Montparnasse. The artists come to the Dôme, they argue about their art, but, by the hour, messieurs! And there is all the hooting of the traffic at the crossroads there, and the trams go clanging past and the children chase each other with cries—messieurs, since I go blind I see it all so clearly, more clearly than I did when I could see Besançon and only remember Montparnasse."

"Wait here a little," said James. "We will find some receptacle in which to put the money, and so return."

The blind man listened to their retreating footsteps and shook his head.

"They will not come back," he said, "it was a jest only. I wish they had not done it. I did not know, until I began to talk, how greatly I desire to be there where I belong."

Ten minutes later he heard their footsteps returning, James' very firm and steady, Charles' lighter and with more spring in them. They came up to him and put down a suitcase beside his stool where he could lay his hand upon it.

"There," said Charles. "We thought you would require a small piece of luggage also, and the notes are inside."

"I think it would be wiser," said James, "not to open it until you are private in your room. There are envious eyes everywhere."

"Messieurs," said the blind man in a voice which was almost a wail, "for the love of God tell me if this is true or only a jest. I will not be angry, indeed I will not, only tell me if it is true."

"It is true," said James in tones of deep compassion, "I swear it, upon my honor."

"The money is there," said Charles, "I give you my word. Tomorrow, if you wish, you may be in Montparnasse."

They shook him by the hand and hurried away before he could speak; when they looked back at the corner, he was gathering up his cap and the stool; clutching the suitcase tightly, he wandered off down a side turning and out of sight.

"That was well done, Charles. That man was honest and truthful, we were fortunate to encounter him."

"Yes, sir. You must allow, Cousin, that as philanthropists we are better equipped than most. If some of these rogues knew the sort of aroma with which they affront a supernaturally sensitive nose they would turn honest for mere shame. Cousin James, that thieves' den from which we snatched Mr. Fowler's despatch case!"

"It reminded me," said James, pulling down his waistcoat and throwing his shoulders back, "of Farmer Hoggeston's mixer when I was a boy. He used to clear it once a year to put on the fields. Sir, you could smell it at Oakwood Han, two miles off, if the wind set that way."

"We have still a vast deal of money," said Charles. "My coat is distended with it."

"Very true. Let us study for a moment this map which Mr. Fowler lent to us; if we were to walk round to the various places of worship doubtless we should find worthy objects for our beneficence."

"Cousin, those blackmailers were grieved and pained when their money vanished, but if they could see it being donated in handfuls to religious and charitable organizations, they would be ferocious. Yes, sir."

"How much have we left, Charles?"

"Two hundred pounds in English money. We gave the blind man one thousand eight hundred."

"It is to keep him for the rest of his life," said James, "and he looks older than he is by reason of his affliction. I am truly sorry for that poor man. If we pursue this road, Charles, we shall presently come upon the Eglise Notre-Dame, which dates from the eleventh century. I assume it to be almost certainly in need of financial assistance."

"Cousin, I will admit that that is a sound assumption. If a building eight hundred years old should not need repair it must surely be so solid as to have no insides. Yes, sir, that is what I think." Charles tilted his hat back, threw open his coat, and strolled along with his hands in his trouser pockets, a very picture of amused indolence. His dark eyes passed in review all whom they met and his mouth curled up at the corners. "Cousin, I feel that tonight will prove amusing, I feel it in my bones. Now, who is this drifting towards us? A character, James, an eccentric, or I am a Dutchman."

Where they were walking the pavement was wider and less thronged; wandering irresolutely in their direction there came a man in a long black coat reaching to his ankles though he himself was unusually tall, well over six feet in height and topping even Charles. The man himself was thin to emaciation but of a cheerful countenance; his coat was threadbare, beneath it he wore striped trousers with a large patch on the left knee, a blue jersey such as seamen wear, and on his head a blue beret. His eyes met Charles' and lit up,

"Good evening", said the tall man in a friendly manner entirely free from impertinence; also, he spoke in an educated voice.

"Good evening," said Charles, "A pleasant evening for a stroll."

"It is, indeed, and I am glad the messieurs find it so also. You are strangers here?"

"We do but lodge here one night," said James, "in the course of our journey."

"I also loved to travel when I was young," said the tall man, who seemed to be in his late fifties, "at your age it is natural and fitting. But now I live here in the one place and I have advantages of which you have no idea, you who come and go like swallows and do not even build a nest, not even for the season. These streets"—he gestured widely with a rather grubby hand—"are my theater, my lecture hall, my club. I see one man rise and another sink, I watch the children grow up and fall in love, fat laughing Colette, serious Martine, dark-eyed Yvonne. There are plots there for many plays, messieurs, when Etienne is discomfited and Georges triumphant and Alexandre makes no conquests. Furthermore, messieurs, there is no charge for admission."

"Monsieur is, perhaps," said Charles, "a playwright?"

"Oh no, monsieur, I am a lecturer on medieval history in the University of Paris."

"Indeed," began James.

"Retired," interrupted the tall man, "retired some years ago." He laughed cheerfully. "This prisoner is no longer in bondage. Punctuality, bah! Regularity, ach! The strict adherence to the timetable, *au diable* with all timetables. Messieurs, there was a time when I even hated clocks, picture that to yourselves."

"Monsieur," said James, "I perceive that you are a philosopher. Will you do us the honor to take a glass of wine with us? There is an adjacent café.

Shall we repair to it?"

"Monsieur, I will not attempt to conceal from you the fact that I cannot return the compliment; all—or nearly all—I had I gave up to purchase this freedom."

"Monsieur," said James, "the invitation came from me and I receive in exchange the pleasure of your company."

They all bowed formally to each other and, strolling slowly towards the café, settled down with more bows at one of the outside tables. James consulted a waiter.

"Permit," said the tall man, "that I introduce myself. René Frachot, at your service."

"Thank you, monsieur. I am James Latimer, from England—"

"And I, Charles Latimer from Virginia. I take it, monsieur, that you no longer hate clocks since time no longer tyrannizes over you?"

"Clocks are now my friends, monsieur, telling me that another happy hour is about to begin. Like the sundial, *Horas non numero nisi serenas.*"

"Monsieur," said James, "can it be that I have at last found upon this earth one perfectly happy man?" He glanced at Charles, whose eyebrows went up in comical dismay.

"Monsieur, the ancients had a saying of which the Latin for the moment escapes me," said Frachot. "It runs: 'Call no man happy until he is dead.' "

"No, monsieur," said Charles firmly. "That whiskered saying is too cautious for my taste. What? If I am happy should I not sing?"

"I doubt not," said Frachot, "that you would, but as to whether you should or not depends, surely, upon the quality of your singing."

James broke into his odd laugh, a little like a barking dog, and the waiter came with the wine.

"I trust, Monsieur Frachot," said James, "that this wine is to your fancy, it is a Chateau d'Arlay. Our waiter here assures me that it is drinkable."

"Monsieur," said Frachot, sipping, "this wine is such as, after we are dead, will be served to us in the gardens of Paradise, when we sit round tables of amethyst and drink from diamond goblets. Messieurs, your health and long lives to you both."

They returned his politeness.

"Tables of amethyst," said James thoughtfully.

"A stone which was anciently said to have the property of preventing drunkenness," said Frachot.

"I was sure," said Charles appreciatively, "that you were not speaking at random."

"Tell me, Monsieur Frachot," said James, "are you so much of a philosopher as to despise money?"

"I may be a philosopher," said Frachot crisply, "but I am not a fool. Money, though less important than the world believes, yet has its uses."

"Let us suppose," said Charles, "that you suddenly became possessed of two hundred thousand francs, what would you do with it?"

"Would you, for example," said James, "go back to Paris?"

"No, no," cried Frachot with a shudder, "never to Paris, never. I have suffered too much in Paris."

"I am sorry," said James kindly. "I have said something to pain you, I did not intend it."

"Humiliation and mockery," murmured Frachot in a tone barely audible. "They can be very cruel, the people of Paris."

"Let us dismiss Paris," said Charles cheerfully. "It is a long way off and there is this to be said, it cannot run after us. We are now in Besançon."

Frachot looked up with a smile.

"Come, monsieur," continued Charles, "you have not yet told us how you would spend your two hundred thousand francs."

"I should buy some new clothes," said Frachot. "My coat is, as you may notice, not what it was. My suit also is not, strictly speaking, a suit. Yes, I should buy some more clothes. But first of all I should have a dinner; not just a meal, which is something to hush the clamor of an empty stomach, but a dinner to be taken slowly, savored with attention, and enjoyed without distraction. I should drink wine with it, not *vin ordinaire* at forty-five francs a glass, but real wine like this." He touched his glass. "I will admit frankly that I like to drink a little good wine, but when one has to choose between food and drink, why then my stomach always wins. Nor would I eat and drink alone; I would share my good fortune with two old friends, who are, like me, in reduced circumstances, *res angusta domi,* Mr. Latimer. The rest of the money I would use with discretion, by degrees. I fear that my plans are not exciting, messieurs, but ambition and I parted company long ago. *Non sum qualis eram,* I am not what I was but I am a great deal happier."

"Monsieur," said James earnestly, "I applaud your moderation."

"Monsieur," said Charles, "you are a wise man and here is your money."

He laid a fat packet of notes upon the table. Frachot stared at them for a moment and then, with a murmured apology, picked up the notes, turned his back upon the table, and counted the money. He turned round to them again and laid two notes before Charles.

"The messieurs have miscounted," he said, plainly finding it an effort to steady his voice, "there is two thousand francs too much." He sat down again and broke into a rather shaky laugh. "Permit me, messieurs, to thank you. When a man of my education and standing—former standing—finds himself compelled to stay in bed while his one shirt is being washed, he is apt to feel a little embarrassed. It is foolish, but there it is; besides, it is tiresome if the weather is fine and one wishes to go out. Tell me one thing, if I am not indiscreet—"

"What is it?"

"Is there need for any precaution in changing these notes?"

James stared and Charles broke into a laugh.

"You need have no anxiety on that score, monsieur. Those notes belong to none but you."

"I do not offend by asking?"

"Certainly not," said Charles. "You do not know us."

"I have never met anyone like you," said Frachot. You are no ordinary men."

"Nonsense," said James with a slight gasp, "nonsense. We are of sound English stock, that is all, though my cousin is American by birth."

"I sympathize for the first time with St. Augustine," said Frachot. *"Non Angli sed angeli."*

"Come, Charles," said James, rather embarrassed, "shall we stroll on a little since we are here for so short a time? Monsieur Frachot, I wish you many happy days."

It was a little difficult to part from the grateful Frachot but they managed it at last and walked on slowly down the street.

"Here is your Eglise Notre-Dame, Cousin," said Charles. "Will you have the good Frachot's small change to put in the offertory box?"

"Those two notes, of course. Yes, why not? Let us do so. We did not spread our benefactions as widely as we intended."

"Why, no," said Charles, "but we spread them a great deal thicker. What, sir, would you have us go about to give all the inhabitants of Besançon sixpence each?"

"We did as we were guided," said James placidly. "Let us return to our hotel."

They found the proprietor standing upon the doorstep and exchanged a few words with him.

"You have inspected our lovely town? Yes, and had a pleasant evening, I trust."

"Thank you, yes," said James. "We talked to one or two here and there. Your charming town has its characters, monsieur."

"We have, as you say, our characters. What town of any distinction has not? I wonder whom you may have met."

"Most notably, one Monsieur Frachot, a man of education and intelligence."

"Our poor Monsieur Frachot," murmured the proprietor. "He was, it is said—he says it himself—a professor at the University of Paris. It is also said that he was discharged for persistent drunkenness. Poor man, he came here where he thought no one would know him; he forgot that a man who addresses a series of classes of fifty or more over a period of years becomes known to a truly enormous circle. But he does not know that we of the town are aware of his history. No, monsieur, there is no one here who would remind him."

"You are good people," said James. "You deserve to flourish."

Chapter IX
Kermesse Zoologique

ABOUT AN HOUR later Monsieur Frachot, accompanied by his two friends the Messieurs Delor and Thevenet, wandered into a small café in the Rue Proudbon, near the autobus depot. They had started out intending to dine and had had a little glass here and there while they discussed where they should have dinner. It was not that they had drunk much, the mistake was in drinking at all upon an empty stomach, and the result was that they forgot all about dinner and just strolled vaguely about from one place to another, quite harmless and inoffensive and perfectly happy. The café was empty when they went in.

"This," said Thevenet decidedly, "is a nice place." He leaned heavily upon the bar.

"I heartily concur," said Delor gracefully, "in what my learned friend has just said." He came to anchor beside Thevenet.

"Barman," said Frachot, "a good sweet red wine, if you please. Normally our palates would prefer a dry wine, but not tonight."

The proprietor, who ran the place with occasional help from his wife, was a little offended at being addressed as "Barman," but he knew his duty and did it. He said he had a very nice muscat if the gentlemen would like to try it, and they agreed.

"Bring on your muscat," said Frachot splendidly, and threw down a thousand-franc note.

"Put it in the dock," said Delor. "You may be sure that we will give it a fair trial."

The proprietor poured out three glasses and set them upon the bar before his clients. Thevenet and Delor picked theirs up at once but Frachot was delayed by having to receive his change. When he did turn to pick up his glass he was mildly surprised to see that a small Capuchin monkey, in a little red jacket with a tiny round cap to match, was sitting on the bar close to his elbow and drinking his wine out of his glass.

Frachot uttered an exclamation, at which the monkey set down the glass carefully, stood up, removed his cap with one little paw and bowed deeply, with the other paw laid over his heart.

"Tiens!" said the innkeeper. "From whence did that species of animal arrive? I do not approve of animals in my bar."

But Frachot had not spent years of his life keeping order in large classes of students to be set back by an innkeeper.

"When you say 'animal,' " he explained, "you make use of a term which includes not only yourself, which is not surprising, but also, believe it or not, my two friends and myself. Am I not right, Thevenet?"

"Certainly," said Thevenet. "Moreover, anatomically speaking, the difference between the barman here and your little friend there is principally a matter of size."

"And in other respects, such as manners," said Delor, "the weight of the evidence is heavily on the side of the monkey. He is polite, he takes his wine like a gentleman, and he does not speak unless he is first addressed."

The innkeeper turned red and began to splutter, but Frachot cut him short by ordering another glass for himself, "since my little friend here has taken a fancy to mine." He pushed the monkey's half-empty glass towards him and Ulysses bowed again and took it up.

At the end of the next round Frachot announced that he had been thinking and the other two turned courteously, if a little waveringly, towards him.

"That very charming little monkey," he said, "did not come in with us, did it? No. Have any of us ever owned a monkey?"

"No," said Delor.

"No," said Thevenet, "though I have had patients who were barely distinguishable from members of the middle group of the primates, particularly *Cynopithecidae.*"

"Do you suggest," said Delor, "that we are being dogged by one of your satisfied customers?"

"No," said Thevenet.

"Your glasses are empty," said Frachot. "Barman, kindly recharge these goblets. Is this monkey a member of your household? Four glasses, please."

The innkeeper controlled himself with difficulty and refilled the four glasses. Ulysses began to scratch but when Frachot checked him he stopped at once. Charles never permitted public scratching.

When the wine had been poured and the innkeeper had been paid he drew a long breath and said that he never harbored such animals in his house, never had and never would. His wife did not either.

"What, no children?" said Thevenet. "How sad, what a disappointment. Perhaps I could advise. When I was at the Sorbonne—"

"We are wandering from the subject under discussion, my dear Thevenet," said Frachot, "if you will forgive me. In any case, this man would doubtless prefer to consult you privately. The point at issue is this. If the monkey did not come in with us and was not here before we came, how did it arrive?

"A salient point of evidence which," said Delor, "has not yet been brought out is that the door has not been opened even once since we came in and it is still shut."

They all turned round and looked at the door, which was, indeed, firmly closed.

"That's right," said Thevenet.

"It follows, therefore," said Frachot, "that this is not a real monkey. It is, to put it in simple words, indubitably phantasmagorical."

"Nonsense, my dear Frachot, nonsense," said Thevenet. "I am, as you know, a lifelong and convinced materialist and what you are saying is, if you will forgive me, absurd. You will be asking us to believe in ghosts next."

"Can you adduce any proof of your statement, Frachot?" asked Delor.

"If," said Frachot, "as seems to me probable, this little animal merely appeared, it should also disappear in the same way. That is logical, is it not?" He turned to Ulysses, who rolled his great dark eyes at him, and Frachot hesitated. "I like him, but logic must be served." He waved his hand carelessly over the monkey's head and said: "Vanish!" in a commanding tone.

Ulysses finished the last few drops left in his glass, set it down upon the bar, quite slowly became transparent, and vanished altogether.

"There you are, Thevenet," said Delor, "what does your dialectical materialism say in face of a proof like that?"

The innkeeper awoke with a start from a moment of stunned paralysis; uttering a strangled howl, he rushed across the room and out into the street. Here he encountered a gendarme of his acquaintance and seized him by the arm.

"Come with me," he said. "Come at once. There is a man in my bar who is making a monkey appear and disappear, and when it is there it drinks wine."

The gendarme looked at him severely and also with surprise, for he knew very well that the innkeeper was a man who drank very little indeed and then only at mealtimes.

"I am not drunk," said the innkeeper urgently, "indeed, I have had nothing. What I tell you is true."

"It does not sound true," said the gendarme. "Vanishing monkeys? You probably have a fever. But I will come."

In the meantime Frachot had suddenly realized what he had done.

"He is gone," he cried, "and I liked him. I want him back. Come back!"

Ulysses came back as slowly as he had gone. While the innkeeper and his friend the gendarme were in the act of peering through the window, they saw upon the bar a monkey-shaped transparency which thickened, rounded, and solidified. More than that, it moved. It held the end of its tail elegantly in one paw and performed a few steps of the stately sarabande, ending with a series of lightning somersaults from one end of the bar to the other. Frachot, Thevenet, and Delor applauded loudly and Delor handed Ulysses his half-empty glass to finish.

"You see?" said the innkeeper.

The gendarme nodded, pulled himself up, and advanced with a steady stride into the cafe.

"Is this monkey the property of any or all of you gentlemen?"

"No," said Delor.

"No," said Frachot. "Does any man own the song of birds, the glory of the evening sky, the flash of fountains in the sun—"

"No," said Delor.

"For of such," continued Frachot uninterruptedly, "is my young friend on the left. He is a *lusus naturae*, a spark from the wheels of Phoebus' chariot, an emblem of our lost innocence." He wiped his eyes.

"It is reported," said the gendarme, "that you allege you can make him vanish."

"I can," said Frachot proudly, "and bring him back again when I want him, too. Pay attention, please, the class." He waved his hand again over Ulysses. "Vanish!"

The monkey, who was getting a little tired of this place, promptly disappeared and the gendarme blinked but stood his ground.

"Now I call him back," said Frachot and did so, but nothing happened, for Ulysses had gone to look for amusement elsewhere. Frachot called several times but with no result, and finally he lost his temper.

"That is your fault, you frightened him away, you flat-footed, long-eared, warty-nosed bum-bailiff! Now I'll vanish you." He drew himself up to his full height and waved his hand majestically over the gendarme's head. "Vanish! Go!"

There was a stunned silence in the café, there was not even the sound of breathing and nobody stirred. The silence lasted till Thevenet turned abruptly, buried his face on Delor's shoulder, and cried: "No, no! I can't bear it!"

Frachot's arm fell to his side and the gendarme moved at once, he thumped himself upon the chest, and the muffled thuds were reassuring. He turned towards the door, going stiffly like a waxwork come to life; as he went he passed a table and tapped sharply on it with his knuckles. This produced several loud, clear raps, a satisfactory proof that he was indeed as solid as he felt himself to be. He opened the door and went out, shutting it firmly behind him, and there was silence in the bar for a long minute.

"Let us go," said Frachot. "I may be mistaken, but I feel that we are unwelcome here, eh Delor? Thevenet?"

"Yes," said Delor.

"Yes," said Thevenet.

They finished their wine and turned to go; halfway across the room Frachot turned back and threw a five-hundred-franc note upon the bar.

"If my young friend should return," he said, "he is my guest." He stalked out.

"Heaven forbid," said the proprietor as the door closed, "and that goes for you three, also."

Ulysses, pleasantly exhilarated with wine and freedom, was skipping along the housetops looking for something or somebody to play with. After all, however devotedly attached one may be to one's master, there are times when one longs for the society of one's own kind. He wandered on, crossing streets by swinging upon telephone wires, until he stopped suddenly and listened intently.

Michel Brochier had been associated with performing animals all his life until a combination of advancing years and a badly broken leg had made continual traveling a burden, when he settled down in Besançon in a roomy stable yard which had once housed the dray horses of a brewery. Here he started a boarding establishment for animals; since he had many excellent connections with traveling circuses, his boarders were mainly performing animals laid up for the winter. In September they were beginning to come in and already he had Ernie the Educated Elephant and six monkeys from the same circus, a performing seal from another, a pair of Australian kangaroos six feet high who were not circus animals but just ordinarily tame, a cage or two of assorted monkeys on their way to different zoos, and another very large one holding monkeys of his own, for he was a dealer as well as a boardinghouse keeper. There were also a pair of sleepy lions and an enormous tortoise. What Ulysses had heard was a few remarks being exchanged between the boarders. He listened with his head cocked to one side, ran quickly along a row of houses, slid down a telegraph pole, and was there among them. He danced with delight before the barred cages and his relations inside were equally interested. Grunts, squeals, and cries of "Eek! Eek!" testified to their pleasure.

The six performing monkeys were the boys for him; they were all of his sort, they had been trained, they had manners which, if not so polished as his own, were yet passable, but they were fastened in behind bars which also kept him out. Tiresome. He clung to the bars and gibbered.

One of the prisoners, accustomed to the keeper entering their cage, drew his attention to the gate which was not locked; it had a strong but simple catch on the outside. Ulysses poked it, shook it, pulled it in different directions, and finally stumbled upon the trick of undoing it. The gate opened and the six monkeys filed out in line astern as they had been taught, each holding the tail of the one next in front. There was a happy gathering in the stable yard with much tail-pulling and general back-slapping until the monkeys tired of it and capered off to release Ernie the Educated Elephant. Their act always came on just after his, it was a fixed habit for him to go out first. Ernie majestically rolled out. There was a rather flimsy gate between the yard and the road; Ernie gave it a gentle push and it fell down flat. He advanced over the ruins.

By this time the other monkey cages had been opened and their occupants, to a total number of seventy-nine, spilled like quicksilver over the town of Besançon. The kangaroos came out together and stayed side by side; with one accord they stood up and looked round, their long ears twitching; with one accord they went out with slow hops into the night, and the performing seal flopped painstakingly after them. Nobody went near the lions, who are not popular with other animals, and the tortoise did not even open his eyes.

It was getting late, the streets of Besançon were emptying, and Frachot, Thevenet, and Delor were making their way homewards. They did not sing because they were not of the sort who make noises, they were not even talking much. They were all three in a pleasant, dreamy condition, getting sleepy and going home to bed. Delightful. When, therefore, they heard most peculiar footsteps which were not so much footsteps as the sort of noise which might be made by somebody slapping the road with a wet sack on the end of a pole, when they looked over their shoulders and saw two well-nourished kangaroos overtaking them with standing leaps, they merely moved on to the pavement to let whatever it was go by as they would have done for any other traffic. They did not even comment and the two kangaroos passed on out of sight.

A little farther on Frachot and his friends came abreast of a narrow turning to the right; Frachot looked at it, shook his head, looked again, and stopped.

"Curious," he said, "very curious indeed are the visual effects produced by cross lighting. One would say, if one did not know better, that there was an elephant standing at the mouth of that alley."

Thevenet shaded his eyes. "I see what you mean. It is a curious optical illusion."

"No," said Delor, "I see it plainly. It is a barrage balloon such as I saw in London when I was there during the war. That large tube which hangs down in front is where they blow in the gas."

The Educated Elephant was severely at a loss. Where was the lighted stage made ready for him to perform, where were the rows of pink faces turned up to him, where was the applause? Where was his trainer and what was this dark, chilly place? Ernie had never been very bright as elephants go, but he was gentle and biddable, he had been very carefully taught, and he had done exactly the same repertoire of tricks for so many years now that the performance was as natural as eating.

"It cannot be a barrage balloon," said Thevenet. "They are only used in war and there is no war. Someone would have told us." He took a few steps forward. "It is a figment of the imagination."

At that moment someone in a neighboring house turned on the radio, cheerful music could distinctly be heard, and the Educated Elephant took heart again. The orchestra, at least, was performing its duties. One started by tossing rubber balls to the audience; he looked about for the rubber balls.

"It is an elephant," said Frachot, and also advanced a few paces, with Delor beside him. Ernie saw them and was further encouraged, it was a poor house but there at least was the front row. The show must go on; he took one solemn pace forward, still looking for something to throw.

"It is a barrage balloon, I tell you," said Delor obstinately. "It has got stuck in that narrow street and there are soldiers behind it pushing it out." Ernie took another pace forward. "There, you see?"

There was, unfortunately, a pile beside the pavement of those oblong granite setts called *pavé* with which the French still cover too many of their roads. When after the lapse of centuries they become so worn that there is an epidemic of broken ankles, they are sparsely replaced. Ernie saw them and neatly picked one up.

"It is, in fact, an elephant," said Frachot.

"It is a figment of the imagination," insisted Thevenet. "We have a slight disorder of the liver. I prescribe—"

Ernie swung the sett and hurled it at them; it missed them by several feet and went through the window of a greengrocer's shop behind. There was a resounding crash and a clatter as things fell down and a stack of melons rolled out into the street. Ernie took the noise to be applause and continued to throw.

"Figments of the imagination," said Frachot loftily, "do not, my dear Thevenet, hurl things. Let us pursue our road."

"I lodge a protest," said Delor angrily, "I shall complain to the Commander-in-Chief. It is the rumbustious and dissolute soldiery—"

But one of Ernie's missiles caught him in the middle and he folded up, dropping the bottle which he was brandishing. There was no crash, for it never reached the ground. Three stupefied gentlemen, clinging to each other, watched with passionate disbelief the portly form of a seal flopping down the middle of the street with a bottle balanced on his nose.

Doors opened, windows were thrown up, and people began to gather. The audience were assembling at last and Ernie moved forward cheerfully. This was going down well, after all, the people were actually shouting. Something else to throw—ah! These nice round things—

The first of a flight of melons sailed through the air as Frachot, Delor, and Thevenet went on their homeward way.

"The town seems, tonight, a little less quiet than usual," said Delor. "Can that be a monkey on that lamppost?"

Frachot nodded. "One would say," he remarked, "a *kermesse zoologique.*"

Chapter X
A Wreath of Monkeys

THE INNKEEPER who had previously entertained Frachot and his friends had had a few more customers in and was thinking of closing for the night when the door opened rather uncertainly with much handle-rattling. He looked across the room and saw to his disgust the small red-jacketed monkey who had so discomposed him earlier in the evening, while behind him an attendant train of six other similar little horrors, clad only in their native fur, filed in one behind the other holding tails as they had been taught. With glazing eyes the innkeeper looked on while Ulysses hopped up to sit on the bar and the others, chattering happily, arranged themselves on chairs round a table, for this was a part of their accustomed act. They all settled down and looked at him.

The innkeeper sighed heavily, took down seven glasses, and filled them with the same muscat, for had he not been paid? He gave Ulysses one, set the others round the table, and retired behind the bar to give himself a stiff dose of cognac. A café keeper must serve all who come, but if there was much more of this he would give up the café and go in for cabbages instead. Cabbages, at worst, only harbor caterpillars.

The six at the table were not very adroit; they were used to handling mugs, not glasses, and it was the first time they had tasted wine. Ulysses finished his glass neatly and handed it back to be refilled. This was a mistake; Charles, who knew Ulysses' limitations, would not have allowed it. Ulysses tossed it off rather hurriedly, set down the glass, put his paws over his eyes, and suddenly rolled off the bar.

The other six instantly scrambled down. Three of them picked up Ulysses by whatever limb came handiest and carried him to the open door; the other three, dutifully holding tails, followed behind in line astern and so all passed into the night.

The café proprietor rushed to the door and leaned out to make sure that they were indeed gone; the next instant he dodged back as two kangaroos, traveling fast, passed by within a foot of him and out of sight.

He was still staring after them when an ungainly movement in the road caught his eye and one of his own advertisements came to life, the familiar Cinzano picture of a seal balancing a bottle on its nose. That, also, passed by.

The proprietor backed inside; slammed, locked, and bolted the door; switched out the lights and rushed upstairs to bed, shouting to his wife that he had retired and that when she came up she could undress in the dark, she was not to switch on the light on any account. He had, he said, seen enough. He then hurled himself into bed and hid his head under the bedclothes.

The proprietor of Besançon's weekly paper had heard rumors that there had been serious irregularities in recent army contracts and that at any moment there would be revelations, scandals, and exposés which would shake Besançon to its deepest roots. He therefore kept a reporter on duty at the telephone waiting for a call from a well-paid friend at garrison headquarters; upon this night the unwilling night watchman was Pierre Champeaux, short, impatient, snub-nosed, and twenty-three. He grumbled about his assignment.

"Nothing," he said to his friend the sports reporter, who was preparing to go home, "ever happens in Besançon, never. Especially after nightfall. Yet the Old Man insists that one stays here all night long attached to this infernal telephone."

"But," said his colleague, "there is no actual hardship in spending a night in a comfortable armchair such as that in which I now see you sitting, and if nothing happens outside you will not have missed anything."

"Yes, I shall. I had a date with a girl."

His friend shrugged his shoulders. "There will be other nights." He took his hat down from its peg and went out.

The office was busy, for this was the time when they "put the paper to bed"; it would be published in the morning. Sub-editors and all their train, compositors, printers, and others swirled through the building upon frenzied errands while the typesetters, who read print mirror-fashion faster than most men can read it straight, sweated over their frames and cursed the compositors, who cursed the sub-editors, who cursed the reporters, and all together united to curse the advertisers, which is most ungrateful, for it is advertisers who make a paper pay. In the midst of all this turmoil Pierre Champeaux twisted his legs round those of his chair and cursed the day he had taken up journalism. Presently his telephone rang and he snatched off the receiver.

"Is that Pericles?" said a careful voice at the other end.

"Yes," said Champeaux, replying to a previously arranged gambit, "and you are Socrates. Well?'

"He has come," said the cautious voice.

"Who? And where?"

"The General." The speaker added a surname and the reporter whistled softly. "He is here at headquarters. He will review everybody and everything tomorrow morning. There will be a demonstration of mortar bombing tomorrow afternoon."

"Good, that is as it should be," said Champeaux cheerfully. "That is what Generals are for. Why this fuss?"

The other speaker lowered his voice yet further. "He has sent for the Quartermasters' records. He has brought a staff of experts with him and they are spending the night going through them. Tell the Old Man that. At once."

"Certainly," said the reporter cheerfully, and put down the receiver. If that were all, he might yet meet Giselle. Before he had time to lift the receiver to call the proprietor's private address, the telephone rang again.

"Besançon *Clarion,*" said the reporter.

"There is," said a solemn voice, "a seal in the cattle trough at the market place."

"The kind one bangs on hot sealing-wax?"

"No. The kind that swims in northern waters."

"Thank you," said Champeaux. "We will send somebody down. Who are you, please?"

"It is balancing a bottle on its nose," said the voice.

"Is it, also," enquired the reporter, "surrounded by a light cloud of performing butterflies?"

"Young man," said the voice severely, "I do not jest. I am a Pastor of the Protestant Reformed Church." There was a click as the speaker rang off.

"Some people," said Champeaux sadly, "think themselves funny." He put back the receiver, the bell rang again at once, and he lifted the receiver once more.

"Is that the Besançon *Clarion?*"

"Oh yes," said Champeaux eagerly. "Is that you, Giselle? Look, I will be with you in—"

"My name is not Giselle," said the feminine voice tartly, "and I desire no impertinence."

"I beg a thousand pardons—"

The lady gave her name and address and added: "I have been trying to ring the police and the fire brigade but both numbers are engaged. There are monkeys in the bathroom. I wish them removed."

"But, naturally, madame. This is, however, only the office of the local paper. May I suggest that perhaps Madame's doctor would be more—"

"How dare you!"

Click!

"This," said Champeaux decidedly, "is a gang of the boys and girls having a game with me. I should have thought I should have recognized their voices, but no. Doubtless they disguise them. Now I ring up the Old Man."

He replaced the receiver once more and immediately the bell rang again.

"Besançon *Clarion!*"

"Please," said a childish voice, "my maman is out and I have just seen two kangaroos go past the house. I was looking out of the window."

"Listen carefully," said the reporter. "Were they wearing tall hats and carrying harps?"

"No. No, nothing like that. Just plain kangaroos."

"Then they were not real and you need not take any notice. You just pop into bed and think about something else." Champeaux rang off and managed, this time, to deliver the message to the proprietor, who received it with a series of noncommittal grunts.

"Will that be all tonight, sir?"

"Yes. No. Wait a minute. Yes, you can go now but call me again in an hour's time."

"Very good," said Champeaux insincerely. He hung up the receiver, seized his hat, and rushed out of the office before any more practical jokers could get at him, but in the passage outside he met one of the sub-editors.

"You've been getting a lot of calls," he said. "Anything interesting?"

"On the contrary. A lot of silly so-and-sos playing practical jokes."

"Some people," said the sub-editor bitterly, "think themselves funny. *What's that?*"

He extended an ink-stained finger and pointed at the window opposite to them. A telephone wire passed by it some six feet away to lead into the building by the side of a window at right angles to theirs, that of the composing-room. Along this wire there passed, swinging by their arms, a procession of monkeys on their way towards the window.

"Someone," said Champeaux dazedly, "rang me up about monkeys, but I thought it was a hoax."

The sub-editor, shouting instructions to shut the windows, all of them, turned and dashed into the composing-room but he was too late. There were yells and excited squeals and then a resounding crash. A compositor, in the act of carrying from the room one of the big *formes* which produce one page of the paper, had been clasped round the neck by a monkey and had dropped his burden. It fell face downwards and all the lines and columns of type, wedged in place after the old-fashioned manner, fell out and were scattered across the floor. Instantly all the other men in the room, with cries of horror, abandoned their work to repel monkeys who flashed about the room, gibbered from the tops of cupboards, threw anything movable, and dodged out of the doors to spread alarm and despondency throughout the building.

"Who let those brutes loose?"

"That was my front page!"

"Get down the town, Champeaux," shouted the sub-editor above the din. "Get the story!"

By this time half the town was up, for seventy-nine unbridled monkeys will destroy any peace. They ran up stackpipes to the roofs or dodged in at open bedroom windows to leap upon already occupied beds or fight their mirrored reflections upon dressing tables. Eldritch screams floated down from upper windows to augment the growing babble in the street below and several people rang up the fire brigade. There were monkeys on the roof, let them be instantly removed. The fire brigade turned out at once with an engine and fire escape, but was then at something of a loss.

"My training," said one of the firemen, "though singularly extensive, did not include catching monkeys. How is it done?"

Several people eagerly told him.

"You need but to go up and look at them. They will all think you are their papa and follow you home."

"Take a butterfly net."

"Throw them a rope and pull them down."

"Offer them some nuts."

"Sing to them!"

"Play the hose on them."

This reasonable suggestion was tried out, but the monkeys merely took refuge inside the houses—some even slipped down chimneys and emerged in fireplaces, bringing soot—and the inhabitants of such houses evacuated them with cries.

Champeaux rang up his office from a street call box.

"The wild animals at the moment infesting Besançon," he reported, "appear to be part of the stock of Michel Brochier, wild-animal dealer. He is not at home tonight, having gone to Autun to visit his daughter, the amiable Madame Claude-Alexandrine Bergerand-Dubois, who has recently been confined."

"Are there lions?" asked the sub-editor.

"Not yet. Kangaroos, but not, hitherto, lions."

"What are the kangaroos doing?"

"They pass by, leaping together, after the manner of kangaroos. No more than that."

"And the monkeys?"

The monkeys, or some of them, were upon the roof of Besançon's biggest department store. It had a number of flagpoles for ceremonial occasions permanently fixed at an angle from the parapet; the monkeys were climbing briskly up these and sliding happily down again. The leading fireman ordered the escape ladder to be run up to the roof.

"Get up these, men," he said. "Get a move on."

Champeaux, making a further report from a shop just opposite, described the scene. "There is also," he added "an elephant which advances with ponderous dignity. The fire chief, gazing upwards, does not see it. Now he does. He climbs up the ladder until his head is upon a level with that of the monstrous pachyderm, which extends its trunk towards him in a gesture of touching simplicity. The fire chief speaks, I hear him. He says: 'I am desolated, monsieur, but I have no buns.' His voice is shaken with emotion. A window opens near by and there is something long which comes out. The blunderbuss of our grandfathers? No, it is a trombone and behind it a dimly lit figure which extends it towards the ear of the elephant. Ha! Did you hear that? He blew a fearful blast. The elephant removes himself at a smart pace, the concourse scattering before him."

Ernie lumbered off up the street at a heavy trot till he reached the green-grocery with the broken window. Here he renewed his energies with a few cabbages, a score or so of cauliflowers, and all the celery in the shop before wandering on again. It was a nice night and there was no hurry.

The girl on night duty at the telephone exchange was, naturally, insulated from the sights and sounds of the outside world and she was not listening in to any of the calls she put through because she was writing to her fiancé, compared with whom the rest of Besançon did not, in any real sense, exist. After a time, however, she had an uncomfortable feeling that she was being stared at; she glanced over her shoulder and saw three small brown monkeys sitting on a bench watching her intently; even as she looked the door swung open a few inches and a fourth sidled in.

She gave one startled scream, rushed out of the office, and locked herself in the toilet.

The monkeys took no notice of her, it was the board which interested them. It was a large, upright thing upon which buzzers sounded, lights went on and off, and a thing like an eye at the top of each column opened and shut when a plug was stuck into one of a row of holes. They had been watching for some time. They scrambled up on her chair and tried for themselves. It was easy. One just pushed a plug in and another and another; when one tired of that one pulled them out again.

Telephone bells rang all over Besançon and the most unexpected conversations were taking place. The sacristan of the Eglise St. Madeleine found himself discussing silk underwear with the proprietor of a ladies' outfitters who was expecting a call from Lyons and could not be persuaded that this was not it; at a particularly involved point in the argument they were inadvertently joined by the night watchman at the railway works, who wanted to tell the fire brigade that there were monkeys all over his cranes.

At the hotel, where the Latimers and the rest of the coach party were staying, the uproar in the streets demanded attention; when it was understood that there were monkeys involved, the staff rushed round the place shutting windows and James and Charles looked at each other.

"Monkeys," said James uneasily.

"It cannot be Ulysses," said Charles, laughing, "for he is only one and there seem to be dozens of them."

They got up from their seats in the lounge and strolled to the front door to stand upon the steps and survey the night. The streets were full of a loose throng of people rushing in groups from one place to another, chattering excitedly. Even as the Latimers watched, the groups parted to let two kangaroos go by; leaping solemnly together, they went on out of sight.

"Definitely not Ulysses," said Charles with a sigh of relief.

"No indeed," agreed James. "This is some menagerie which has broken loose. Shall we return within, Cousin? There may be lions also and we are not armed."

"True, true. Not that we need arms to protect us, but the animals might alarm the ladies." They turned to go in. "Look up there, Cousin! High up."

Upon a concourse of telephone wires high above the houses, a wreath of monkeys capered across the moon.

Besançon is very much a garrison town, with four or five barracks and no less than six forts upon the circle of hills which hem in the town, besides the Citadel, which closes the loop of the River Doub as a clasp closes a necklace. The visiting General was staying in the visiting General's quarters in one of the barracks, a pleasant one-story building upon one side of the parade ground, at right angles to the entrance gate. He had retired early to his quarters, accompanied by his financial staff and a quite appalling pile of Quartermasters' records.

The Educated Elephant had still, in the recesses of a dim but conscientious mind, a sense of duties unperformed. He was strolling about looking for a show ground. When, therefore, he came to a pair of wide gates standing open with a large expanse of gravel inside and, at the far end, a brilliantly lighted verandah with men toiling busily upon it, he stopped and his great ears went up. He watched them for a few minutes; they were arranging round missiles in neat piles. Ha!

In point of fact, they were fusing mortar bombs in readiness for next day's practice.

Ernie put himself in motion and rolled majestically in at the gate. The sentry tried to stop him but Ernie drew a long breath, placed the end of his trunk against the man's face, and blew. The sentry sat down with a bump which shook him to the teeth and Ernie walked on. The men working on the verandah looked up to see an elephant advancing and shouted, waving their arms; he took this to be encouragement and broke into a trot.

The round missiles had each a short handle projecting from it, very convenient to hold; Ernie picked one up and swung it thoughtfully and all the soldiers immediately fled. Quite right. Stagehands off the set. Ernie whirled the bomb round three times and let go.

It sailed up into the moonlit air, turned, and came down again to burst with a shattering crash upon the roof of the General's quarters.

Chapter XI
The Educated Elephant

THE EXPLOSION was heard all over Besançon, and even the rollicking monkeys blenched. Ernie, with a scream of terror, rushed out of the gate and through the streets straight to Michel Brochier's yard, where he walked into his own stable and put himself to bed. When, therefore, the General in shirt and trousers—for he also was preparing for bed—struggled out of a window from the ruins of his quarters, there was nothing to be seen except a few heads peering round corners and the sentry nervously emerging from his box.

The General was, of course, a regular soldier and had been trained to project his voice. His remarks were clearly audible over the whole of the parade ground and in every room of the buildings surrounding it, from which officers, noncommissioned officers, and men emerged in every stage of undress from practically scratch to the Colonel, who wore a dressing gown over pajamas. The sentry resumed his beat with a smartness which would have been a credit to the palmy days of Versailles. One would say clockwork.

The General did not. He said that a dastardly attempt had been made to assassinate him, probably by Communists, and that the sentry should be shot forthwith. The Colonel, when he had managed to recognize his distinguished visitor under a thick coating of soot and ceiling plaster, ordered the gates to be closed and asked if any unauthorized person had been seen. When the Sergeant in charge of the working party fusing bombs said well, no, only an elephant, the General's comments passed beyond the confines of the barracks to be heard two streets away, and there followed a shocked silence in which it was possible to hear the rising tumult in the streets of the town below.

"Listen!" said the General. "I tell you it is a Communist rising. Turn your men out, Colonel, and patrol the streets."

The Colonel saluted. "Blow the *alerte!*" he said.

The order was transmitted. "Blow the *alerte,*" said the hierarchy of officers in descending order until it reached the French equivalent of an R.S.M. "Blow the *alerte,*" he said. "Where the inextinguishable blazes is that metaphorically unborn child of misdemeanor, the bugler? Come here! Stand there! Blow the *alerte!*"

For a few moments there was no sound but bounding feet on the gravel as the regiment rushed indoors to get dressed and equipped, and then the boy fitted the bugle to his lips, drew a long breath, and blew. The high silvery notes soared up into the night sky to be heard by the sentries of Fort de Brégille,

Fort Beauregard, Fort Griffon, and the rest; one after another they took up the call until all the forts of Besançon were crowing against each other in thin, high notes like cocks at earliest dawn and the sound ran round the hills.

The Colonel took the General by the arm. "Come to my quarters," he urged. "Bath. Coffee. Cognac—"

"Hell and damnation," snapped the General, "look at my quarters now! The place is on fire."

"No, no," said the Colonel, who had come out without his glasses. "It is only the dust which is still rising."

But there was a burst of flame, the fire-fighting squad was called out and came, running, with buckets to form a chain from the nearest tap. The General watched them sourly.

"Is there a fire brigade in this town?" he asked.

"But certainly, *mon Général.*"

"Let them be summoned. This has been arranged in order to destroy the Quartermasters' records."

But the telephone appeared to be out of order and a despatch rider was sent into the town to deliver the message in person. He came back a quarter of an hour later to say that they would come at once. He had had to hunt for them in the town; they were all out chasing monkeys.

"Chasing—" said the R.S.M.

"Monkeys, *mon Sergent.*"

"Indeed," said the R.S.M. in such a comparatively mild voice that the despatch rider nearly asked him if he did not feel well. The Sergeant walked across to the sentry at the gate.

"Did you," asked the Sergeant, "see any kind of unusual animal about just before all this uproar started?"

"Certainly, *mon Sergent.* An elephant."

"You saw it, too," said the R.S.M. ominously.

"Certainly, *mon Sergent.* It rushed in at the gate, knocked me down with one swing of its trunk, trampled over my prostrate body, and rushed on. Before I could pick myself up there was a loud bang and it rushed out again."

"Why did you not fire at it?"

"What?" said the soldier, horrified. "When it might have been government property?"

"Listen," said the Sergeant. "That was not an elephant. It was a Communist."

"What?" said the sentry feebly.

"You heard me. A Communist."

"A—a Russian Communist?"

"I have not been informed," said the Sergeant, "of its exact nationality."

"Who says so?" asked the sentry mutinously.

"Don't take that tone to me," said the R.S.M. sharply. "The General says so."

"Oh," said the sentry blankly, "does he?"

"So now you know," said the R.S.M., "and any more back chat about elephants from you and you'll find yourself on a charge for being asleep on guard." There came to their ears the sound of motor-lorry engines being started up and the yard began to fill with men, properly dressed this time. The R.S.M. went away to see to it.

One cannot have it said that a distinguished General has turned out a regiment to repel a Communist rising because an elephant has strayed on to the parade ground.

The Besançon fire brigade leader received the despatch rider's message with relief amounting to enthusiasm. Fires were his job, not wild animals, and here was an order from the commanding officer of a regiment concerning a fire which had involved a General. He saw himself being thanked, rewarded, decorated by the General in person and, best of all, getting away from those infernal monkeys. At his frenzied urging, the fire engine gathered up its hose and roared off up the street, with the escape hot upon its tail and winding down the ladder as it went.

Champeaux telephoned again, not waiting in his excitement for the official reply: "Besançon *Clarion*."

"A disastrous fire has broken out—the General's life endangered—our intrepid fire brigade has dashed to the rescue, leaving, in its haste, a number of its personnel marooned upon a high roof. Their plaintive cries can be heard in the street below. 'Ladders,' they cry, 'ladders. Our duty calls and we cannot answer it.' The concourse below makes suggestions: they should slide down the stackpipes, they should slip down the chimneys, they should obtain umbrellas for use as parachutes—"

"No doubt," said a deep voice at the other end, "the ultimate outcome of such activities will come to be my concern in due course, but why ring me up now?"

"Who are you?"

"I have the honor to be the Custodian of Besançon Municipal Cemetery."

Even as Champeaux dropped the receiver he heard the siren at the railway works start up with a rising howl, rise to its top note, and go on and on and on. The reporter dashed into the street and ran towards the sound, but it was difficult to get along. The rumor of a Communist rising had spread; in addition to the crowds on foot the streets were further impacted by cars containing whole families and such valuables as they could snatch up in haste. The prudent citizens of Besançon were taking to the woods.

Champeaux reached the gate of the railway works at last. The siren, which was upon the roof of a tall, narrow block of office buildings, was worked by a cord which passed down the wall to the ground. Someone had swiveled a searchlight upon this cord and there, just below the roof, was a small monkey in a little red jacket and cap. Ulysses had run up the cord to escape the night watchman and was too terrified even to vanish. He was, besides, still not very clear in the head. The crowd had started by laughing but was now becoming annoyed, and at this point the first of the lorry loads of soldiers from the barracks pushed through to the gate.

"Where," they said, "are these disorderly rioters that we may deal with them?"

"There are no rioters," the night watchman explained through the grille. "There is only a monkey on the rope. Look."

The soldiers looked and laughed. "Why don't you go up and get him down?"

"What?" said the night watchman indignantly. "Me?"

There was an angry snarl from the crowd. "Shoot the little beast down and let's get some peace."

The soldiers hesitated. "That's someone's pet," said the Corporal in charge, "dressed up like that. Probably valuable."

One of his men made a suggestion in an undertone. "We might shoot, we needn't hit him. Put a bullet alongside him. Might frighten him off."

The Corporal nodded. "You're not a bad shot yourself, you do it. Careful, now."

The soldier loaded his rifle, steadied himself against the cab of the lorry, took careful aim, and fired. Ulysses saw the flash, the bullet smacked into the grimy brickwork beside his head, and he promptly vanished. The siren stopped with a descending howl and there was silence.

"Didn't see it go," said the soldier, staring.

"Never mind," said the Corporal, "it's gone. Over the roof, no doubt." The lorry moved on.

The coach party left early the following morning since they had before them the mountainous run to Andermatt. As they drove through the streets, the cleaners were busy sweeping up broken glass, tiles, and other debris; near the market place the coach passed a hand truck pushed by two men, and the amiable features of the performing seal nodded solemnly over the side. For some miles out of the town the coach met loaded cars returning from woods and pastures, the citizens of Besançon were coming home.

"I wonder whether all the animals have been recaptured," said James.

Charles laughed. "Ulysses was out on the ran-tan too, Cousin," he said in a low tone. "He came in very late, very dusty, and rather sorry for himself."

"Serve him right," said James severely. "He should behave himself more seemly."

The coach went on steadily climbing, in sweeping curves, the foothills of the Jura Mountains; they drove through dusty Pontarlier to pass into Switzerland at Les Verrières. The moment they had crossed the frontier it was noticeable how much cleaner and neater were the houses, the villages, and even the roadsides.

"The Swiss," said James approvingly, "had always a commendable degree of self-respect."

"Most praiseworthy," said Charles, "but why the cats?"

"Cats?"

"In the fields. To every field one cat or even more."

James leaned across his cousin to look out of the window and saw that it was quite true. Nor were the cats idly sleeping in the sun, they were alert and prowling.

"To diminish the number of field mice?"

They drove on through Neuchâtel to lunch at Berne; to admire the numerous fountains in the streets, each topped by a carved figure, dramatic or grotesque, and to pay a short visit to the immemorial bears. Early in the afternoon the coach began to climb in earnest while all about their road the cold giants of the Swiss Alps looked down indifferently upon the crawling beetle below, until they entered a valley closed at the end by a mountain with a zigzag line scored upon its face and here and there supported by massive terraces.

One of the party leaned forward to ask a question. "Mr. Fowler! Is that a road, high up, ahead of us?"

"Not only a road," answered Fowler, "that is our road. It is called the Susten Pass."

"Oh! Are we going right up there? Ooh!"

Up and up, with the driver swinging the long coach round one hairpin bend after another, right and left and right alternately, occasionally running through short tunnels of dripping rock, while the valley dropped away below them until the houses looked as small as matchboxes scattered upon a green rug and the grazing cattle shrank to the size of small dogs and then became indistinguishable altogether. Up and up, with the passengers exclaiming at the first sight of snowdrifts beside the road, and still up till there was the snow all about them and, away on the right, a frozen lake with a glacier eternally sliding into it by inches in the year; on every hand were waterfalls, spouting white and swaying in their fall.

There was not much traffic on that road, mainly private cars cautiously descending in an intermediate gear or standing at some of the wider viewpoints to cool their brakes. As the coach came up to one of the sharper bends, there was the sound of a two-note horn upon the next stretch above and the coach driver immediately pulled in to the side of the road to let pass a yellow bus with the emblem of a post horn painted upon its sides.

"Now I find that strange," said James, addressing the courier. "In my young days traffic going uphill had always the right-of-way."

"It still has," answered Fowler, "with that one exception. Everyone, going up or down, must give way to the postal bus. Of course, they carry the mails. Excuse me."

The driver had been balked of a sufficiently wide sweep to take the corner; he stopped halfway round and backed while the courier leapt down into the road to direct him.

"All right, Michel. All right. Another yard. All right. Stop now."

The passengers in the back seats were, naturally, sitting on the overhang of the coach; they looked down from their windows and saw nothing beneath them but the valley a mile below. There were a few quiet exclamations and Charles laughed.

"What amuses you, Cousin?" asked James.

"Some of our rear passengers repenting their sins and promising amendment of life."

"I dare to say that, in their condition, we might have felt the same," said James kindly. "This little experience may even have a permanently salutary effect upon some, who knows?"

The courier sprang into his seat and the coach moved on again; there was a general feeling of relief as they crossed the wide, level space at the summit and started carefully down the other side. The sun came out, and it became perceptibly warmer as the southern valley opened and spread before them. The little town of Goeschenen lies at the foot; as they approached it, the Rome Express slid by upon the adjacent railway lines, bound for the St. Gothard tunnel and the South.

More questions from the coach passengers. "What's the St. Gothard Pass like, Mr. Fowler? Is it as bad as the Susten?"

"It's a better road," said the courier cautiously.

"But I suppose we've done with those awful corners for today?"

"There are one or two more," said Fowler cheerfully, "between here and Andermatt. But we haven't much farther to go, now."

The hairpin bends between Goeschenen and Andermatt are far worse than anything on the Susten, largely because the road has either not been rebuilt, or is in process of being so. However, the coach had to back only once and the passengers took the strain better that time; they ran into Andermatt as the dusk was falling.

There was the usual delay while the members of the coach party were allotted rooms; the Latimers, being the newest recruits, went out to the front door while this business was going on and looked up at the green hills above them, tree-clad on their lower slopes.

"I think, Charles, there would be some pleasant walking upon those green slopes. It is a pity that we are not longer here."

Charles agreed. "There is indeed, James, something in this air which fills one with the urge to climb mountains. I wonder whether—"

But he was interrupted by the courier, who, with the hotel proprietor, had come out to find them.

"Mr. Latimer—Major Latimer—I am most terribly sorry, but the proprietor here tells me that he is a room short. Some people are not moving out so soon as had been arranged. Would you mind very much being housed for the night at a small *pension* just down the road? It is a decent, clean place and you would, of course, have your meals here."

The proprietor added his apologies, he was most upset at having to transplant guests of their quality, but the only room he had vacant was unsuitable at the moment. It was not clear as to why the room was unsuitable and James assumed that it was probably small and dark or in need of redecoration.

"I am sure," he said, "that any arrangements which you and Mr. Fowler make for our accommodation will be quite admirable, but indeed we are not unreasonably fastidious, we are seasoned travelers. Even if your spare room is not one of your best I have no doubt but that it will serve us well enough."

The proprietor continued to display embarrassment, Fowler grinned covertly, and Charles' curiosity awoke.

"Tell me frankly, sir, what is the matter with this room of yours? Is it over the kitchen? Has it no window, no light, or even no bed?"

"On the contrary," said the proprietor, "the room is one of my best, upon the first floor with superior furnishings and a balcony."

"In that case," began James.

"But it is haunted," said the proprietor. Fowler laughed and the proprietor, turning upon him, said it was no laughing matter. "One of my best rooms," he mourned. "The loss! It is true it is only intermittently haunted, there are times when it is quite wholesome and pleasant, but only yesterday morning a most respectable married couple vacated it at two o'clock in the morning in their nightwear and refused to return even to pack their clothes."

"But that is delightful," said Charles.

"Delightful?" said the proprietor.

"Certainly. Delightful. We are something of experts in these matters, are we not, Cousin? Yes, sir. I will go so far as to say that we revel in them. Cousin, you will bear me out."

"Assuredly," said James. "We are phantasmophiles."

"Golly," said Fowler.

"Come, sir," said Charles, as it were, shooing the proprietor towards the stairs, "lead on to your haunted chamber."

Chapter XII
The Quiet Man

THE ROOM to which the Latimers were shown was large and pleasant. Its balcony looked across at the wooded hillock where the little white church looks down upon its parishioners and the last colors of the sunset still hung in the western sky. The Latimer luggage was brought up, the porter was tipped, and the door closed behind him.

"I say," said a hesitant, rather husky voice, "what are you two fellows doing here? Have you been sent to keep me c-company?"

The Latimers turned from the window. The young man was half lying in a comfortable attitude as one may lounge upon a bed, raised upon an elbow and with one foot just touching the floor. He was sandy-haired and freckled, with a snub nose and an obstinate mouth; the only thing at all remarkable about his appearance was that he was not lying upon anything but was apparently suspended in the air. "I haven't met anyone like you," he continued, "since I became one myself. It is quite a relief to have someone to talk to. I have tried so often but they only scream and run away."

"We were not sent, except in so far as all our actions are guided, as you know," said James. "For all we know, this meeting is accidental. Who are you and why do you stay here if you do not like it?"

"My name is Henry Mortimer," said the ghost, "and I am staying on here in the hope of c-c-clearing up a certain matter connected with my premature decease."

"And can you not attain your end?"

"No. I have made no progress so far."

"I hope that you may soon be more successful," said James politely.

"Sir," broke in Charles, "would you oblige me by taking a seat on something? Forgive me if I incommode you, your state of incomplete transference is one of which we have no experience and I allow that you may be entirely at your ease. But to see you hanging in the air as in an invisible hammock—"

Mortimer smiled and apologized. "The bed used to be this side," he explained, "I k-keep on forgetting they have moved it. Stupid of me. Bad form, too, showing off." He rose to his feet, crossed the room, and sat down upon their bed. "Is that better?"

"A little lower," said Charles, inspecting him, "you are not quite touching the quilt. Not too low, you are going through it. It must be plaguey awkward to be in your condition."

"You look solid enough," said Mortimer a little enviously.

"We are," said James. "We are, in all material respects, human. We eat and drink and occupy space so long as we are materialized. The only thing which we can do which mortals cannot is to vanish." He suited the action to the word. "And reappear again, of course." He did so. "We have no intermediate stage like yours."

"That's very odd," said Mortimer, staring. "Did you say vanish? To me the only difference was that you did not cast a shadow."

"By Jove," said James, "now that is odd."

"Whereas in your case," said Charles, "You are always in the same condition, are you? You cannot appear and disappear at will?"

"Why, no," said Mortimer. "The only thing is that some people c-can see me and others c-cannot. The last people in this room saw me very plainly but they were infernally rude about me. They told the landlord that I made faces at them and smelt of sulphur. As though I would!"

"Deuced disconcerting," said Charles. "Yes, sir. I opine that you suffer severely from frustration."

"I am like a prisoner in a glass box," said the young man violently. "It isn't fair. I didn't do anything wrong. I was slandered and murdered and I c-can't even tell anyone about it."

"With every sympathy for your unhappy predicament," said James firmly, "I must point out that it is entirely your own doing. You are like a man who is sent upon a journey but who, instead of completing it, springs out at an intermediate station and refuses to go on. It is no wonder that you have no place and no company. I have heard of the state you are in, it is called Limbo."

The young man wilted before this blast and the softer-hearted Charles was sorry for him.

"Perhaps we may be able to help you," he said. "Sir, if we can, we shall be happy to do anything possible. Eh, Cousin James?"

"Certainly," said James, feeling that he had been a little harsh, "certainly. My comment had to be made, but pray believe that we are your true friends. Allow us a little time to think it over, and if any course of action commends itself to you, pray inform us."

"In any case," said Charles, "it is now the time when we should go in to dinner with our companions. I confess your mountain air has given me an appetite. I take it, sir, that you do not appear for meals?"

"No," said Mortimer. "I do not require food. How nice to feel hungry!"

"Take heart," said James. "There must be some way out of your troubles."

"After dinner," promised Charles, "we will return here. Sir, I suggest that later this evening we should all repair to some other hotel here and take a glass of wine together. You are too downcast, you live too retired, you need your faculties to be restored. You should divert yourself and make merry sometimes; drive dull care away, Mr. Mortimer. Yes, sir, that is what I think."

Mortimer smiled wanly. "What, in my c-condition?"

"Oh, perk up, sir," said Charles. "With our help you might manage something."

"Besides," encouraged James, "you may feel yourself stronger after dark."

When they returned to their room they said that there was a good place to which they had been recommended, the Schweizerhof. A good bar, music, and cheerful company.

"I know the place," said Mortimer. "My partner always stayed there whenever he came to Andermatt and I have been in there with him once or twice."

"Perhaps," said Charles, struck by the strong distaste in his tone, "You would rather go elsewhere?"

"On the c-contrary," said Mortimer, "I should like to go there again. I might even chance to see him and I should like that very much," he added in a sarcastic voice. "By the way, you said something about your c-companions. Are there, then, a number of you going about together?"

"Dear me, no," said James. "Our companions are just ordinary mortals and have no notion that we are any different. We are, in fact, upon a coach tour."

"You've got a nerve!" said Mortimer, laughing. "I never heard of such a thing. What are you doing, then, just taking time off for a holiday?"

"Oh no. We should never have the impertinence to suggest that. No, it is a long story, with which I need not trouble you, but there is a small matter in Italy, involving our family, to which we are allowed to attend and we are making our way thither."

"Well, Mr. Mortimer," said Charles, "how do you find yourself now? Shall we venture forth?"

They all went out together, down the stairs and into the street. Some of the coach party, loitering in the hotel entrance, spoke to James and Charles as they passed but took no notice of Henry Mortimer. There were a good many people about in the village, strolling about or standing in groups; the Latimers and their companion made their way between them, talking as they went. Mortimer named the hills, dark against the translucent evening sky, and described the avalanche of earth and stones which had done such damage to the village a year or two earlier; he seemed happy to be out and was walking confidently, looking about him, when suddenly his face fell and he was plainly disconcerted.

"What is it?" asked Charles.

"I am not normal, you know. I feel all right, but did you notice that man in the green hat? He walked right through me. I don't like it."

"I am sorry for that," said James kindly, "I did not notice. Did the process give you any pain or—er—disarrange you in any way?"

"Oh no. Not at all. A faint quivering sensation, not unpleasant. He nearly fell over the monkey, too; he didn't seem to see it."

"Monkey?"

"A small monkey which appears to be following us. Someone's pet, it wears a jacket and—oh, now I see. Is it yours?"

"My cousin's," said James.

They turned into the Schweizerhof, entered the lounge, and strolled up to the bar. There were a number of people already there and Mortimer looked about among them.

"Do you know anyone here?" asked Charles.

"No. But someone I know might possibly come in."

The bartender came to them and Charles ordered three glasses of red wine.

"Three, monsieur?" said the barman in surprise.

"Yes, please. We always order three," said Charles airily. When the wine came he pushed one glass in the direction of Mortimer, who was upon his left, picked up his own, and said: "Your health, sir. And yours, Cousin James."

"Chin, chin," said Mortimer mechanically. Then, in a suppressed wail: "I c-can't pick it up!"

"Pardon, monsieur?" said the barman.

"It's my hand," said Charles hurriedly. "Rheumatism, you know. I must use my left."

"Monsieur has my sympathy," said the barman. "This rheumatism, what it gives us! Monsieur has it in the one hand only?"

"Writer's cramp, actually," said Charles, beaming upon him. "I am a poet."

"Indeed! Most interesting. The sparkling lyric of the noble epic?"

"Cookery recipes," said Charles blandly, "translated from the Chinese. Would you care to hear one or two?"

The barman said that at some other time he would be honored. He hurried away and Charles was able to turn his attention to Mortimer.

"Pray, sir, what ails you? Sir, I cannot describe the distressing effect produced when you slip sideways into the bar like that. It is as though you had been bisected at the midriff and set upon the bar like some memorial bust—worse, for you don't keep still."

"It is that monkey," said Mortimer, looking down over his shoulder.

"Cousin Charles," said James firmly, "if that animal of yours sees fit to materialize now I shall be very seriously annoyed. One at a time is enough, upon my soul."

"It's all right," said Charles, "I won't allow him to appear. It is only our guest who sees him."

But Ulysses, excitable and inquisitive like all monkeys, was taking an enthralled interest in Mortimer. Charles could prevent him from materializing but he could not suppress him altogether.

"He's dancing round me," said Mortimer nervously, backing into the bar until he coalesced with a plated coffee urn. "Does he scratch?"

The bartender came back, eyed Charles a little dubiously, and lit a spirit lamp under the coffee urn exactly in the middle of Mortimer. This horrid sight distracted Charles' attention from Ulysses, who jumped up and down with cries of "Eek! Eek!"

"Where," said the barman, "did that noise come from?"

"Me," said Charles with a hand to his mouth. "I am a sufferer from hiccoughs. Eek!" The barman moved away.

"Mr. Mortimer," said James in low but firm tones, "pray dissociate yourself from that lighted urn at once. The sight is inconceivably distasteful. It gives me heartburn." Mortimer returned to their side of the bar and James went on: "It is happily plain that no one among the present company is percipient, for the sight of Mr. Mortimer lit up under the ribs like a turnip-head on Halloween is more than flesh and blood could endure unmoved."

The lounge was gradually filling up as guests from various hotels and *pensions* drifted in; they were for most part young and athletic, they had come to Andermatt for mountain air and exercise and they were still energetic. An orchestra of three began to play dance music and the vacant space in the middle of the room filled with whirling couples.

"A gay and cheerful scene," said James approvingly. "It always delighted me to see young people engaged in innocent enjoyment."

"I always enjoyed it more if I engaged in it myself," said Charles. "I should even now ask one of these ladies to honor me but that I fear to make a public laughingstock of myself in these new-fashioned dances. Mr. Mortimer, pray tell me, what is the name of this dance?"

"Two-step," answered Mortimer, who appeared to be sunk in gloom.

"And the one before was a—"

"Slow fox trot."

"Fox trot! Pray sir, do young people nowadays never tread the stately minuet or the graceful gavotte?"

"Never heard of them."

Charles turned his brilliant smile upon Mortimer. "Why, sir, cheer up! I would add 'Never say die' but that the expression would be a trifle unsuitable. What ails you at the sight of happy people?"

"I used to dance this with my fiancée," said Mortimer glumly.

Charles turned towards James and spoke in his ear. "Cousin, I am truly sorry for this poor man but he is plaguey melancholic. Nay, Cousin, such a mood as his is mephitic. I wish I could put him in better spirits. Do you think that if I held the glass he could drink the wine?"

"No, for heaven's sake! Think what the public would see, wine pouring from a glass in your hand, and where would it go? Consider, he has no physique in which to absorb it. They would think you tipsy, that is all, ask us to leave, perhaps, and it would do him no good."

"You are in the right, James, as always."

"Let me talk to him upon some interesting topic," said James, "it may serve to divert his mind." He passed behind Charles to stand next to Mortimer; the appearance produced to the ordinary beholder was of two men at a bar with a space between them. "My cousin has, in my opinion, monopolized your company most unfairly. Mr. Mortimer, let us converse together a little with your good leave."

Mortimer shrank back into the bar, for the dignified and authoritative James alarmed him; Charles begged to be excused and motioned him to emerge again. "We shall have our bartender emptying ashtrays into you if we are not careful."

"Dust and ashes," said Mortimer with a bitter little laugh, "appear to be my portion."

"Oh, come," said James, "there is no need to be so downcast. Smooth, Mr. Mortimer, the ruffled brow of care. Tell me, do you collect birds' eggs?"

"Birds' eggs?"

"As an aid to the study of nature."

"No," said Mortimer, whose eyes kept straying towards the door.

"I used to when I was a boy," said James. "It was at once healthful and instructive. Botany, too, what a fascinating study."

"No doubt," said Mortimer, "but I hardly know one plant from another."

"Perhaps your interests were engaged by one of the more learned sciences," pursued James. "Astronomy? Physics?"

"Good gracious, no. I had enough swotting to do reading up law."

"But surely", said James, "you had some hobby for your leisure hours."

"I spent all my spare time," said Mortimer, "in the company—" He broke off short as the outer door swung open and a man came in, a small, neat man with a heavily lined face. James and Charles Latimer looked sharply as he crossed the room to stand at the far end of the bar; one would have said that there was something about him which affected them unpleasantly.

Mortimer stiffened, like a terrier when he sees a rat. He made a rush at the newcomer.

"Perkins, at last," he said in a voice loud enough for the Latimers to hear every word. "Perkins, you fiend. I've been waiting for this and now at last I've got you—"

But the small man took not the faintest notice nor did anyone else in the group round the bar. The newcomer ordered a double brandy; from his appearance one might deduce that he was in the habit of ordering double brandies or their equivalent, as there is no mistaking the signs of habitual intemperance. The barman served him and he sat upon a high stool, with his elbow upon the bar, sipping his drink and exchanging casual remarks with those nearest to him. The Latimers noticed that he did not seem popular with the rest of the company for no one came up to greet him; on the contrary, there was a plain tendency to drift away, leaving a clear space in which the unfortunate Mortimer raved and stormed without producing the slightest result.

"He cannot hear him, Cousin James."

"Nor see him," answered James. "No one is aware of the poor young man's presence except our two selves."

"But," objected Charles, "when he complained that he could not lift the glass the tapster heard him plainly. Why was that?"

James shook his head. "Perhaps because he was addressing us and we in some sort acted as a connecting link. I do not know the conditions of his state. Or, perhaps it is because he desires vengeance upon this man for a personal wrong that he is prevented from communicating with him. It would be so, Charles, for that is not allowed; even he must know that."

Charles nodded.

"You pushed me over," sobbed Mortimer, "murderer. As though that wasn't enough, you blackened my name. You said I had made away with the c-clients' money when you'd stolen it yourself. Liar and thief—"

The small man turned towards a group of three young men standing near him and said: "That right you're having a shot at the St. Annaberg tomorrow?"

"We had thought of it," answered one of them, "but it depends on the weather, of course."

"We probably shan't go after all," said another.

"Too much like work, you know," said the third, and they drifted away together.

"Don't know what the young men of the present day are coming to," said the small man, addressing the bartender.

"No, monsieur. Indeed, no."

"When I was their age . . ." and so on.

"The unfortunate Mortimer is steadily going mad," said Charles. "Look, Cousin, he is trying to strangle the man—Perkins, is it? And to none effect. It is uncanny this encounter."

"I think it should be stopped," said James. "How say you, Charles?"

"I am of your opinion, yes, sir. And since we alone can see him, I opine that it is for us to act."

They finished their wine and sauntered along the bar to the place where Perkins sat, to all appearances alone. James addressed him.

"Sir, a word with you, if we may?"

"Certainly," said Perkins genially, "as many as you like. What are you having?"

"Thank you, nothing at present. Sir, there is an unfortunate young friend of ours who is desirous of speech with you."

"Desirous of speech, is he?" mimicked Perkins. "Then why doesn't he come up and speak to me?"

"He is speaking to you," said James, "but you are unable to hear him."

The band had just stopped, with a clash of cymbals; several people near by heard James' words and frankly stared.

"I don't get you," said Perkins. "What d'you mean I can't hear him? I'm not deaf. Who is he?"

"Henry Mortimer," said James, and there followed a rather dreadful pause. It was a story often told of Perkins that he was the man whose young partner had jumped over a cliff while they were walking together two years earlier, young chap named Mortimer. Besides, some of the staff remembered him. The chatter and laughing stopped abruptly and there was silence in the room broken only by the voice of a deaf lady who did not know how audible she was.

"That poor man is the color of green peas, why? He can't be seasick in Switzerland."

Somebody hushed her and Perkins told James sharply not to be ridiculous, Henry Mortimer was dead.

"Yes," said James quietly. "I think it would perhaps be better if we discussed this matter in your private room."

"Nonsense," said Perkins, "nonsense. I don't know what you're talking about and I have no wish to continue this absurd conversation."

"He says you killed him," said James in a low voice.

Another voice broke in upon the argument; a hesitant, rather husky voice, and since it was speaking to the Latimers it was plainly audible to all present.

"I only want him to c-confess," it said.

An elderly waiter who was passing with a tray of glasses, stopped abruptly and dropped the tray with a crash.

"Axel!" cried the head barman. "What are you about?"

"That was his voice," mumbled the waiter, feverishly scraping up broken glass. "I go home."

Perkins slid heavily down from his stool.

"Gentlemen," he said, addressing the Latimers, "I think we had better go up to my room, after all."

Chapter XIII
Green Ink

PERKINS SAT DOWN sullenly in the chair before his dressing table; since it was the only chair in the room the Latimers had to stand but they did not seem to mind and Perkins did not apologize.

"I brought you up here" he said roughly, "because it looked as though you were going to make a scene and we can't have that in public. I suppose you knew my late partner, one of you certainly mimicked his voice very well. Quite upset poor old Axel. By the way, you ought to pay for those broken glasses. Well now, the joke is over. Are you clearing out of your own accord or do I telephone for the police?"

"There is no need," said James, "we can go very well without the help of the police. Look." He and Charles, standing close together, very slowly thinned out and disappeared, only to return equally slowly. "As you see, we can go but we can always come back."

By the time they were palpably solid again Perkins was grasping both arms of his chair and his face was greenish white, but he was not prepared to give in.

"This is some trick," he said contemptuously. "You two should go on the halls, you'd be a riot. Get out!"

"We are going away from the subject," said James. "You have not to trouble with us. We are only intermediaries for your partner Henry Mortimer since he cannot communicate with you direct."

"You fools, he is dead and done for."

"Mr. Mortimer," said James, addressing a point exactly in front of Perkins, "you must have realized by now that this man can neither hear nor see you. If you will address yourself to us—"

The husky voice answered at once and it was plain that Perkins heard it.

"He has got to make a written c-confession and c-clear my name. He invited me to c-come out here with him and we used to go walking together. The last time, we went by a path that goes round the top of a precipice; when we were just above it, he asked me for a light for his cigarette because his lighter wouldn't work. I held my lighter for him with both hands round the flame on account of the wind and he hit me in the stomach. I staggered back and he pushed me and I went over."

"But why?" asked Charles.

"Because we were partners. Solicitors. He had been embezzling the c-clients' money and got in a mess with it. So he said I'd c-committed suicide because I was guilty and when he got home he took steps to prove it. Now he must make a written c-confession signed and witnessed."

"You heard that," said James to Perkins. He was white and shaking but he still fought back; after all, one does not confess to murder, embezzlement, and perjury without a struggle.

"So what?" he said, though he could hardly speak. "Do you propose to indict me in court on the indirect testimony of a ghost?"

"No," said James. "I think you had better write that confession. Do you want us three close about you, night and day, without pause, for the rest of your life? Consider, sir. If for the future, all your days will be haunted like this, what will your dreams be like?"

"After I'd gone over," said Mortimer, "he picked up my lighter. I dropped it. He still has it, he used it just now."

Perkins' hand went halfway to his pocket and fell again.

"Sir," said James, "there is nothing left for you now but to make what amends you can since, one way or another, you cannot hope to escape retribution."

There was a long pause.

"You win," said Perkins abruptly, "I'll write it." He opened an attaché case and took out a pad of writing paper. "In point of fact, this is all Mortimer's fault for being such a gullible fool. Anyone less of a nitwit would have spotted something was going wrong long before." He took out his fountain pen and began to write. "What's the date? The seventeenth?"

He glanced over his shoulder and saw that only James was with him, Charles had gone.

"I locked the door," said Perkins, "when we came in and the window is shut."

"My cousin," answered James, "has no need of open doors. Go on with your task."

Perkins shuddered and turned again to his writing.

When he had finished, James took up the paper and read it through.

"I think that that covers everything," he said. "Mr. Mortimer, do you agree?"

"I agree," said Mortimer's husky voice. "I don't know your name but please believe that I am eternally grateful." The voice died away, leaving the last syllable lingering on the air as though it had been left behind by someone who had gone away. James went across to the bedside table and picked up the house telephone.

"Mr. Perkins speaking," he said, and gave the room number. "I should be most grateful if the manager and the undermanager would kindly come up to this room at once. I have an important document to sign and I want my signature witnessed. Yes, at once, please. Thank you very much." He replaced the receiver, crossed the room, and unlocked the door.

"Now remember," he said, returning to Perkins' side, "though you may not see us we shall be close beside you until this business is finished. No monkey tricks."

"No monkey tricks," echoed another voice behind Perkins' chair. He spun round to see the taller and leaner of his two terrifying visitors smiling grimly down upon him; as though that were not enough, the tall form held in its arms a small brown monkey in a little red jacket and cap who was clinging affectionately to his owner's coat collar and staring at Perkins with great dark eyes.

Perkins gasped, there came a knock at the door, and at once the room emptied, leaving him alone.

"Come in!" he cried "Come in quickly, come in!"

The manager, with as much surprise upon his face as hotel managers ever permit themselves to show, entered the room followed by his second-in-command.

"Monsieur wished to see us?"

"Oh yes, yes," babbled Perkins. "Yes, thank you. I'm jolly glad to see you. Come right in and shut the door."

The manager, knowing Perkins' habits, immediately jumped to a conclusion which was, actually, a little unfair. This guest was exceeding the permitted limits, he must be humored for the moment and persuaded to go to bed. In the morning, if there was not a marked improvement in his behavior, his room would, with fluent apologies, be required for someone else, nor would there be a room available if Monsieur Perkins wished to return at any time in the future. Certainly not.

"There was, we understood, some matter in which we could serve Monsieur? Some affair of a signature?"

Perkins took himself in hand and explained, as he had so often explained before to inexperienced clients, the procedure of witnessing a signature. "The contents of the document are no concern of the witnesses; it is usual to cover up the writing as I am doing now. Your duty is merely to certify that you saw me actually sign my name with my own hand. Like this."

He signed his name, rather shakily, upon the uncovered portion at the foot of the sheet; the manager and the undermanager signed below as witnesses, and Perkins blotted the wet ink. He took up an envelope, folded the sheet and slipped it inside.

"Excuse me," said the undermanager, having received a glance from his senior, "I do not think that Monsieur looks at all well. He is pale, his hands tremble," which was perfectly true.

"Let Monsieur," said the manager, "retire early to bed this evening. You have, perhaps, walked too far; our strong air is sometimes exhausting. Let me send up a little something on a tray—"

" No, no," said Perkins with a shudder, "I'm not spending the rest of the evening moping up here. What d'you take me for? I'll just put this document away and come down."

"Monsieur shivered just now, I saw it," said the undermanager in a tone of kindly commiseration. "He probably has, without knowing it, a fever."

"Be advised, monsieur," urged the manager. "What says your English proverb? A stitch in time saves the camel's back? Monsieur does not wish to be taken seriously ill—"

"I am not ill at all," roared Perkins. "Don't pester me!"

The two men immediately retired, with apologies, and shut the door behind them. As they went down the stairs, the manager said in a low tone that they would see how he was in the morning and the undermanager nodded.

Perkins was left alone, holding the envelope in his hands. Here it was, in his power; he would tear it into small pieces and burn them in the ashtray, it would not take long. It might take several minutes, though, and he did not want to sit alone in that room for several minutes. Besides, the chambermaid usually came along at about this time to turn the beds down and she might think it odd if he were burning bits of paper in an ashtray. Besides again, he wanted a drink urgently, at once, for it was quite true that he did not feel well. A tendency to gasp for air and an odd fluttering sensation just below his ribs. He would put the thing in a drawer now and deal with it later on. He pulled open one of the dressing table drawers, put the envelope in, shut the drawer again, and sat looking at it No, better finish the job now. He pulled the drawer open again.

The letter was not there.

Perkins gasped noisily once and yet again and fell back in his chair with his head hanging over the arm.

The chambermaid came along the passage ten minutes later upon her evening rounds; she knocked at Perkins' door and, getting no answer, entered. She was an elderly woman and well trained; she did not scream. She looked intently at the scene before her, felt Perkins' pulse, if one can be said to feel something which is not there, and walked quickly out of the room, locking the door behind her. The rest of the rooms upon that floor would have to wait awhile; she pattered down the stairs to the manager's office and spoke to him in low, urgent tones.

The Chief of the Andermatt Police had had a long day; at last he had been able to clear his desk of the accumulation of papers which had cumbered it and could go home. He looked with deep satisfaction at his empty blotter; it was not every day that one could clear right up like that. He glanced at the clock and decided to have one cigarette before leaving; this packet was empty but there were some more in the pocket of his coat hanging upon the door. He got up from his desk and crossed the room for them, standing by the window to light one while he looked carelessly up and down the street before sitting down again. When he returned to his desk there was an envelope upon it, squarely in the middle of the blotting-pad.

It was addressed "To the Chief of Police, Andermatt," and along the bottom of the envelope was written: "The Confession of the Late Mr. Joshua Perkins." The writing was thin, slanting, and pointed, one would say an old-fashioned hand, and the ink was his own green ink, which he always used. Furthermore, it was still wet.

He looked at it for a stunned moment and then quite automatically turned it over and blotted it. After another short interval for incredulity, he opened the envelope and read the contents, which interested him greatly. The document was commendably brief and he read it again; he was just reading it for the third time when his telephone rang.

"Andermatt Police!"

"This is the manager speaking from the Schweizerhof Hotel. One of my guests has just died suddenly of heart failure."

The police chief's eyes rested upon the paper before him; it was headed "Schweizerhof Hotel" and was dated that day. The late Mr. Joshua Perkins—

"What's the guest's name?"

"Mr. Perkins, of Winchester, England."

"Oh. Who says it was heart failure?"

"The doctor. He says he's not altogether surprised. He said I'd better ring you up; I don't know if you're interested at all, or will you take this as a formal intima—"

"I am interested," said the police chief in tones of heartfelt sincerity. "I am coming straight round to you now. Tell me, did you—"

"What?" asked the manager after waiting a moment.

"Nothing. I've forgotten. Never mind. It will do when I come."

It was a fine sunny morning when the Latimers came down for an early breakfast at their own hotel and the manager was waiting for them in the hall.

"I trust," he said nervously, "that the gentlemen had a quiet night and slept well?"

"Excellently well, I thank you," said James.

"Sir," said Charles, "I will let you into a secret. When I encounter such comfortable beds as yours, Rip Van Winkle is my maternal grandfather. Yes, sir."

"And you had no—er—unpleasant disturbance?"

They took him, each by one elbow, into a quiet corner and spoke in low tones.

"Reassure yourself, my good man," said James. "You may, in future, let that room with the utmost confidence. You will have no more trouble there, believe me."

"We told you," said Charles, "that we were experts in these matters. We attended to it before we went to sleep."

"Then you saw—and, perhaps, heard—"

"We both saw and spoke to that poor unquiet spirit," said James solemnly. "He had something he wanted to say; he has said it and that is the end. He has gone beyond."

"If at any time," said the delighted manager, "there is anything I can do for you I beg you to give me the felicity of doing it. There will always be room for you here, no need to book in advance, send me only a telegram stating your time of arrival and the house is at your disposal."

After breakfast there was still a little time before the coach was due to start and the cousins strolled out into the long, winding street that is Andermatt. Children ran heartily about, the postal van came through sounding its two-note horn, "Hoo-hah! Hoo-hah!" and a small wooden cart drawn by a dog and accompanied by a young girl turned in towards the kitchen premises of the Hotel St. Gotthard; the guests would have cabbage with their lunch. Some of the coach party were clustered round the window of the souvenir shop opposite the St. Gotthard Hotel and a group of three girls together were uncomfortably addressing picture postcards on the top of a low wall. The air was diamond-clear but warm and smelled of roasting coffee, damp moss, and pine trees. A herd of fawn-colored cows with soft fur inside their ears filed past, each with a bell hung round its neck which rang musically "Di-dong, di-dong" at every step.

"Idyllic," said James, drawing a long breath, "Idyllic."

"A pastoral symphony in full operation," agreed Charles. "Yes, sir, I opine that such a scene as this recalls the golden age."

"It is all," said his cousin, lifting his eyes to the hills, "the *disjecta membra poetae.*"

Fowler the courier, on his way to speak to them, caught the last few words and faltered in his stride, but Charles had turned to meet him and it was too late to retreat.

"Charming little place, isn't it?" said Fowler. "Have you ever been here before?"

"Why, no, sir," answered Charles. "This is my first visit to this enchanted spot but I understood my cousin to say that he was here upon a previous occasion."

"Many, many years ago," said James absentmindedly. "We came by *diligence* and did not lodge here, we did but change horses. It was raining, I remember."

"Indeed," said Fowler faintly, and then looked sharply at James to see if the remark were a joke, but the elder Latimer's eyes were fixed upon the blue lift above.

"Is that an eagle? Or what the natives call a *Lämmergeier?*"

"I am sorry," said Fowler, "I haven't the slightest idea. I am no ornithologist." The winged speck above them wheeled about and James moved away to keep it within view. "Your cousin," said Fowler, with a rather forced laugh, "has excellent sight for so old a gentleman. The horse-drawn *diligence—*"

"My cousin was ever a wag," said Charles hastily, "and motley is his favorite wear." He also seemed to speak with a divided attention, and was looking over the courier's head up the street towards the way they had come; Fowler murmured something about starting in half an hour and took himself off while Charles went after James.

"Cousin," he said rather breathlessly, "a truce to your eagles. Do you not sense something?"

James brought his eyes down to his cousin's face, vividly alive and sparkling with fun.

"Why, I believe I do," he said. "Yes, Charles, by Jove, you are in the right. They are near; where are they?"

"They are drawing nearer," said Charles, "they must be upon the road. Will they of necessity pass this spot or is there some other—there they come."

The long bonnet of a Rolls-Bentley came slowly round the corner by the bridge and dropped to a footpace to let an oxcart go by.

"We had best stop them there, Charles," said James hastily. "They do not expect to see us and their unguarded comments might be embarrassing before our fellow travelers."

"Such as Jeremy crying 'Good Lord! We buried you last year!' "

The Rolls came on a few yards, suddenly faltered, and came to a stop. The street was narrow and Jeremy, with a gesture of horror, leapt out and opened the bonnet; Sally followed him more slowly. By the time James and Charles Latimer with long strides came up to them, there was an interested little crowd, mainly of children, round them and a garage proprietor saying that beyond a doubt it was the ignition, but beyond a doubt, monsieur.

Sally looked round to see the elder Latimers arriving, hats in hand; her eyes widened and they saw her gasp. Then her face lit up and she held out both hands to them.

"My dear child," said James, "my dear little Sally, what a privilege for us to meet you again, and Jeremy, too. Such a delightful reunion."

Charles lifted her hand and kissed it. "I told you, did I not, that we should meet again? Yes, ma'am, I surely was a true prophet. No wonder the sun shines so bright today."

"Isn't this fun?" said Sally, sparkling at them, "Isn't this nice? Cousin

James and Cousin Charles, I am so glad to see you, I can't tell you. Jeremy darling, look who's here."

Jeremy straightened up and turned, his mouth opened and his eyes rounded, his fingers relaxed and the spanner he was holding fell with a clatter upon the Rolls' front mudguard, and still he neither stirred nor spoke but only stared upon them.

The garage proprietor broke into a laugh. "One would say that Monsieur had seen a ghost."

"Jeremy," said Sally, "wake up, darling."

Jeremy came to himself with a start.

"Why, sure," he said, rather uncertainly. "Guess I was daydreaming, or something. Cousin James, how are you? Cousin Charles, you look well." He shook hands with them; if his smile was a trifle strained, his manner was normal enough. "What a strange thing, meeting you in an out-of-the-way place like this! Are you staying here or just stopping overnight?"

"We are delighted," said James, "to find ourselves once more in your pleasant company. No, we did but lie here last night and we are to leave again almost at once. We are upon a coach tour."

"A coach tour?" said Sally. "'You? Surely not!"

"A coach tour, ma'am," said Charles. "A conducted party of persons of both sexes escorted by a courier who points out places of historical or architectural interest as we pass. Cousin Sally, I have truly been absorbing culture and you will find me vastly improved, ma'am."

"Where are you going?" asked Jeremy.

"To Lake Como—"

"But that is where we are going," cried Sally. "My Uncle Quentin, father's youngest brother, has a villa near Menaggio and we have been asked to go and stay there."

"A very delightful spot," said James. "I passed through it once, many years ago, in the course of a tour of southern Europe."

Jeremy laughed almost naturally. "We are, believe it or not, a sort of rescue party. Poor, dear Uncle Quentin has gotten himself tangled up with—"

He was interrupted by an outburst of hooting as a lorry behind desired to pass and could not.

"Oh, nuts! And Rollo's having a fit."

Some recollection evidently struck him for he stopped suddenly with one foot on the running-board to regard his cousins with plain disquiet, but the garage proprietor, who had been tinkering with the engine, broke in.

"Try the starter, monsieur, I beg of you. There was a little spot on the contact breaker—"

"Get in, both of you," said Sally, jumping into her seat, "or the police will come. Quickly!"

James and Charles scrambled into the back seat, the Rolls started, and Jeremy drove slowly on, with the garage man trotting alongside.

"A few yards farther, monsieur, and you can pull off the road. She is all right now, yes?"

"She seems to be. Contact breaker, did you say?" Jeremy drew a long breath and spoke over his shoulder to the elder Latimers in the back seat. "To tell you the truth, I was remembering other times when Rollo stopped when she saw you two coming, but maybe it was the contact breaker after all."

Chapter XIV
Frontier Post

"OVER THERE," said James, "upon the other side of the way, is our coach. Our companions are assembling for the start. Charles, we cannot be so discourteous as to keep them waiting."

"You are in the right, Cousin," said Charles, not attempting to move. "Yes, sir, I suppose we must rejoin our party."

"But you can't go off with them when we're going the same way," said Sally, "that would be silly. Wouldn't it, Jeremy? You're coming with us. Aren't they, Jeremy?"

"Of course," said Jeremy. "The idea of you going off when we're here. We'll be glad to have you with us."

"Thank you, thank you! Then we must lose no time," said James, getting out of the Rolls, with Charles hard upon his heels. "We must settle our account—"

"Collect our baggage," said Charles. They dashed across the road and hurriedly explained matters to the courier.

"Our young relatives of whom we spoke—we have met earlier than we anticipated. They have kindly invited us to accompany them. Sir, we owe you a sum of money if you will kindly—sir, besides the money, our grateful thanks—great courtesy—prodigious kind of you—"

While James settled with the courier and Charles helped Michel the driver to get their suitcases out of the luggage compartment, Sally and Jeremy sat in the Rolls waiting for them and there was a long pause.

"Nice meeting them again," said Sally.

"Yes," said Jeremy, "yes. Sure it is."

"It'll be such fun having them with us."

"Yes, yes. Cigarette, Sally?"

"Yes, please."

He lit hers and his own and relapsed into silence again.

"Jeremy. You don't mind their coming with us, do you?"

"Not if you want them along, honey. What you say goes."

Sally slipped her arm through his. "You always used to enjoy their company, didn't you? You were always so pleased to see them."

"Yes, that's true enough. Nice guys."

"Then what—"

"But then I didn't know they were ghosts," burst out Jeremy. "I don't believe in ghosts, but there they are! Solid as you or me. I don't get it, Sally. What's a man to think?"

"What does it matter? Ghosts aren't what you thought them, that's all."

"Umph," said Jeremy.

"What you mean is that you don't believe in transparent figures gliding about with their heads under their arms rattling chains. Nor do I, that's silly. But if this is what ghosts are really like, what's the matter with it?"

"Well," said Jeremy doubtfully.

"Nice, amusing, cultured, friendly people. Relations of ours, too. I tell you what, Jeremy, I wonder how many ghosts we do meet without knowing it? I mean you can't tell."

"There is that. But I still don't like it; it isn't natural, if you get me. They shouldn't do it, if you see what I mean."

"Why worry? Don't think about it. They're so funny and so helpful—I tell you what, Jeremy darling!"

"What?"

"They'll be terribly helpful dealing with Poppy. If we get stuck they'll think of something."

"Ah," said Jeremy, relaxing at last. "Now you've got something. I don't mind telling you now that I've been stalling over the fascinating Poppy, but if they'll lend a hand it will be quite different. We'll give them the facts of the case and they can give us good advice and we'll all pitch in together. Yes, ma'am, as Cousin Charles says."

"That's right," said Sally.

When, therefore, James and Charles came back to the Rolls they found the others laughing and Jeremy sprang out of his seat to stow their cases in the locker.

"Come along," he said, "that's right. Cousin James, will you get in? Would you like a rug? It's cold on these passes. Cousin Charles, let me move that case, you've no room for your legs. All O.K.? Right, let's go. Sally has a story to tell you."

The Rolls started, Jeremy drove slowly down the narrow street between the wooden houses, and the elder Latimers sat on the edge of the rear seat to hear what Sally had to say. She turned in her seat to face them and hesitated.

"I hardly know where to begin—do you know anything about this business? I don't know how much—"

"We only know that there is some sort of family difficulty," said Charles, "about someone called Quentin. You said you wished we were here to lend a hand, so here we are."

Jeremy threw up his head. "But she said that before we met you. At St. Denis-sur-Aisne, she said that."

"Just so," said James cheerfully. "Before we go any further into this matter, may we thank you very sincerely, my dear young people, for the very beautiful floral tribute you so kindly gave us? It was quite delightful of you and we were most touched. A really moving scene, I do assure you. How say you, Charles?"

Jeremy shuddered visibly and the car swerved.

"It surely was," said Charles, "yes, sir. Cousin Sally, ma'am, I took the liberty of plucking one of those lovely pink roses for my buttonhole and James here reproached me most sternly. But, Cousin Jeremy, I don't think you'll hold it against me?"

Jeremy swallowed awkwardly.

"Well, no," he said. "I mean, no, certainly not. I mean they were for you, if you get me. All this is beyond me. Takes a lot of getting used to, as you might say. I mean—"

"Oh, darling!" said Sally, laughing.

"I guess I haven't got much imagination or something," said Jeremy apologetically.

"Pray do not let it trouble you," said James. "Indeed, it is we who should apologize for involving you in such a situation though, in point of fact, it is commoner than you think."

"Don't worry," said Jeremy. "I'll get used to it. And," he added emphatically, "this doesn't mean I don't like having you two around, because I do. We had a darn good time together before and we can again, but—if only I didn't know you were ghosts!"

"Try to forget it then, Cousin Jeremy," said Charles very kindly, "and for our part we will, if possible, do nothing to remind you. We did nothing before, did we? No, sir. We will be very careful, eh, James?"

"Certainly," said James, "certainly. Let us now dismiss the subject and tell us instead the sad story of Uncle Quentin."

"Just one thing more," pleaded Jeremy. "Promise me just one thing."

"What is it?"

"Don't—please don't—suddenly vanish before my eyes. Maybe I'm a goof and a hick but I just couldn't stand it!"

"Of course not ," said Charles stoutly. "We should not entertain such a thought for a moment. Never, before you or Cousin Sally. No, sir."

"We should not think of such a thing," said James. "Most unkind and discourteous. You have our word."

"Thank you," said Jeremy. "I feel better. Now, Sally?"

"When Uncle Quentin was a young man," said Sally, "he fell madly in love with a girl named Poppy. They were engaged to be married at one time and then she jilted him and married a man named Thompson, George Thompson. He had a candle factory and was very well off."

"Did she do this of her own accord?" asked James. "Or under parental pressure?"

"I don't know what made her do it," said Sally, "but I believe her parents died young."

"And George Thompson was very rich," put in Jeremy.

"And Uncle Quentin?" asked Charles.

"Wasn't. Not then, he's got plenty of money now."

"Of course," continued Sally, "any man with the backbone of a rabbit would have thrown her out of his mind and married somebody else. Not he. He sat down and indulged his broken heart for twenty-five years."

"One does not receive the impression of a man of strong character," said James disapprovingly.

"Quentin, the human jellyfish," murmured Charles. "Or do I do him injustice?"

"He has his good points," said Sally. "He's terribly kind and generous and sympathetic, he's traveled quite a lot, he's read a great deal, and he's very hospitable. We're all very fond of him, actually. Aren't we, Jeremy?"

"Sure," said Jeremy, "sure we are. You can't help liking the guy. If only somebody'd managed to operate on him and slip a nice stiff length of three-eighths steel rod down his spine, he'd be a real man."

"About eighteen months ago," said Sally, "Mrs. Thompson was left a widow."

"We all thought," said Jeremy, "that after a decent interval Uncle Quentin would gather up the broken fragments of his young romance, stick them together again with the glue of belated matrimony, and live happily ever after. But things didn't turn out that way. Not at all."

"He wrote to her, I believe," said Sally.

"No doubt," suggested James, "the obligatory letter of condolence upon such melancholy occasions. Had they been in the habit of meeting in the interim, do you know?"

"Oh no. He couldn't have borne it. Well, they wrote and then they met. Oh dear!"

"I opine he found some changes in the scenery," said Charles, and Jeremy burst into a yell of laughter.

"You've said it! Talk about a built-up area—"

"Jeremy, darling! Really! Well," said Sally, "of course there was that, too, but the real trouble was that she wanted to manage him. He's rather the helpless type and she thought he wanted looking after."

"Bossy," said Jeremy. "Bossy as the Pavilion at Brighton. All over."

"Whereas actually he had a nice house in Cheshire with servants who'd been with him for years and everything just as he liked it and he didn't want to be improved."

"Who does," said James, "however much we may need it?"

"She came and stayed at a hotel within walking distance of his place," said Sally, "and she used to drop in to make sure that he was comfortable."

"She wanted to know," said Jeremy, "whether he wore wool next to his skin. And whether he changed from summer to winter underwear not later than September the first."

"She liked to change his library books for him because she didn't think he kept abreast of modem trends in literature," said Sally.

"I don't want to give you the idea that he isn't a perfect gentleman in every way," said Jeremy, "but he does like onions. The thin kind you eat raw. She doesn't. She tried to wean him."

"She wanted to know exactly what steps were taken to ensure that his linen was properly aired."

"Oh, dear me," said James. "Had he a housekeeper?"

"Oh yes," said Sally, "a former cook who'd married his butler, and when Poppy asked about the laundry they both gave notice after twenty years. What made you ask?"

"I had one," explained James, "after my poor wife died. When my sister Emma was left a widow she came home from India to stay with me for a time, and after a little she enquired of my housekeeper what happened to all the fruit which was brought in from the hothouses. Mrs. Bigglestock gave me notice at once."

"And I suppose you couldn't get anyone else," said the girl who was born in 1931.

"I made no effort to do so," said James drily. "Emma took me over."

Jeremy laughed and said that it almost sounded as though he were in a position to sympathize with Uncle Quentin.

"I think," said Sally, "that it was those two old dears giving notice which finally made up his mind for him, for when she called round the next afternoon he wasn't there. He'd gone to Italy."

"Bang," said Jeremy, "like that."

"He that fights and runs away," said Charles, "will live to fight another day. Yes, sir."

"Yes, fine," said Jeremy, "but that's just where he isn't doing so well."

"You cannot possibly mean," said James, "that she was so lost to all sense of propriety as to pursue him to Italy?"

"And how!"

"He went to a small hotel, an *albergo* they call it," said Sally, "at Menaggio on Lake Como. He'd known it years before. When he got there he found that the proprietor had grown old and was thinking of selling the place so Uncle bought it, put in a manager to run it, and lives there himself in a little private suite. About a month ago he went downstairs on his way out for his usual walk when whom should he meet in the hall—"

"You've guessed it!" said Jeremy.

"Poor man," said James, "poor man."

"And when she told him that she was actually staying in the same hotel, his knees gave way and he had to be revived with cognac," said Sally.

"She said it was an overwhelming uprush of bliss," said Jeremy. "That's just what she said."

"So after he'd wrestled with his problem for a fortnight or so and made no progress, he wrote home and told the family all about it."

"The beleaguered garrison appeals for a relieving force," said Charles. "Justifiably, in my opinion. What, shall the house of Latimer be held up by a large-sized female picaroon with a name like Poppy? Never let it be said."

"We four," said James, "should avail for the purpose, I believe."

"Quentin," said Jeremy, "here we come."

Towards the end of the run they passed through Lugano and were approaching the frontier at Candria when a sudden thought struck Jeremy. "I say," he said, "have you two got passports or don't you—er—know about them?"

"Of course we do," said Charles with dignity. "Yes, sir, and we bear them upon our persons. Here is mine."

"They are very nice passports," said James. "They were made for us in Paris. Pray, Cousin Jeremy, do not gape upon me after that manner, you remind me of the bulls of Bashan in Holy Writ. Besides, you might misdirect your delightful automobile."

Jeremy pulled up at the back of a short line of cars waiting to pass the barrier and wiped his forehead.

"Excuse me," he said. "I thought I heard you say that they were made for you in Paris. Guess my ears are going back on me."

"Not at all," said James. "Upon our previous visit we found that our Paris hotel required to see them, so, as we could scarcely go to England, we purchased them from a most helpful man who lived near the Place de la Bastille. Here they are."

Jeremy examined them closely and said that they looked all right to him and he only hoped the frontier police would think so too. He collected his own and Sally's passport and the car's papers and got out of the Rolls to walk across to the office. Halfway across he turned and came back.

"If there is any trouble," he said, "I suppose you could, at a pinch, vanish?"

But there was no trouble at all. James and Charles watched with interest the process—one might almost call it the ritual—of passing customs. It was true that they had gone from France into Switzerland on the coach, but the passing of a touring coach merely in transit through a country is the barest formality; for the real thing one should drive one's own car. The barriers, heavy red-and-white-banded poles hinged and counterbalanced at one end, rest their other ends upon a forked support in the middle of the road; a car drives up to the barrier and stops and the driver, his hands full of passports and carnets or triptyques, leaps from his seat and hurries into the office. After a decent interval he comes out again only to be joined at once by one of the customs officials who spend long hours on their feet walking from car to car. The official makes sure that there are not more passengers than there are passports and then asks to have the luggage compartment opened. He may ask to have the luggage inside it opened, too, but this is seldom seen to happen. When it does, the customs people have probably been tipped off beforehand. If all goes well, the customs man steps back, the driver slams the lid of the boot and hops back into the car, the barrier rises majestically into the air, the customs man salutes smartly, the driver and passengers wave back, and the car goes on its way. Another of life's milestones has been passed.

"Well, that's the Swiss side," said Jeremy, "and all's well so far. Now for the Italians."

A short distance along the road brought them to the Italian frontier post; just before they reached it there was a rudely imperious blast from the horn of a car behind and an open tourer, chauffeur-driven, overtook them. The chauffeur did not give the Rolls more than just enough room and immediately cut in front of it because a lorry was approaching and the road there is none too wide. The indignant Jeremy had to apply his brakes and pull in uncomfortably close to the rock face.

"Will you look at that!" he said angrily. "And what's the big idea, anyway? He's got to stop at the frontier post like anybody else, so what?"

"A common fellow with no manners," said James. "He should reprove his servant at once, but I see no sign of his doing so."

The touring car stopped at the barrier and the Rolls drew up behind; the chauffeur alighted from the tourer and proceeded, with the immense dignity displayed only by really superior menservants, towards the office. His master, a stout, middle-aged man with a forbidding expression and a dust coat over his suit, remained in the car. He seemed to be rearranging things in a small attaché case beside him.

In the back of the Rolls there was an excited "Eek! Eek!" James muttered something inaudible and Sally looked round.

"What was that funny squeak, do you know?"

"I think it was a passing bird, ma'am," answered Charles, looking up and about him.

"It sounded so close," said Sally. "Oh! Whatever's happening over there?"

The farther barrier had just been raised and was vertically in the air; the official who was working it had just uttered a cry of horror and was watching his hat going quickly up the pole in the grasp of a small monkey in a red jacket. The Italian finance police wear wide-brimmed hats turned up at one side with an eagle's feather stuck in them. Monkey and hat reached the top of the pole and it could plainly be seen that a determined effort was being made to pull out the feather. The policeman uttered a few Italian remarks and brought the pole down smartly; just before it hit its rest, the monkey dropped the hat and disappeared under the touring car. The whole episode was over in a matter of seconds and the owner of the touring car had paid not the faintest attention to it. He had taken from his attaché case a small linen bag tied round with tape at the top and was surreptitiously trying to stuff it into a pocket of his dust coat.

A movement beside him caught his eye and there beside him on the seat was the same little monkey with his busy paws among the things in the open case. The man reacted promptly but unwisely; he hit out at the monkey with the linen bag, which slipped from his fingers into the corner of the seat.

Ulysses dodged the blow, seized the bag, and dived over the side of the car with it. The man leapt out, bawling to all present to catch the brute, but in vain, for Ulysses dodged the various bystanders and ran up a rainwater pipe to the roof of the customs shed, where he sat on the ridge tile contentedly playing with his new toy.

The chauffeur came out with his documents duly stamped to find his employer dancing with rage in the road and addressing Ulysses in that form of French which is called the argot and is not, as a rule, used by persons who can afford uniformed chauffeurs. The servant took one horrified look at Ulysses' plaything and instantly abandoned his sepulchral dignity.

"Run, André, run," he bellowed at his employer, and immediately began to run himself. He was at once tripped up and sat upon by a policeman and his employer was also gathered in before he had taken three strides. The police did not know for what they were arresting these men but they had tried to run away and there must be a reason for that. Then they all gathered in the road and looked up at Ulysses, who had found an interesting piece of tape round the neck of the bag and was trying to pull it off.

A moment later he succeeded, and since the bag was upside down, its contents slithered down the roof of the customs shed, glittering as they came, and pattered into the roadside dust as little sparks of white and colored light.

Instantly there was a cordon round the jewels in the road; police were hurriedly picking them up like hungry hens amid the homely corn while others
removed the chauffeur and his employer, kicking and scratching, to a place of
seclusion. When the excitement had settled down, an enthralled Jeremy
emerged from the crowd dragging a policeman with him.

"Come along! You have to inspect the car anyway, don't you? Now, for
heaven's sake tell me—Oh, you can't speak English? Too bad—*parlez-vous
francais?* Good. Describe to me, monsieur, the cause of all that excitement, I
beg of you. And the jewels, to whom do they belong?"

The policeman, panting slightly, dabbing with his handkerchief at a bleed-
ing scratch on his left cheek and grinning from ear to ear, said that it was
almost certainly the outcome of a jewel robbery at one of the biggest hotels in
Lucerne two nights before. They had been informed and descriptions circulated, though not of these men. There was a reward offered, but a most handsome reward, monsieur.

"And who will get that?"

The policeman hesitated, laughed, and shrugged his shoulders.

"We hope that it may be divided among us here but it should, in justice,
go to the monkey, should it not?"

"Certainly," said Jeremy, "but I expect you need it more than he does.
Incidentally, where is the monkey? He is not, it appears, to be seen."

The officer looked up at the roof, which was, indeed, entirely monkey-
less.

"He has run off," he said indifferently. "Probably gone home."

Charles leaned across the seat to murmur in James' ear.

"The doing of good deeds is doubtless infectious, Cousin. Even Ulysses
has now earned his holiday."

Chapter XV
The Hotel of the Patient Fisherman

THE ROLLS CAME slowly and carefully down the hairpin bends into Menaggio and turned off the Como road to pass the harbor and enter the town square,
the Largo Cavour, which has for one of its sides the Lake of Como and an
expanse of such beauty as makes a man catch his breath. The sun was shining
and the blue water spread the blue of the sky at their feet; across the lake the
mountains soared into the sparkling air while away to right and left of them
one lovely tree-clad promontory after another stepped forward into the water.
By mutual, silent consent, Jeremy stopped the car and all four went to lean on

the railings above the water to look upon such loveliness as is scarcely to be matched in Europe.

Eventually Jeremy straightened up, said "Ah!" and broke the spell. "Now, then. Where is this Albergo del Pescatore Paziente?"

"Let's ask someone," said Sally. "Ask one of these patient fishermen, he ought to know," for there were several men whose rods leaned over the railings while their owners smoked cigarettes and talked to their friends, with an occasional glance at the brightly colored float bobbing in the water below. Jeremy nodded and came back a moment later to say that it was quite near by, along the front just before one reached the Grand Hotel Victoria, and they found it without difficulty since it was the only house there with a frontage close to the road. It was a square white house, small for a hotel, with three slim cypress trees on either side of the porch. Above the roadside wall was a newly painted notice board bearing the hotel's name and a spirited painting of an empty fishing basket, English pattern.

Jeremy asked: "Is Uncle a painter?"

"Oh yes," said Sally, "but only of signboards. For inns, you know. He says they're the only sort of pictures that are really useful."

"He has something there," said Jeremy, drawing up at the door. James and Charles Latimer sprang out of the car to hand out Sally and to wait, hat in hand, while she hesitated in the doorway.

"Jeremy! What do I do if the first person I meet is Poppy?"

"You won't," he said, glancing at his watch. "At this hour she'll be in the dining room feeding her face. Lead on, honey."

The hall was wide, shadowy, and pleasantly cool, with a curving flight of stairs winding up at the far end. A door opened under the stairs; a bald-headed little Italian came out and looked inquiringly at them.

"Are you the manager, Signor Buscari?"

"At your service, signora."

"I am Mrs. Jeremy Latimer and—"

"Ah! Signor Latimer's relatives? Ah! Come this way, quickly." Buscari ran across the hall on tiptoe, with a gesture for silence. "Up the stairs, quick! You are all the one party, yes? Good, good, he is expecting you. I am to take you up to him at once. He is in bed."

"In bed!" said Sally. "Is he ill?"

"No, no. Now you are come, he will get up. It is only to ensure himself a reasonable privacy, you understand. A lady cannot enter a gentleman's bedroom, can she? No, no. But you will defend him, yes. Magnificent. This way."

The conspirators hurried down a passage and round a corner to be faced with a closed door. Buscari knocked upon it in a plainly prearranged pattern of taps and a voice inside asked who was there.

"It is I, Buscari, with your relatives who have come."

"Nobody else about?"

"No one, signor."

Buscari unlocked the door with his passkey and ushered them into a small sitting room; a farther door led to a bedroom and in the doorway there stood a short, stout figure wearing a dressing-gown over pajamas. He was bald on the top of his head, the rest of his hair was sandy, turning to gray, he had a gray mustache with a pathetic droop at the ends and large, wide-open blue eyes. He was standing upon one foot and resting a hand upon the doorpost; in a word, he was poised for flight. He saw Sally and his face lit up.

"Dear Uncle Quentin," she said, and went across to kiss him.

"Dear child, how good of you—Buscari! Is that door locked?"

"Most securely, signor."

"That is right. Dear Sally, I am so glad to see you. Jeremy, my boy, how are you? And these—"

Jeremy introduced James and Charles Latimer. "Cousins of ours. We met up with them in France—no, I mean Switzerland—and they came along too."

"Sir," said James, "this is indeed a pleasure."

"I am honored," said Charles, "to make your acquaintance. I hope I see you well."

"Pleasure's mine," said Quentin Latimer. "Cousins, eh? I thought I knew most of my cousins. Tell me, where do you come in? You can't be old Roger's boys, you're not old enough."

"No, sir," said James. "We—"

"Cousin Charles," broke in Jeremy, "is a relative of mine. He comes from Virginia." He wiped his forehead and threw an appealing glance at Sally.

"Oh, the American branch," said Quentin, "yes, yes. But you," to James, "are an Englishman, surely?"

"Uncle Quentin," said Sally determinedly, "could we not sort all that out some other time? Tell us now why you lock yourself in here like this and why aren't you dressed since Signor Buscari says you aren't ill?"

"She means to marry me," said Quentin, and his eyes went from side to side.

"Mrs. Thompson?"

"Good Gad, Sally, who else?"

"I just thought I'd make sure," murmured Sally, and the manager said in an apologetic voice that there was, of course, also the Contessa.

"Oh yes," said Quentin in an offhand voice, "of course. Charming woman. But she's all right, she's married."

There was a momentary silence until Jeremy spoke for all four visitors. "What d'you mean," he asked, " 'she's all right, she's married'?"

"She's got a husband," explained Quentin. "I mean she isn't a widow and there's no divorce for R.C.s so she can't marry me. That's what I meant. Look here, do sit down. I can't think what's become of my manners. Sally dear—"

They sorted themselves out upon various chairs, except Buscari, who remained standing by the door, thus reminding Sally of either the Swiss Guard at Versailles or the even more famous Sentry of Pompeii or, possibly, both.

James cleared his throat impressively. "But, sir, I cannot conceive how a woman can marry a man against his will. Sir, 'tis against the course of nature."

"It isn't against the course of Poppy," said Quentin, "you wait." He took hold of either end of his mustache and pulled it violently.

"But, sir," said James again, "would it not be possible to explain to the lady in simple but unmistakable terms that you have no intention of marrying anybody?"

"I have. She won't listen."

"Write her a letter," suggested Sally.

"I have. She said I didn't really mean it."

Charles moved in his chair and spoke in a voice which sounded a little choked, as by some emotion. "Marry somebody else," he said.

Quentin abandoned his mustache in order to thump the table. "Now that, my dear, good American cousin, is the first sensible suggestion anyone has made to me since Poppy was left a widow. The only trouble is that I don't want to marry at all."

"Why should you," said Sally, "if you don't want to?"

"Life," said Quentin violently, "is like this. When you're young you fall in love with a girl, and if she throws you over you think you're going to die. But do you? No. You go on living without her and, as the years pass, you build up a life for yourself in which there is no room for a wife. Make no mistake"—he thumped the table again—"you don't realize this. You go on telling yourself how happy you would have been if you'd had her, until when she's left a widow you say to yourself: 'Ha! My dream at last!' And then you meet her." He swept both hands over his bald head and his extraordinary blue eyes looked vaguely past them out of the window.

"And then the roof fell in," said Jeremy.

"Eh? Just so. That's all."

"Is she still living here?" asked Jeremy.

Signor Buscari, by the door, uttered a low moaning noise.

"Well," pursued Jeremy, "why don't you give her notice? Tell her you want her room."

Buscari gave a loud sardonic laugh.

"Well, throw her out, then."

"Signor," said Buscari, "that is easy to say, but to do, no. She says she does not wish to go. Am I, in my own person, physically to push her? Signor, it would be as if I were to push the statue of St. Peter at Rome. You have not seen the lady." He sighed gustily. "Besides, it would be assault."

"Send for the police," said Sally.

"On what grounds, signora? If a person commits a crime in a hotel one may send for the police to come and arrest the offender, but she commits no crime. Alas, she even pays her bills punctually. I cannot, signora, have her ejected without legal cause; I keep a hotel, not a private house."

"Let us," said Charles, "combine to frighten her away." Sally looked quickly over her shoulder to see his long, dark face alight with mischief, but Quentin was not impressed.

"I tried that," he said. "I am something of an amateur conjurer, gentlemen. Mice"—he paused—"mice running upon the carpet, mice in the sofa upon which she habitually sits." He sighed. "She likes mice." He paused for thought. "Perhaps that is why she likes me."

"Oh, keep your heart up, Cousin," said Charles. "Sir, we will investigate your problem and between us we will find a solution. Yes, sir. Now we are all here you have no longer to face your troubles alone."

"Cousin Quentin Latimer," said James earnestly, "in the words of Milton, 'hence, loathèd Melancholy.' Nay, perk up, sir, *ne cede malis,* Mr. Latimer. We will abate your nuisance, our word upon it."

"I hope so," said Quentin doubtfully. "Sometime, when we have a moment to spare, you must tell me where you come in the family and why you talk like Sir Charles Grandison."

"Get dressed and come down, Uncle Quentin," said Sally. "We want to see what we have to deal with."

"I will," he said, "I will. We will dine together, Buscari, in the dining room in half an hour."

"Attaboy, Uncle Quentin," said Jeremy.

"Call for me, Jeremy, my boy, on your way down," said Quentin. "Tap on this door as you heard Buscari tap just now. Open the door, Buscari, and lock it after you."

The dining room at the Hotel of the Patient Fisherman looked upon the lake through a wide bay window in which there stood an oval table. Buscari was standing beside it overseeing a waiter who was laying it afresh, with a spotless tablecloth and shining glass and silver, for five people. All the other guests in the hotel, except one, had finished their meal and gone; the one remaining was a very large lady, stiffly corseted but still ample and with elaborately waved hair. She was sitting at a small table by herself and the manager walked across to her.

"You will take coffee, signora, in the lounge as usual?"

"Not tonight, thank you, I will have it here."

Buscari bowed, turned away, and spoke to the waiter. "Coffee here for the signora," but the lady called him back.

"Some more guests arriving?"

"They have arrived, signora."

"I meant, of course, newly arrived."

"Naturally, signora."

"What nationality?"

"I have not yet seen their passports, signora. Excuse me." As the waiter came with the coffee, Buscari went out into the hall and found the elder Latimers standing there together.

"Would you care to come in, gentlemen?"

"Thank you," said James, "but we will await the rest of our party before going in."

Buscari came close to them and spoke in the tones of a conspirator.

"She is there—alone!"

"Say you so," said Charles in the same tone. "The lady who was asking the questions, I suppose."

"Every night," muttered Buscari, "she finishes fast and hurries to the lounge for her coffee. The chairs—they are all good but not all of equal comfort, you understand? But tonight, no. She lingers, why? No one has told her anything. It is sorcery." He "made horns" as Italians do to avert the evil eye; the two middle fingers closed over the palm, the first and fourth extended.

"Nonsense, my good man," said James. "No doubt our valises were brought in through this hall? She saw the labels."

Sally came down the winding stairs followed at a short distance by the shrinking form of Quentin and the encouraging presence of Jeremy. James bowed and Charles went to the foot of the stairs to meet her.

"Ma'am, you look as fresh and comely as though it were morning instead of the end of a long day."

"You always say such nice things, Cousin Charles." Then, dropping her voice, "Have you seen her yet? Is she in, do you know?"

"In the dining room, ma'am," murmured Charles, "waiting for us. She saw our luggage, I believe."

Sally flashed him a look and then composed her features, drew herself up, and swept in through the door which Buscari was holding open. Charles and James followed her, and last of all came Quentin, with Jeremy's arm flung affectionately round his shoulders. "I'm glad I brought my car," Jeremy was saying. "This is a lovely part of the world. We must plan several trips together; Venice maybe, I've always wanted to visit Venice, Queen of the Adriatic. How far is it to Venice?"

On the far side of the room Mrs. Thompson rose to her feet and Quentin would have checked in his stride but for Jeremy, who swept him on towards the table in the window so that he could only bow hurriedly in passing. They put him at the head of the table, with Sally on his right hand and James on his left. Buscari and two waiters circulated on the outskirts and Jeremy talked on.

"There was quite a bit of excitement at your Italian frontier post this afternoon. They caught a guy trying to get through with some stolen jewels! No, there was no shooting—"

The soup was served and Buscari was handing the wine list, the two waiters withdrew and there was a gap in the defenses. There came a rustling sound and a high, gay voice broke in.

"Oh, Quentin, do forgive me, I just had to ask how you were! I am so glad to see you well enough to come down."

All the men at the table rose with the usual hovering effect produced by one's chair pressing the back of one's knees. Quentin said: "Thank you, much better, thanks," and dropped his spoon on the tablecloth.

"Oh, please don't stand up—don't stand upon ceremony, as one might say, mightn't one? Really, there is no need to be so formal with me, as Mr. Latimer will tell you. Quentin dear, perhaps it would be as well if you were to introduce me, would it not? Then we shall all know each other, shan't we?"

Quentin's hunted eyes passed round the table.

"This is Mrs. Thompson, Sally. My niece, Mrs. Latimer, Mr. James, Mr. Charles, and Mr. Jeremy Latimer."

"Quite a gathering of the Latimer clan, as they say in Bonnie Scotland. Now please all sit down and I will sit just out of everybody's way here by Mrs. Latimer—Buscari, bring another chair—and we can all get to know each other. You know, I cannot help thinking it's particularly providential that so many of Quentin's family should happen to have come just now. Isn't it, Quentin?

"Er—partially," said Quentin accurately.

"Partially!" cried Mrs. Thompson with a burst of silvery laughter. "Dear Mrs. Latimer, aren't men funny? Never know what unexpected thing they'll say next, do you? Oh, thank you, Buscari. Especially dear Quentin, he's such a humorist. You don't mind my making myself at home close to you, do you? I feel that the sooner we get to know each other the better, under the circumstances."

"Are you sure," said Sally, "that you are not in a draft there? The open window—"

"Now isn't that thoughtful of you? Not at all, thank you, on such a warm Italian night. That's what I always say about Italy, our warm nights are so typically Italian, if you see what I mean. So romantic, too, especially when it's moonlight as it is tonight; it really makes one go all soft inside, if you understand my feelings, which are, perhaps, natural under the circumstances."

"Sally," said Quentin, "what will you have to drink? We have a particularly good Asti which I can recommend unless you would prefer a hock.

Buscari, there is some of that 1934 hock left, isn't there? Or would you—"

"Whatever you suggest, Uncle Quentin."

"The Asti, please, Buscari."

"At once, signor," said Buscari. The waiter was serving grilled lake trout to Sally and Buscari was following behind with a small tureen containing a thick cream sauce. As he passed behind Mrs. Thompson's chair he tripped over something, uttered a cry of horror, and dropped the sauce tureen bodily into her lap. She sprang up with a shriek and instantly disorder ruled the scene. The Latimers all rose, making pawing gestures with their napkins, though as Mrs. Thompson was at once the center of a whirlpool of waiters there was nothing they could do.

"That I should do such a thing," howled Buscari, vigorously rubbing the dress with his napkin.

"My dress—completely ruined!"

"My life is over," declaimed Buscari. "There is nothing left to me but suicide!" He went through the motions of tearing his hair, but as he was almost entirely bald the process could not have been painful.

"Your lovely dress," said Sally, who had been well brought up. "Is there a cleaner's in Menaggio?"

"Cleaners," snorted the lady, "cleaners, my foot! The only place for this dress is the dustbin!" She turned upon Buscari. "Clumsy oaf! Ham-handed fool!"

"Signora," said Buscari in a broken voice, "how shall I ever atone?" He wrung his hands.

"Indeed, madam," said James in his throatiest voice, "your unhappy predicament must touch all hearts, but would it not be better to retire? That apron of glutinous viscosity must be monstrous uncomfortable."

She glared at him and then forced a smile. "I think you are right," she said. "We shall meet again under, I hope, happier circumstances." She stalked out of the room followed by Buscari, still apologizing and mopping up from the carpet the trail of drips which marked her line of retreat.

The moment she had gone Jeremy, scarlet in the face, sat down with a bump and laughed till the tears ran down his face.

"I was waiting for that," he crowed, "the minute I saw the fish procession draw near. Who ever saw a maître d'hôtel following around with the sauce while his understrapper serves the dish?"

"Do you mean to imply," said James, a little shocked, "that the fellow did it on purpose?"

"Certainly he did, Cousin," said Charles, "and prodigious neat, too. His apologies were as good as a play. Yes, sir, he is an accomplished actor."

"What beats me, Uncle Quentin," said Sally in a shaking voice, "is why you felt you had to send for us at all when you'd got Buscari beside you. I mean he seems to me to be most resourceful."

"You'd better eat up your fish," said Quentin, "before it gets cold."

"But—" said Sally, wide-eyed.

"All I shall get out of that," said her uncle, "is an insistent demand for Buscari to be dismissed."

"But, surely," began Jeremy, "you won't—"

"Think of the arguments," said Quentin, shaking his head mournfully, "think of the blandishments." He shuddered and suddenly raised his voice to a bellow. "Buscari!"

"Signor," said Buscari, rushing into the room.

"Bring me some whiskey. And, Buscari—"

"Signor?"

"If I dismiss you tomorrow morning, take no notice."

"Very good, signor."

"I may do so several times," said Quentin, cheering up. "Repeatedly, in fact."

"Very good, signor."

"But you will continue to take no notice."

"It would appear more natural, signor, if I were to register considerable emotion. I can weep," said Buscari proudly.

"Do so, then."

"Very good, signor."

Chapter XVI
Dueling Pistols

"YOU KNOW," said Jeremy thoughtfully, "it's all very well to laugh, but it isn't going to be easy to dislodge that dame."

The four Latimer cousins were sitting upon the lakeside wall in the morning sunshine.

"Would not," suggested James, "your uncle consider shifting his quarters?"

"No," said Sally. "He doesn't want to, so he won't. Besides, what would be the use? She'd only follow him."

"Into a monastery?" asked Charles.

"That suggestion," said James, "is ingenious, as are all your suggestions, Charles, but scarcely practical politics. We Latimers were ever Evangelicals."

"Here come those two who were in the dining room for breakfast," said Sally. "The Conte and the Contessa. Buscari is so proud of having them."

"Is that right the Contessa's been making passes at Uncle Quentin?" asked Jeremy.

"Some men," said James, "might not too violently object." He pulled down his waistcoat.

"She certainly is easy on the eye," said Jeremy. "Looks like her clothes had been melted down and poured over her."

"Like poor Mrs. Thompson last night," said Charles.

"The Contessa walks beautifully," said Sally. "She seems to float along."

"So she does, Cousin Sally," said Charles. "I guess that when she was your age she was quite a belle, yes, ma'am."

"That would be quite a while back," said Jeremy thoughtfully, "but Uncle Quentin—"

"Be quiet," said Sally, "they'll hear you."

The Count and Countess came level with the Latimers and Sally looked round with a smile and a bow, to which the Countess immediately responded.

"Ah, good morning! You are enjoying the air of our lovely Lake Como? Ercole, these are the relations of our delightful Signor Latimer. It is so good for him to have members of his own family with him."

The Count bowed jerkily and said that he was enchanted. He was a short, roundabout man with a red face and he seemed to have something on his mind, for his eyes and his attention were wandering

Jeremy said that as they found themselves in the vicinity they thought they would just stop by a few days with Uncle Quentin. After a few minutes of desultory conversation the Count begged to be excused; he had to see a man on a little matter of business. He bowed deeply to Sally and to his wife, turned on his heel, and trotted briskly away.

"My poor husband," said the Countess. "Business, always this business."

Sally suggested that it was a necessary evil.

"But not romantic," said the Countess. "When I married my husband he was—picture it to yourselves—a slim, smart young officer in the Army. Not tall, I grant you, but a spine of steel and a heart of fire! Then he has to leave the Army and engage in business." She opened her eyes very wide and pulled down the corners of her mouth. "Madame, it has ruined him!"

James murmured something about unfortunate speculations falling to the lot of most men at some time, but she cut him short.

"No, no! He is very successful—that is, reasonably successful. He is, how do you say in English, a good provider? Yes. But I speak of the immortal spirit, the fire in the soul of man. It cannot survive under the—the—mess of business—"

"Slag heaps?" suggested Jeremy helpfully.

"Slag heaps, thank you. When he was in the Army he was my hero. Now he is the man who pays the bills. It is a descent, yes? I dress in silk but my heart is hungry."

"Jeremy," laughed Sally, "be warned in time."

"Sure, honey, sure. If you see any signs of me disappearing under a slag heap, you just jerk me out."

"I must go," said the Countess vaguely. "I have some tiresome letters—we shall meet again. One moment—you are all English, no?"

"No," said Sally, "only Mr. James Latimer and I. Major Latimer, here, and my husband are American."

"Indeed. Most interesting. There is something about the English, is there not? The famous buccaneer spirit is not dead." She smiled brilliantly upon them all and drifted gracefully away.

"Uncle Quentin," said Sally breathlessly, "a buccaneer?"

"Ma'am," said Charles, "if we are to laugh in comfort had we not better walk a little?"

"Look," said Jeremy, "did you see where that poor little guy's business took him? Straight into that *albergo* over there on the corner."

"I cannot find it in my heart to blame him," said James.

There were other guests in the Hotel of the Patient Fisherman. There was a group of half a dozen Scandinavians, bronzed and athletic, who kept to themselves and spent their days going for long walks. There was a middle-aged French couple who admired the scenery of Lake Como but disapproved of the humidity of the climate. The ground was, too often, damp; one got one's feet wet. There were a number of Italians who had come up for a breath of mountain air from Milan, Turin, Pavia, and other cities of the plain, but there was only one other Englishman, a tall, loose-limbed man with thick gray hair and strong glasses.

"Dr. Williams," said Buscari. "A quiet man. A little—just a little—a friend of the signora Thompson. He is the only other man she ever talks with."

"Couldn't we swivel her off," began Jeremy.

"No, no. She is immutably faithful," said Buscari sadly.

The presence of the four Latimer visitors made Quentin Latimer's life a great deal easier. No longer was he waylaid in passages, buttonholed in doorways, or met upon the stairs, at least, not alone and unprotected; one of the four was always there, and even Poppy's iron nerve would not uphold her to the point of urging matrimony upon Quentin before an interested audience. They were always haling him out for a run in the Rolls or a row upon the lake or holding Poppy Thompson in earnest talk while Quentin walked away with Sally. He cheered up noticeably and his appetite returned, but while Mrs. Thompson remained in the field the problem remained unsolved.

"You know," said Jeremy, "we're getting no place fast. She can stay here forever, but we can't, and when we go—"

Quentin had gone up to bed and the four Latimers were in conference in the deserted lounge.

"This situation," said James a little irritably, "is the height of absurdity."

"Some really brave guy," said Jeremy, "should take the bull by the horn—or maybe I ought to say the cow—and tell her she's wasting her time. Suppose we told her he wasn't worthy of her and she should look around for someone else."

"Cousin James," said Sally, "is the one to do that."

"No, no," said James. "No, no, no, no."

Sally looked hard at him. "Cousin James, you're turning pink. You're blushing. What have you been doing?"

James threw his head up. "I must confess I did not intend to admit to a humiliating failure. Sally, my love, your eyes are too sharp."

"Cousin James," said Charles, "unfold this story. No, sir, you cannot now withdraw."

"Out with it," said Jeremy.

"I did but try to intimate tactfully that she was wasting her time upon a man so immutably averse to matrimony as Mr. Quentin Latimer. I was most polite. I said that it was surely a pity to squander her years of splendid maturity to no effect. I said that there were numberless men of irreproachable family and good financial standing who would be proud and happy to see her gracing the head of their table." He stopped, cleared his throat, and took a sip of wine. "I scarcely like—"

"Go on!"

"She thought I desired to supplant him. She was kind and even tender, but very firm."

"My Lord—"

"She said that she had loved him long. She—"

He was interrupted by a shriek of anger from somewhere in the hotel, followed by the sound of furious altercation.

"What in hell's that uproar?" asked Jeremy, getting up.

"It's Poppy," said Sally, running towards the door.

"That is the voice of the Contessa," said James, following her.

"And that of il signor Conte," said Charles. "Sir, I opine that a rift has opened in the matrimonial lute—"

They gathered upon the stairs since the quarrel was proceeding on the floor above.

"You abandoned female," said Poppy.

"You," said the Contessa, "are a barefaced husband hunter. Poor Signor Quentin—"

"Signor Quentin to the devil," said the Conte. "Sir, you are an unprincipled libertine! Margharita! To your apartment. I have a word to say to this English milord."

"Uncle Quentin!" gasped Sally. "Jeremy, do something! Cousin Charles, what is happening?"

"Signor Conte," said Quentin's high voice, "ladies, ladies! There is some terrible mistake. The most excellent Contessa only came to my sitting room to look at my stamp collection. I have a complete set of New South Wales including the health stamps."

Jeremy and Charles dashed up the stairs to find a babbling group outside Quentin's sitting room door.

"Your stamp collection to the devil," shouted the Count. "You have mortally offended my honor. Take that." He flipped Quentin across the face with his handkerchief. "I shall expect to hear from your seconds in the morning. Sir, I will skewer you like a sausage."

"Not if he chooses pistols, signor," said Charles.

The Count showed his teeth, seized his wife by the arm, and hustled her down the passage out of sight. There came the sound of a closing door.

"My poor Quentin," cried Poppy, "you are the victim of a designing woman. You have been led astray, you have—"

"Don't be a fool, woman!" snapped Quentin. "You know perfectly well she's married."

"She says so," said Poppy pointedly.

"Bah!" said Quentin. He spun into his room and slammed the door; the key turned audibly in the lock.

"Quentin!" cried Mrs. Thompson. "Quentin! Open to me." She tapped upon the panels of his door and another door opposite flew open to disclose the French gentleman in a striped nightshirt. He bowed politely to the company in the passage but his face was red with anger.

"Mesdames! Messieurs! Without wishing in the least to impair your child-like enjoyment, may I humbly suggest that you should continue your parlor games elsewhere?"

"Monsieur," began Charles, who happened to be nearest to him, "I am desolated—we are all desolated—to think that our careless revelry may have disturbed your rest and that of your charming wife—"

"My wife sleeps," said Monsieur, and shut the door firmly.

"I'll say," said Jeremy in an awestruck whisper, "she must be the one and only original Sleeping Beauty——"

The door flew open again. "And she wishes to continue to sleep!" The door shut.

Sally took Mrs. Thompson firmly by the wrist and towed her towards the stairs. "Come away," said Sally, "all of you, at once. This is most unseemly."

"You hurt my wrist," said Poppy Thompson, jibbing.

"Now I've got a sensible suggestion to make," said Jeremy, urging her on from the rear. "Why don't we all go down to the lounge and have a drink?

Apparently we aren't too popular on this floor."

"No," said Poppy, stopping abruptly. "I shall retire. I am very seriously upset. This is my room." She opened a door at the head of the stairs. "Good night. I hope that you will all sleep well. I, of course, shall not close my eyes, but that is quite unimportant." She went in and shut the door after her; the key also turned audibly in the lock.

"Tweet, tweet," said Jeremy softly, "twee!"

The four Latimers went quietly down the stairs, Sally leading, but three steps from the bottom she sat down suddenly, covered her face with her hands, and leaned against the banisters. Her shoulders shook and small squeaky noises could be heard.

"Sally!" said Jeremy bending over her. "Honey, you aren't ill! What is it?" And Charles, taking three steps to a stride, passed him to go upon one knee below her.

"Cousin Sally—"

Sally lifted a scarlet face and eyes running with tears. "I'm not ill," she gurgled, "I want to l-laugh. If I can't laugh out loud I shall burst." She clapped both hands over her mouth.

"Come on," said Jeremy. He lifted her to her feet, Charles took her other arm, and between them they ran her into the lounge and put her in a chair while James shut the door behind them.

"What you want," said Jeremy to Sally, still bubbling with laughter, "is a long, cool drink of something. I'll go see what Buscari's got in his cupboard." He went out of the room and James spoke to Charles in a low tone.

"A very distressing scene. It is not to be wondered at if our little Sally is a trifle hysterical. You look shocked and bloodless yourself."

"It is a hot night," said Charles, pulling himself together. "As for our little cousin, I opine she is merely amused."

Sally sat up. "I am so sorry," she said. "I couldn't hold out any longer. Oh dear!"

"The scene certainly had its humorous aspects," said James. "You are certain that you are not distressed?"

"Far from it, you are all so good to me," said Sally. "Cousin Charles, thank you." She held out her hand and he bent over it and kissed it. "Do you really suppose that the Count means to fight a duel with Uncle Quentin? Surely not. People don't in these days, do they, even in Italy?"

"Ma'am," said Charles, "I do not take him to be one of nature's warriors. I calculate that the fresh air of morning will cool his fevered passions. Yes, ma'am, that is what I think."

"Depend upon it, Sally," said James, "we shall hear no more of this absurd duel."

But he was mistaken, the duel was not cancelled in the morning. The

Count said nothing about it but he had no need to speak since the next move was with his adversary. Quentin Latimer, however, turned obstinate.

"Back out?" he said angrily. "Certainly not. What, an Englishman ask for mercy from a tubby little Italian? Certainly not. He insulted me and, what is far worse, he grossly insulted his charming, intelligent wife. Why, she actually knew an 1850 lilac-blue twopenny without the pick and shovel when she saw it."

"But, Uncle Quentin—"

"I won't kill him if that's what's worrying you. I'll just put a ball into his arm or leg to teach him how to behave."

"But, Cousin Quentin—"

"Are you thinking I shan't hit him? I fought in the First World War, sir. Are you suggesting I can't handle firearms?"

According to the rules of dueling, the choice of weapons is left to the one who has been challenged and is usually pistols or rapiers. There is a story of an Australian army officer who, when challenged, chose felling axes, after which the appointment was cancelled. Quentin Latimer chose pistols, but when it became known that what he had in mind was a .45 revolver such as he had carried in the First World War, Buscari firmly undeceived him.

"No, no, signor. No, indeed, it cannot be allowed. It is not according to protocol. When duels are fought with pistols, the pistols used are dueling pistols, if I make myself clear, signor."

"And what distinguishes dueling pistols from all others?"

"They come in pairs," said Buscari, "in a wooden box lined with velvet, having depressions carefully shaped to accommodate the pistols themselves, the ramrod, the cleaning rod and brushes, and other necessary appendages."

"Kind heaven," said Quentin, "I asked you what the pistols were like, not the packing."

"The barrels are longer than is usually the case with pistols," said Buscari, "and octagonal. Or hexagonal."

"What? Inside?"

"No, no. Outside. And they have no sights on them."

"No sights? No si—I think I shall insist on .45 revolvers," said Quentin. "These things sound dangerous."

"Oh no, signor. One sights the top of the hammer in line with the end of the barrel—the front end. Then one allows for—"

"Did you say 'hammer'?"

"Certainly, signor. To explode the cap."

"Just a minute, just a minute," said Jeremy. "Do I gather correctly that these pieces of artillery are fired by a percussion cap on a nipple?"

"That is quite right."

"Then are they——I mean, they can't be—you can't possibly mean they're muzzle-loaders?"

"As a rule, yes, signor, though not, perhaps, invariably."

"My God!" said Jeremy. "I beg your pardon, Cousin Charles."

"Among the fittings in the box," continued Buscari, "is a small can or cup, usually of brass and sometimes finely decorated, affixed at right angles to a short length of rod with a knob at the other end. This is the powder measure."

"And you fill that up with gunpowder, do you, and pour it down the spout?"

"Signor?"

"Down the barrel from the front end? Yes, I see. And then ram the bullet on the top."

"A wad," said Buscari. "A wad, then the ball. The bullet is round all ways, like a ball; that is why it is called the ball," said the expert.

"Buscari," said Charles, "I opine you have had considerable experience in these matters, yes, sir. How come, if the question is not an intrusion?"

"When I first left school, signor, I started my career in the household of one of the Ministers of State of that day. He made, as you might say, a hobby of it. One of my duties was to load his pistols when he practiced in the gallery."

"Your master," said James, "had a shooting gallery?"

"Oh no, signor. The picture gallery."

"We seem to be getting away from the matter in hand," said Charles. "You pour the powder into the barrel. How big is it, for mercy's sake?"

"About," said Buscari, looking wildly round him, "about—" He snatched his fountain pen from his pocket and unscrewed the cap. "About that size."

"Half-inch bore?" said Jeremy.

"Half an inch," agreed Charles. "Oh, my stars! Cousin Quentin, do you still wish to go on with this duel?"

"What? I wasn't listening, I was thinking. Cousin James, will you do me the favor to act as my second?"

James bowed formally. "Sir, I understand that that is a request which no gentleman may refuse except under the most stringent circumstances. Sir, I am honored."

"That's all right, then, you carry on. You know the drill, I suppose, I don't. Buscari, have we any dueling pistols in the house?"

"No, signor, but—"

"Get some, then. I suppose you'll have to go to Milan, or is there a gunsmith in Como?"

"It occurs to me to doubt," said Buscari, "whether a gunsmith would stock dueling pistols in these days. I should be more confident of obtaining what the signor wants from an antique dealer."

Jeremy said: "Oh, Caractacus!" and leaned heavily upon Charles' shoulder.

"I don't care where you get them," said Quentin. "Excuse me, I've got some stamps to stick in." He went up to his room, Buscari went about his business, and the three remaining Latimers looked at each other.

"Look," said Jeremy, "I suppose these two old guys must pop off at each other? I know it's one hell of a joke, genuine antiques and all, but they might hurt each other."

"Leave it to us," said Charles. "James and I will see to it that no harm is done. James, do you indeed know what formalities are to be observed upon these occasions?"

"I think so. When I was a lad there was an elderly gentleman who used to dine at my father's table, who had himself fought several duels and acted as second in several more. After the ladies had retired the old gentlemen took pleasure in telling us about it."

"If in any doubt, Cousin," said Charles, "you can call upon the experienced Buscari, can you not?"

Chapter XVII
My Hero!

JAMES WENT UPSTAIRS and tapped upon the Count's door. There was some sort of reply from within; he opened the door and entered. The Count was sitting in an armchair drawn up to a small table by the window; on the table before him were a bottle of wine and two glasses. James stopped just inside the door and bowed.

"Signor Conte, I have had the honor to be appointed by Mr. Quentin Latimer to represent him in this matter. If you will—"

"What matter?"

"The duel to which you challenged him."

"Oh. The duel."

"If you will be so good as to nominate some gentleman to represent you, he and I will make the necessary arrangements together."

"Oh. Yes, very well. Will you kindly ask Buscari to come up to me and bring another bottle?"

"Sir," said James, stiffening. "I am not—"

"And the monkey, too," said the Count, refilling his glass.

"Monkey?" said James, taken aback.

"A small monkey who has given me the pleasure of his company the last two days. I have not seen him this morning."

"Signor Conte, I am not your lackey. I see a bell push in the room; if you wish to summon the staff kindly avail yourself of it." James stalked out of the room and found Charles waiting for him in the hall.

"Well, Cousin James?"

"Charles, the disgusting fellow is tipsy!"

"What, at this hour of the morning? But, Cousin, it was plain from the outset that such was his failing. Maybe the prospect of mortal combat has aggravated his thirst. How say you, James?"

Buscari came across the hall on his way upstairs and they called him over.

"Buscari," said James in a low tone, "the signor Conte is, I regret to say, not sober. I went to see him about—"

"Signor," said Buscari simply, "he never is. I would not be understood to suggest that the signor Conte is ever completely squizzo—"

"Completely—"

"Squizzo. An English word, no? I have it wrong, then."

"Never mind," said Charles, beaming upon him. "It is an excellent word, pray continue to use it."

"I thank the signor. To return, the signor Conte is always a little"—Buscari teetered slightly—"*comme ci, comme ça.* A little misty. But always the perfect gentleman."

James, who disapproved of intemperance, raised his eyebrows and Buscari hurried on.

"But this last few days—a week—he has been worse. I think, myself, he is grieved that his wife, the signora Contessa, makes the big eyes at my signor."

"Cousin James," said Charles, "we sure must hand it to our cousin Quentin. He certainly has something, yes, sir."

"Yesterday and again today," pursued Buscari, "the Conte has ordered two glasses to be sent up. He has, he says, a little monkey who comes and drinks with him. Gentlemen, there is no monkey there when I or my waiters enter, nor do I admit monkeys to my hotel. Yet—" Buscari's shoulders practically touched his ears.

"Sad," said James.

"Deplorable," said Charles.

One of the underservants appeared at the service door and murmured something to Buscari.

"Excuse me," said the manager. "His bell is ringing non-for-stop." He galloped up the stairs.

"That animal of yours," said James severely, "is encouraging the man in his evil courses."

"You are in the right, James, as always," said Charles. "Since we cannot see him when we are materialized unless he materializes too, I had not missed him."

"Steps," said James, "should, I suggest, be taken, my dear fellow."

He received no answer and looked round, but Charles was not to be seen.

"Discipline," said James thoughtfully, "discipline."

A few minutes later a short procession came down the stairs: it was headed by the signora Contessa undulating bonelessly from step to step, behind her came the signor Conte, red-faced and glassy-eyed but composed, carrying a pearl-gray Homburg hat and a rolled-up umbrella, and Buscari. James drew back and bowed distantly as the nobility swept past, almost imperceptibly bending their heads in reply; they went out of the front door into the sunshine and Buscari came to a halt.

"I took the liberty," he said, "of suggesting to the signor Conte that sobriety was needed for straight shooting and the signora Contessa very obligingly agreed with me. They have gone to take the air."

"I should have thought," said James, "that you would have preferred to have him tipsy as causing less risk to your signor. Much as I applaud your action on moral grounds," he added hastily.

"Signor, I gave that idea some thought, but I concluded that he would be safer sober. He will at least try to aim the weapon, he will be fully conscious of his danger and probably suffering from an overhang. Whereas, if he were lighthearted and carefree, who knows but that he might aim the thing straight?"

"I see your point," said James, "and I doubt not that there is something to be said for it. Has he appointed—"

"Heavens," said Buscari, frantically hauling Italian currency notes out of the till at the reception desk, "I shall miss my bus. I am for Milan for the weapons. What did the signor please to ask?"

"Who will be his second?"

"Me," said Buscari. "Me, at your service when I return."

"What," said James, "against your patron?"

"*Sciocchezza!* The patron will assassinate him with his eyes shut and both hands tied behind his back." Buscari rushed towards the door and turned upon the doorstep. "Consider the reputation of my hotel, the glamor, the *cachet*. The hotel to which gentlemen come to settle their affairs of honor! The manager, they will say, is a man of education, of experience, of discretion. My name will be glorious, I shall receive the very best *clientèle*. My God, the bus!" He ran out of the door.

"If Jeremy were here," said James to himself, "he would say: 'Nuts. Just plain nuts.' By the way, we shall have to take a doctor with us, it is always done."

He went up to Quentin's room, made himself known through the door, and had it opened for him.

"I assume, my dear fellow," said James affably, "that you have a regular medical attendant?"

"What, me? Good Lord, no. If I feel off-color I take a handful of liver pills. What's the matter? Aren't you well?"

"Perfectly, thank you. The question arises in connection with this duel. We shall have to take a doctor with us."

"You'd better ask the Count," said Quentin cheerfully. "He's the one that's going to need a doctor."

"Since he is not a resident in these parts—"

"Or, I tell you what. Ask the poltergeist fellow, he's a doctor of medicine. Or was. He's on the premises."

"The—excuse me—polter something?"

"Poltergeist. He goes in for 'em."

"Pray excuse my stupid ignorance, Cousin. What are poltergeists? I never heard the word."

"Bogies. Hobgoblins. A sort of ghost."

"Indeed," said James, deeply interested. "Does this Dr.—"

"Dr. Williams. You've met him. He's staying here. Eight feet high and two feet wide and his hair wants brushing."

"I know the man. Does he see ghosts?"

"According to Williams, you don't see poltergeists. You hear them and feel them and occasionally smell them, though, as I told him, in Italy that isn't poltergeists, it's drains. They don't appear, they throw things and stick pins into people. Don't believe a word of it, myself."

"Most interesting," murmured James, "most."

"Not at all. Poppycock, my dear fellow, poppycock."

James went away and encountered Charles just outside the door.

"May I take it, Cousin," said James, "that you were present and heard that?"

"You may, Cousin, you may. And how! That conversation, James, was pregnant with fruitful suggestions. Yes, sir."

"So it appeared to me. As a means of frightening away our cousin's undesired inamorata—"

"A few loose trifles flying inexplicably through the air, a few pins—"

"We cannot stick pins into a lady, Charles," said James severely. "We may be no longer mortal but we are still gentlemen of refined tastes."

"We will consult this Dr. Williams."

But Dr. Williams and Mrs. Thompson were sitting side by side upon deck chairs under the great cedar on the Patient Fisherman's lawn, and the cousins went out for a stroll before lunch instead.

After lunch they were more fortunate; they came into the hall to find Dr. Williams, with a smile of delighted benevolence upon his rough-hewn features, regarding with approval the entry of two children, complete with parents and baggage, into the hall of the Patient Fisherman. The boy was about thirteen years old, brown-haired and thin-faced, with a beaky nose and a mischievous grin; his sister was some two years younger, with black hair in two long plaits, a round solemn face, a rotund figure, and a mouth which turned down at the corners. They were staring about them while their father signed the register and their mother fussed with the luggage; presently the children's eyes met those of Dr. Williams and he said: "Hullo!"

The boy said: "'Allo!" and grinned; the girl frowned and looked away; their parents collected them and swept them upstairs.

"Sir," said James with a pleasant smile, "I perceive you to be one of those amiable persons who enjoy the society of children."

"I do, yes," said the doctor tolerantly, "but it is not altogether for the charm of their innocent prattle that I rejoice to see them here."

"No, sir?"

"Not altogether," said the doctor.

James was not really interested; he had been fond of his own children but other people's were to him merely creatures who should be seen and not heard. He abandoned that subject.

"Dr. Williams, I believe? My name is Latimer. May I, sir, without appearing intrusive, enquire whether you are a doctor of medicine?"

"I was, though I retired from practice some years ago to take up other interests. If you require medical attention, my dear sir, the local medico is a good fellow and most conscientious."

"I am assured of it," said James, "but the case is not what you think. Sir, should we stroll across and take a view of the lake?"

"Certainly, certainly. Personally, I could never tire of looking at this lake and, besides, there is a little something in your manner which I find intriguing."

The three men strolled out into the sunlight together and crossed the road to sit on the lake wall.

"Well, sir?"

"I have said, Doctor, that my name is Latimer and this is my cousin, Major Latimer; we are both relatives in varying degrees of Mr. Quentin Latimer, who owns this place."

"I assumed that you were, I have seen you at his table. A dear good chap but never looked a yard beyond the end of his nose in all his life. Eh?"

"Sir," said Charles, "I will maintain that that summary is nothing short of masterly."

"Our cousin," said James, "has been challenged to a duel."

"What? Gobbless my soul. Who by?"

"That Italian Count—"

"What, the one with the wife?"

"Even so. He—"

"Then she's at the bottom of it."

"Dr. Williams," said James, "your perspicacity is quite amazing."

"Rubbish. When she was a schoolgirl she dodged the column and went to the cinema to see Theda Bara. She's been Theda Bara ever since."

The allusion was, naturally, lost upon the Latimers, but they did not say so.

"I am my cousin's second," said James, "and have been entrusted with making the arrangements. One of the necessities, my dear sir, is a doctor. Sir, will you serve?"

"No it isn't," said the doctor, "it's a surgeon. Never mind, I don't suppose they'll hit each other and I only hope they don't hit me. I'll play."

"I am prodigious obliged, sir," said James. "It is most kind of you—"

"No, it isn't," said the doctor. "I wouldn't miss it for anything. Besides, I imagine the atmosphere will be most helpful."

"Helpful?"

"Together with the arrival of those children. I see you do not understand me; I gather that you know little or nothing of the phenomena known as poltergeists, usually associated with the presence of adolescent children. I am making a prolonged and detailed investigation into this branch of the occult. Gentlemen, if it will not bore you unendurably, I should be more than happy to discuss some of my cases with intelligent, educated men like you. If you're sure—"

The Latimers, in tones ringing with sincerity, said that they would be more than interested, they would be enthralled. "The occult!" said James deeply. "It draws me."

"Splendid, we'll get together after supper. I tell you who is also interested. That sensible woman, Mrs. Thompson."

Shortly before eight the following morning a group of people approached the hotel by the back entrance, from which a track led straight up to the hillside. The group was headed by an ancient and rickety wooden door borne horizontally by four bearers, Dr. Williams, Buscari, and two Italian laborers; upon it, covered with a frowsty blanket, reposed the person of the signor Conte with a dramatically bloodstained bandage round his head. Behind the bearers and their burden came James and Quentin Latimer, walking side by side like chief mourners. They had, in fact, been taking turns at helping to carry the Count.

The *cortège* entered through a gate in the wall and proceeded decorously along the center path towards the garden door; before they had gone halfway, the garden filled with all the hotel employees, including the outdoor staff—

one man and a boy—and those who were theoretically off duty. They swirled round the casualty uttering cries of pity, they clustered round Quentin Latimer with congratulatory squeals and patted him tenderly to find out if he also were hurt.

"So demonstrative, these Italians," said James to Charles, who had strolled from behind a clump of bushes.

"You are in the right, James. A gay and animated scene, yes, sir. But what is that I hear?"

It was a scream like that produced by a highly feminine railway engine approaching, at express speed, some point of danger. It was not continuous, it was broken to allow the screamer to draw breath. Just as one can tell by the sound that the whistling engine has entered some tunnel or passed round some curve, the assembled company could tell when the screamer scampered down the stairs and rushed across the hall. Even as the bearers set down the Count in order that a fresh relay should take him up, the Contessa appeared in the doorway in a *négligé* of green satin with her long black hair streaming wildly about her.

"Ercole! My husband! He is dead."

"No, no, ma'am," said James in a loud, firm voice. "He has a cut on the head, that is all. He—"

The Contessa advanced and the company fell back to make way for her. Quentin Latimer went forward, hat in hand.

"Madame, I assure you—"

She fixed her eyes upon him and hissed: "Assassin!"

"But he is not dead."

"Not—Ercole!"

"For pity's sake," said the Conte, lifting weak hands to his head, "be quiet, Margharita! Every sound—"

"My hero!"

"Now she will cast herself upon his body," said James. "There, I said so. It is upon occasions like this that one realizes how naturally grand opera takes root in the soil of Italy. Sir, it is in the blood."

Jeremy came out, slipped his arms through theirs, and led them away down the garden.

"Blood," he said, "would seem to have been shed, unless that's red paint on the Conte's headdress. Don't tell me our uncle really winged him."

"Why, no, Jeremy," said James. "Sir, I protest that that was a rare show I should have been sorry to miss. I took my principal upon the field punctually at seven, the doctor followed immediately upon our arrival, and Buscari brought his principal up at seven minutes past. Buscari and I retired to a short distance and loaded the weapons."

"Wait a minute," said Jeremy, "wait a minute. Cousin Charles, you were there too, I take it?"

"Why, yes, but I—I would say—that is, they could not see me."

"I get you," said Jeremy bravely.

"We led our principals into the middle of the ground, placed them back to back, and told them that, upon the word of command, they were to step out, take fifteen paces forward, turn, and fire."

"And I'll bet the Count ran like a stag and turned like a top," said Jeremy, "while our uncle proceeded—"

"With perfect dignity," agreed James.

"Buscari was horrified," said Charles. "He set off after his principal crying 'No!' The Conte turned as you said, Cousin Jeremy, and Buscari collided with him. Sir, though I say it, if I had not been quick it would have been Buscari who came home upon that door."

"Didn't the gun go off, then?"

"Oh no," said James. "Charles took it from him. It was found lying beneath them."

"Beneath—"

"They fell down," said Charles, "and rolled together. Furthermore, sir, I will maintain against all corners that Buscari pulled his nose."

"The Count's nose," said James. "I told your uncle that he was fully entitled to fire, but he would not. Of course, since he was walking away he was not in a position to see what had happened. He said that the poor gentleman had met with a little accident."

"Go on," said Jeremy, "go on."

"Buscari took the pistol away and very properly came to consult with me," said James. "We decided that it would be better to place them thirty paces apart and that I should count one, two, three. This was, accordingly, done."

"On the way back to their point," said Charles, "I heard Buscari tell the Count that if he fired before the appointed time he, Buscari, would twist the Count's head round till it came off in his hands. Yes, sir, that was what he said and, in my opinion, sir, the Count believed him."

"This time," said James, "they did fire and both, of course, missed."

"Why 'of course'?" asked Jeremy. "I understand that Cousin Charles' movements were not—not observable, but I guess that you, Cousin James, must have been in full view. Or do I still not understand how you work?"

"I walked away behind a tree," said James. "Dr. Williams was farther off behind a rock and Buscari, at some distance, had thrown himself flat. They were both, of course, watching the combatants and had no leisure to observe me."

"Besides that," said Charles, "if they had seen James vanish and appear again they would only have thought him to be on the other side of the tree. We used not to be so careful but we are acquiring discretion."

"I advanced with an air of authority," said James, "and—"

"I'll bet you did," said Jeremy.

"And asked them both if honor were satisfied. The Count said yes but Cousin Quentin said no, so we reloaded."

"The next bout was a little unfortunate," said Charles. "You understand, Cousin, that James and I were not attempting to aim the pistols, we merely deflected the barrels slightly at the right moment. Sir, it was curst unfortunate that one of the hens from a nearby cottage should have chosen that moment to flutter across."

"One of you shot her down?"

"Not only one. I maintain, James, that it was your shot took out her tail feathers; mine, sir, got her squarely between the eyes."

"It may well be so," said James placidly, "you were ever a marksman, Charles. I asked again if honor were satisfied, but Cousin Quentin said that the first two were only sighting shots and that he had the hang of his weapon now. So we reloaded again."

"And the Count?" asked Jeremy.

"Did not seem too happy, Cousin. Charles and I were both beginning to be sorry for him at this juncture since, when all is said, he had had some provocation, though on your uncle's part quite unwittingly."

"She did it on purpose," said Jeremy, "the Contessa, I mean. She was all set to pep up the poor old Conte, she practically told Sally so."

"So I thought, also," said Charles, "and if he went back to her unscathed and Quentin also bore no scars—"

"She probably wouldn't have given him credit for fighting at all," said Jeremy.

"Just so," said James, "but to ensure that he should be hit in a nonvital spot was beyond our powers. So we suffered them to engage in one more bout and then there were no more balls."

"Not really?"

"No, really. Buscari could only obtain six."

"I cannot take it upon myself to say where the last two went," said Charles. "James and Buscari advanced together, flapping white handkerchiefs, and announced that the contest was now over and honor would have to be satisfied—"

"Or else," said Jeremy.

"Or else, as you say, but no blood had been shed and there was the Contessa still to satisfy. The Conte was so delighted that he rushed across the field of battle with arms extended, calling Cousin Quentin his brother-in-arms, his comrade, his friend, when sir, would you credit it? He tripped and struck his head upon a rock."

"No, I wouldn't," said Jeremy. "Which of you worked that?"

"Charles tripped him up," said James. "Cousin, I thought you had killed him."

"Oh no! Cousin," said Charles reproachfully, "You should know me better. He had some scratches, 'tis true, but most of that blood was the hen's."

Chapter XVIII
Roman Holiday

THE EXCITEMENT died down by degrees, the Count was carried to his room to receive the more detailed attentions of Dr. Williams, and the rest of the participants gathered in the dining room for breakfast. The duel was not discussed since Quentin was very plainly no longer interested and the elder Latimer cousins had no wish to introduce the subject. James had warned Jeremy and Sally.

"With your concurrence," he said, "let there be no milling over the matter, no detailed discussion, I beg. Charles and I, believe me, are not so skilled in dissimulation as to ensure that, under close examination, we might not let slip some item of information which would lead to a discovery of our secret."

"Then we'd better keep Poppy off with an electric fence," said Jeremy. "Cousin James, that dame'd get secrets out of a Trappist monk."

"She doesn't believe in ghosts," said Sally. "She told me so. Isn't it silly?"

"Not even in Dr. Williams' poltergeists?" asked Charles.

"No, though I believe he has done his best to convince her."

"Perhaps we may be more successful," said James, and Sally turned round eyes upon him. "Charles and I have been sitting at his feet absorbing his wide and curious store of knowledge."

"You mean you're going to—"

"Cousin Sally," said Charles, "will you assure me upon one point, if you please? If unaccountable things happen, will you promise me to remember that it is no strange occult influence at work but only James and me playing tricks? For, ma'am, if it is going to cause you one moment of alarm, we will not touch it, no, not to save Cousin Quentin from a dozen such women. Let him marry them all sooner than that."

"Charles speaks for us both, my dear little Sally," said James. "Not for the world—"

"As though I should be frightened when it's you and Cousin Charles! Can't I do anything? I'd love to help."

"You can scream," said Charles. "Yes, ma'am, a few really piercing shrieks at the right moment might just turn the scale; she would be sure then that it was not illusion if you also see it. Pray, Cousin Sally, can you scream?"

Sally drew a long breath and Jeremy clapped his hand over her mouth. "Not now, honey, please. Keep it for the appropriate moment. Yes, Cousin Charles, she can. Spiders are what sets the machinery in motion."

"There shall be no spiders," promised Charles.

Accordingly, at breakfast time, James announced that he and Charles thought of making a short expedition together if Quentin would not think them rude. "While we are within reasonable reach of Rome we should consider ourselves barbarians indeed if we did not seize the opportunity to visit the Eternal City. The Colosseum, the Arch of Titus, the Baths of Diocletian, the Trajan Column—"

"Take my advice," said Quentin.

"I am all attention?"

"Wear comfortable shoes. You'll need them."

"Yes," said Charles. "I reckon that there will be opportunities for pedestrian exercise. Sir, your advice is good and I shall take it."

"When are you going?"

James glanced at his watch. "In about an hour's time."

"Enjoy yourselves," said Quentin, "it's more than I should do. Ruins, ruins, ruins. Beside the heat. You can have the Baths of Diocletian."

"Indeed, Cousin," said Charles, "if what you say be true, we may be very glad of the Baths of Diocletian."

"We shall see you again, then," said James, "in two or three days' time."

They went up to their rooms and were presently seen walking together towards the square to take the bus for Como. Presumably they caught it, for the Hotel of the Patient Fisherman saw them no more at that time though their rooms were retained by them.

Mrs. Thompson, like many other stout people, found excessive heat very trying; the afternoon of the day when Charles and James Latimer left the hotel was oppressive in the extreme. She told Sally that it was simply too hot to live and that she was going up to her room to lie down. Sally agreed, saying that a cool shower would be pleasant but that as there were no shower baths in the hotel she and Jeremy were going to bathe in the lake. Mrs. Thompson hesitated but was perhaps restrained by the too figure-revealing properties of a bathing-dress; she said that the idea was tempting but was too much trouble. "What I should really like," she added with her tinkling laugh, "is to have someone bring the lake and pour it over me."

"Haven't I read somewhere," said Jeremy, "that some of your English nabobs in the old days in India—"

He broke off because his eye had been caught by a sort of shimmer in the air above the lady's head; it descended rapidly in the shape of the contents of a bucket of water and soaked Mrs. Thompson to the skin. Her screams awoke everyone in the hotel, and even Quentin unlocked his door to ask whether there had been another duel. The Scandinavians were out for one of their nice long walks and the French couple's bedroom door remained obstinately closed, but heads poking round corners revealed the passionate interest of the Italian guests and the staff were bunched together about the service door, the cook holding a poker. Dr. Williams came hastily down the stairs to be confronted with one dripping lady and a pool of water in an otherwise dry hall.

"Somebody threw it at me! These wretched Italians with their practical jokes—"

"But there wasn't anyone around," said Jeremy.

Buscari, hastily roused from his siesta, came running; he was in his shirt sleeves, collarless and barefoot. Mrs. Thompson turned on him.

"This is another of your tricks—"

"Signora, I protest! I have not the faintest—where did all that water come from?"

Dr. Williams took the lady by one damp arm.

"I warned you," he said. "I told you this morning that something like this would probably happen. Those children-—"

"My children," said their mother, suddenly appearing upon the staircase, "were asleep on their innocent cots till roughly awakened by this unseemly noise. Maria weeps." She turned on her heel and disappeared again from sight.

"But where did the water come from?" asked Buscari.

"From the ceiling, more or less," said Sally in a rather choked voice. "Mrs. Thompson, you did say you wished—"

"But the ceiling is dry," said Buscari.

"Not all over my new dress," said Poppy. "And my hair, it was set only yesterday—" She wrung out the hem of her skirt.

"Most interesting," said the doctor. "Highly gratifying. I consider myself privileged to be on the scene of such a striking example of poltergeist activity."

"Then I hope that in future your poltergeists will pour their water over you," said Poppy tartly. "That should gratify you even more." She dabbed at her hair with an ineffectual handkerchief.

"It would indeed," said the doctor. "I should count it—"

Jeremy pulled his wife back as another bright shimmer appeared directly over the doctor's head and water enveloped him as from some unseen cistern. Sally, mindful of Charles' wishes, let out a healthy scream which startled the passersby upon Menaggio's promenade, and Poppy, uttering what was but a pale squawk in comparison, scuttled away upstairs and locked herself in her bedroom, beating by a short head the hotel cat, which had been attracted by curiosity to the scene of tumult. The doctor stood perfectly still where he was, the water running off his clothes to form a second pool upon the tiled floor.

"This water is cold," he said in a surprised voice.

"This mess must be cleared up at once," said Buscari authoritatively. "Fernando! Rodrigo!"

The servants rushed out from the kitchen quarters, uttered loud cries of stupefaction, and rushed away again for the necessary equipment.

"But surely," said Sally, "you did not expect the water to be warmed?" She giggled regrettably and controlled herself, "Mrs. Thompson did ask for lake water, you know."

"The wonder to me," said Jeremy, "is there weren't some fish in it, too. You know, those sardine things."

"Mrs. Thompson," said the doctor, not moving from his damp spot, "also expressed a wish for water to be apported to me. And it was."

"Seems like to me that Mrs. Thompson has a pull with the occult," said Jeremy.

The servants returned with mops, pails, and cloths; going down on their knees, they started operations round the feet of Dr. Williams, who took not the faintest notice of them.

"Point well taken, my boy," he said. "Mrs. Thompson is undoubtedly in some measure a focus for these manifestations."

"Doctor," said Jeremy, "you should cultivate the lady if she brings results that way."

"I shall, I shall." The doctor turned his earnest gaze upon Sally. "You asked just now why I should expect the water to be warm. It is a characteristic of telekinetic apports that they are often warm or even hot to the touch; the late Harry Price in his book *Poltergeists over England* quotes a case in which cold water was rendered boiling."

"Signor Doctor," said Buscari in an imploring voice, "May I beg that you will permit my staff—"

"What? Oh, yes, yes," said the doctor, moving a few inches. "Tell me, did either of you see the water approaching? Did it come from the direction of the door by a circuitous path?"

"Oh no," said Sally, "it just fell straight down."

"Splosh," concurred Jeremy. "Why?"

Dr. Williams took hold of the lapels of his coat.

"Apports seen passing through the air," he said, "seldom follow a straight course as a stone normally does when thrown; the path of their travel is more usually in a curve on the horizontal plane. Also, the speed—"

"Excuse me," said Jeremy. "Just a minute. That word, 'apports' was it?"

"Apports are objects brought from a distance by other than human agency."

"And the other word you used, tele something?"

"Telekinetic, from telekinesis. The supranormal movement of objects."

Buscari lost patience.

"Signor Doctor, a perfectly normal movement of your distinguished person to, for preference, your bedroom would obviate the probability of your contracting pneumonia and enable my staff to get on with their work."

"What? Oh, I see, I hadn't noticed. Mopping-up operations, eh? Certainly, certainly. I'd better go and change.

"Come with us and have a swim in the lake," said Jeremy, "you can't be any wetter."

"Some other time, thank you. If I were to rush across the road fully dressed and jump in the lake, some fool would be sure to try to rescue me. With a boat hook, probably. Most painful. See you at dinner."

Dinner was well attended and everyone in the hotel was down punctually; even the Conte, with his head wrapped in nice clean bandages, exhibited with his Contessa an air of high social superiority which did not mask a plain determination to know what, exactly, was going on. Last of all came Poppy Thompson escorted by the doctor; she was, naturally, greeted with a number of enquiries after her health.

"Thank you," she said, bowing gracefully to right and left, "thank you all so much. So kind. No, I am none the worse for my unexpected baptism. I think that in future I shall expect the hotel to provide me with an umbrella. Buscari, you heard me?"

"Certainly, madame, certainly. Provision shall be made without delay," said Buscari with a winning smile.

Mrs. Thompson walked across the room to her usual table and Dr. Williams drew out her chair for her to sit down.

"All the same," she said to the room in general, "I shall not rest until I have found out who is respons—"

She sat down as she spoke; there was a sharp crack and a splintering noise. Mrs. Thompson, under the natural impression—shared by the company present—that her underpinnings had given way, rose hastily, clasping herself amidships.

The doctor uttered a loud exclamation, bent forward, and picked up something which lay transversely across the seat of the chair. It had been a neatly rolled umbrella, but the chair seat had a shallow concave curve from side to side and the lady's weight had done the rest. The doctor held up the umbrella but it wilted in the middle like a candle in the heat and emitted small grating sounds.

"That," said the Conte, springing to his feet, "is my umbrella. Mine. My English Fox-frame best snakewood silk-covered umbrella. It has a gold band upon it bearing the arms of my not undistinguished family. In a word, it is mine."

"Please note, everybody," said Dr. Williams in a loud, firm voice, "that the umbrella was not there when I drew out the chair for the lady."

"Who," demanded the Count, in a voice less firm but a great deal louder, "is responsible for this outrage?" He glared at everybody.

"There was no one anywhere near the chair," protested Buscari, almost in tears, "except the doctor and the lady who sat."

"Precisely," said the Contessa, in a carrying, well-bred voice. "And as the doctor had nothing in his hands the umbrella must have been brought in by the lady."

"She could," said one of the Scandinavians judicially, "have concealed it under her skirts."

Sally, at the oval table in the window, pushed away her plate and laid her head on her arms.

"How dare you?" said Mrs. Thompson.

"Poppy, Poppy," said Quentin plaintively, "remember that these ladies and gentlemen are my guests. Conte, I am sorry. I will get you a new and even better umbrella from the Army & Navy Stores—in London," he added, in case the Conte should be numbered among the barbarians.

"That one," said the Conte magnificently, "was the precious gift of my noble wife. It is irreplaceable."

Charles and James Latimer, unseen but present, communicated inaudibly with each other.

"That duel, Cousin, has gained the day. It has worked the miracle."

"You are in the right, Cousin. The married lovers once more adore each other, yes, sir. Another good deed!"

"We must all face the fact," said the doctor, once more assisting Poppy to sit down, "that Mrs. Thompson is in some sense under the protection of some agency which delights to carry out her lightest wishes."

"Phoo," said the Contessa.

"Before saying 'Phoo,' " said Mrs. Thompson, turning in her seat, "it would be better to consider that what the doctor has just said is undoubtedly true. It would be wiser, perhaps, to remain on civil, if not friendly, terms with me."

"Phoo," said the Contessa again, for she did not lack courage. There was an awestruck pause and Sally lifted a flushed face to see what happened. A moment's silence was broken by a soft thud as one exquisite crimson rose fell into the Contessa's lap.

"Dinner," said Buscari, who could bear no more. "Rodrigo, forward. Fernando, bring in the soup. Ladies and gentlemen, dinner is served."

Among the Italian guests was one who had given as his own the impressive name of Orsino Monteverde. He liked it, it sounded well, and though he did not adorn it, it had its effect upon porters, servants, and the more credulous among hoteliers. He had used so many names in his time that he had almost forgotten his own; this one pleased him so much that he was in the habit of referring to himself by it in the third person. "No one can say that Orsino Monteverde ever" did this or that, or "Orsino Monteverde would never" something else. Buscari, however, not being in the least credulous, distrusted the narrow eyes and sidelong looks, the long sharp nose and the thin-lipped mouth. James and Charles Latimer wrinkled their noses when they first saw him, and exchanged glances with each other.

"A spiv if ever I saw one," said Buscari to his headwaiter, Fernando.

"One would know him for a spiv even if one had never seen one before," said Fernando. "What will you do?"

Buscari lifted his shoulders. "Keep our eyes open, that is all. He says he is only here for two or three days."

Orsino Monteverde was not in the least impressed by the poltergeist manifestations, he took no notice of them, he did not even think about them. He had never heard of poltergeists and he disbelieved in the occult; some joker was playing tricks, that was all. When any of his fellow guests mentioned the subject to him, he raised his eyebrows and smiled condescendingly.

"Orsino Monteverde is not the man to be disturbed by childish practical jokes."

On the night when the umbrella came to grief he received a telegram by previous arrangement with a friend; it called on him to return instantly to Rome, as a hitch had arisen in the settlement of his father's estate. He showed it to Buscari and asked to be called early with coffee and rolls in his room. "This nuisance is always occurring," he said languidly. "It is true that my father, the late Prince, was no businessman, but what do we pay attorneys for if we must do their work for them?" Sometimes his father was the late General or even the late Admiral; in point of fact, he was very much alive and kept a boarding house for sailors in one of the more regrettable streets in Naples.

Buscari said that tiresomenesses occurred in the most distinguished families and asked if the guest would care to have his bill now—asking pardon for the sordid suggestion—it would save time in the morning.

"Certainly, at once, please," said the alleged Monteverde, and produced a roll of notes which almost made Buscari wonder whether he had been uncharitable. Monteverde preferred, for his own reasons, a clean, quick, unhampered getaway before the other guests were about in the morning. "Coffee at six, do not fail me," he said as Buscari handed him his receipted bill.

"I will attend to it myself in person," said Buscari, and went away to deal with another impending departure, his odd-job man, a most superior person whom Buscari would be sorry to lose. This man had come to Buscari in tears to say that his—the odd-job man's—mother had been taken desperately ill in Verona and was calling for him, he must go.

"Of course," said Buscari kindly, "at once. Go and comfort your respected mother, and when she is well again you shall return, Giuseppe. Spend this evening instructing in his tasks your successor, of whom I have not much opinion, and leave early tomorrow morning. I trust you will find your revered parent much restored. Come to my office and I will give you your wages."

Giuseppe thanked him with genuine emotion. In point of fact, he had no mother anywhere except, we trust, in heaven, but he had to make some excuse. He had, at one time, served in the Conte's household, where he had been saddled with a theft he had not committed and sent to prison. Some genuine thefts had followed his release but, as he was not a thief *par métier,* he was soon caught and sent to prison again. Here he decided that he was on the wrong road and that there should be no more of this. He had lived honestly, though poorly, ever since. Now, here was the Conte, whom it was not always possible to avoid, and once or twice he had looked at Giuseppe sharply. If once the Conte remembered when and where he had seen the man before, he was not likely to hold his tongue.

Giuseppe knew that he could get a better post in Milan if only he had the clothes for it. He had got as far as buying a good secondhand suitcase but, alas, the good clothes were still to seek. His pay was small and clothes are dear; he had only the suit he was wearing and some overalls. However, perhaps someone in Milan would lend him some money with which to buy a suit. He sighed and weighted his good suitcase with some newspapers and a couple of bricks. One must keep up appearances.

Orsino Monteverde, having provided himself with a passkey, slipped out from his bedroom soon after one in the morning and made the rounds of the hotel bedrooms. He moved like a cat and more expertly, he did not awaken anyone. By three o'clock he was back in his bedroom with a quite useful collection of jewelry, watches, cigarette cases and other valuables, and a very fair amount of loose cash. He had already packed his cases; he put his newly acquired property into a briefcase and retired to bed for three hours. At six a waiter came into his room with a tray of excellent coffee and rolls and drew up the blinds.

"The signor has a fine morning for his journey," he said.

"It would be finer still if I did not have to go," said Monteverde sleepily, and roused himself to drink his coffee.

When he had undressed he had left his clothes on a chair at the foot of the bed; it was hidden from him as he lay by the high footboard, and it was not until he actually got up that he saw that there was nothing there. No clothes, that is; the chair was nakedly in evidence.

"I must have hung them up," he said uneasily. "I was tired when I'd finished."

He looked inside the wardrobe but it was quite empty except for a few scraps of tissue paper and some coat hangers stamped "Albergo del Pescatore Paziente, Menaggio."

"That waiter," said Monteverde, "must have taken my suit away to brush it, the fool! But why did he take my underclothes as well? Dopey, like all the rest."

He flung back the lids of his suitcases but they were even emptier than the wardrobe.

"I've been robbed," said Monteverde. "Me! While I was out of the room last night some sneak thief crept in and scoffed my togs. That's what. No, while I was asleep; the clothes I had on's gone, too." A frightful thought struck him and he leapt at the drawer in which he had left his comfortably heavy briefcase. It was still there and he snatched it out, but it was no longer heavy. It was deplorably light, for it, too, was quite empty.

Chapter XIX
Four Umbrellas

Monteverde staggered to the bed, sat down heavily upon it, and held his head in both hands.

"Since I've no longer got the stuff," he thought, "I can ring the bell and complain I've been robbed."

He thought this over for a few minutes.

"No, I can't. Buscari will call the police and they will come and look at me. I can't have that, they are looking for me already for that job at the Continentale in Rome. I can't have that."

He looked wildly round the room. His dressing gown was still hanging on the door and his washing and shaving gear were still on the washstand. They were all he had except the cheerful cerise-and-green-striped pajamas he was wearing. Another hideous thought rose up and struck him down once more.

"My money! It was in my coat pocket—all the money I have—"

A quarter of an hour later he roused himself from a state of stupor and rose unsteadily to his feet. He would go and have a bath; a nice hot bath was always soothing. Stimulating to the intellect, too. Nothing like a hot bath when you are trying to think out something. He put on his dressing gown, gathered up towel and soap, and tottered along the passage to the bathroom. Thanks to Quentin's English ideas, there were plenty of bathrooms and the water was always hot. He lay in it and soaked luxuriously, feeling more cheerful. He would persuade Buscari not to call the police, so damaging to the good name of the hotel. Buscari would provide enough money, in exchange for Monteverde's forbearance, to supply him with simple necessities and the railway fare to Naples. Monteverde writhed, how his father would laugh. However, everyone slipped up sometimes.

He got out of the bath, picked up his towel, and glanced round the steam-filled room. His dressing gown and pajamas—he had hung them on the back of the door—it was only the steam which prevented him from seeing them. They must be there.

They were not.

A long melancholy hoot filled the room as Monteverde flung open the window for air. He stuck his head out in time to see the early steamer for Como—he should have been on it—leaving the landing stage. The *Garibaldi* had an unusually festive look this morning; a gay splash of color flared on the forestay. The steamer put on speed and the decorations extended themselves in the wind. Cerise-and-green in three-inch stripes. His pajama trousers.

His strengthless fingers fell from the window sill and Orsino Monteverde slid down the wall to lie unconscious upon the bathroom floor.

At about this time it occurred to Buscari that Monteverde had not left the hotel; perhaps he had gone to sleep again. He sent up his newest and youngest waiter to find out. The waiter knocked at the bedroom door, received no answer, and entered.

"Signor, by permission—"

But the signor was not there and his empty suitcases were standing wide open. Empty. Then presumably the signor had changed his mind about leaving. The waiter looked in the wardrobe and glanced into the drawers of the chest-of-drawers. Empty, all empty. "What the devil," muttered the waiter, "has he done with his clothes, for we all knew he had plenty? He cannot be wearing them all at once, including his pajamas and dressing gown."

The waiter went out of the room, shutting the door behind him; on his way to the stairs he passed the bathroom door. He tried the handle but the door, as he half expected, was locked, so he tapped on the panels. Signor Monteverde! Was Signor Monteverde within? He was answered by a most peculiar noise between a howl and a whine. He tapped again.

"Signor Monteverde?"

The same noise again. The waiter trotted along the passage, ran down the stairs, and approached Buscari.

"I cannot find the signor Monteverde. His suitcases are in his room, empty. There are no clothes in the room at all, it is cleared out."

"Nonsense," said Buscari sharply. "The signor has gone, that is all. It does not matter, he has paid his bill."

"But the empty suitcases—"

"Someone else's, put there in error."

"And there is also a dog in number two bathroom, second floor. It is howling and whining."

"A dog? I do not permit animals in my hotel. Why did you not bring it down?"

"Signor"—the waiter hesitated—"it has locked itself in."

Buscari looked at the boy sharply. "That remark is completely idiotic and you know it. I thought you had a little sense, if only a very little. The owner is in the room with it, of course."

"But no one answered and I tapped twice, thinking that the signor Monteverde might be there. Fallen asleep, perhaps, in his bath."

Buscari pinched his chin.

"I suppose," he said, "I had better go up myself. The matter of the dog, at least, must be looked into."

He went upstairs, with the waiter at his heels, and knocked at the bathroom door; there was no reply and he turned the handle. The door was, indeed, locked.

"I said," began the waiter.

"Silence!" said Buscari, and laid his ear to the panel. "There is something in there," he said. "It grunts."

"Blessed saints," said the waiter, recoiling. "The dog has turned into a pig!"

Buscari produced his passkey, unlocked the door, and flung it open. Two long, naked legs were laid prone across the floor; the rest of the body could not be seen for it was under the bath. It was, in fact, looking for its dressing gown. Buscari snatched the towel from the chair, laid it centrally across the body, and signaled to the waiter. Together they laid hold upon the body's feet and drew it out; it rolled over, sat up, and uttered a most heart-rending groan.

"Signor Monteverde! Are you ill?"

Monteverde shook his head, covered his face with his hands, and whined nasally.

"There," said the waiter.

"Shut the door," said Buscari, looking round the room for what was not there. "Signor, where is your dressing gown? Your pajamas?"

Monteverde pointed violently towards the window with a stabbing gesture of one lean forefinger. "To Como," he said. "To Como. To Como. To Como."

"Fetch Dr. Williams," said Buscari.

Dr. Williams came, observed, and administered an injection.

"That'll quiet him down," he said as the babble of "To Como" died down into an indistinguishable mutter. "Fetch a mental specialist. This isn't my pigeon. The man's bats."

In due course the mental specialist came and, later yet, removed Monteverde for skillful treatment. It is to be hoped that he recovered and decided to live a better life; in any case the Albergo del Pescatore Paziente saw him no more.

Giuseppe the porter sat in a third-class compartment of the train to Milan with his good suitcase in the rack over his head. He wanted a handkerchief and took down the case to get one out. Somehow the case did not feel quite the same; bricks bump about. He opened it and found it neatly and tightly packed with extremely good clothes; suits, silk shirts, socks, ties, underwear. On the top lay a sheet of paper folded in half; upon it was written in block capitals a message in simple and elementary Italian.

> THESE CLOTHES ARE FOR YOU. WE THINK THEY WILL FIT.
> WE HOPE YOU GET YOUR JOB. GOOD LUCK.

James and Charles Latimer, in the privacy of their locked and darkened rooms, had looked over the loot from Monteverde's briefcase and had knitted their brows.

"This little gold watch bracelet is certainly Sally's, I have observed her wearing it."

"You are in the right, Cousin James. This gold cigarette case is the Count's and this diamond ring is Mrs. Thompson's."

"No, no, Charles. That is the Contessa's, depend upon it. This gold pocket watch is the doctor's—"

"Oh no, Cousin. The doctor's has a second hand, I opine for counting pulses. Yes, sir, a tool of his trade."

"I am by no means assured, but you may well be right. In that case, whose—and all these other things—'

"And all this assorted money—"

They had brooded over the problem.

"I have it, Cousin James. Let us return these things and the money haphazard among the different rooms. The guests will amuse themselves sorting it all in the morning. Yes, sir, that is what I suggest."

"Upon my soul, Charles, you have hit it. We will not even select Jeremy's and Sally's or it may be thought that they had a finger in this pie."

"Moreover, it will save time; we have still enough to do. James, do you undertake the distribution while I go for the umbrellas. I will take some of this thief's money to pay for them. Sir, it stinks of dishonesty. Pah!"

"How much have you there? Many thousands of lire. Charles, it must be worth several thousands of pounds sterling with the lira at twenty-five to the pound—"

Charles had laughed. "I fear, Cousin, that the lira is but a shadow of its former self; I believe that today it is more nearly a thousand to the pound.

Nonetheless, there is more than enough here for our umbrellas. What do you purpose to do with the remainder?"

"The poor box in the church, Charles. I remember with shame how little we did for the cause of religion in Besançon after all our talk."

"Very true. Well, shall we go?"

The guests of the Patient Fisherman came down to breakfast in a state of considerable excitement.

"Your poltergeist has been at it again, Dr. Williams!"

I know," said the doctor. "I have myself been presented with a gold face-powder container, presumably the property of a lady—"

"My compact!" said the Contessa. "My Ercole gave it me."

"Two lipsticks," continued the doctor, "one gold, one not; a silver cigarette case, and five thousand lire."

"I've got a gentleman's gold watch," said Sally, "and a—"

The babble became general.

"I have lost a cigarette case and this I have is not mine—"

"A diamond ring and a jade brooch—"

"A gold bracelet—"

"Ladies and gentlemen," said the doctor, raising his voice, "if our good friend Buscari would clear one of these tables we could lay out all the stuff and sort it more conveniently."

It was done and the result looked like a counter in a better class pawnshop; it was quickly dispersed, everyone claiming his own. The money was a little more difficult since few people know exactly how much they have at any given moment and are apt to be optimistic, but it was shared out at last.

"There," said the doctor, beaming upon everyone, "now we are all happy, aren't we?"

"*Non!*" said the Frenchman emphatically.

"Not altogether," said the Scandinavians cautiously.

"Not at all," said the various Italians. "Completely not."

"I cannot understand it," said the doctor. "Here you have the almost unexampled privilege of observing the most remarkable exhibition of poltergeist activity of modern times, and you—"

"I go at once," said the mother of the children, "taking my family."

"Oh no!" cried the doctor. "Let all the others leave, but not you. It will be too disappointing if you go; I couldn't bear it just when we were getting on so well."

"Sir," said the children's father.

"At least tell me where you are going and I—"

"*Sir!*"

"What? Oh Lord. My good man, I—"

"Come, Serafina. Come, children. Buscari, we will breakfast in our rooms and leave directly thereafter. My bill, please."

"Mamma. Are we going away? Must we go away, Mamma?"

"Come, my treasure."

"Boo-hoo-oo!"

"Maria weeps," said her mother accurately.

The party left the room and Dr. Williams wiped his brow with a large handkerchief.

"Did that cockeyed laboratory assistant really think I'd fallen for that horsehair pincushion of a woman, his wife?"

"Your remarks, my dear Williams," said Quentin, "were notably ambiguous."

"But it's the children!" wailed the doctor. "When they go it will all stop, and I shall never never have such another chance!"

"Buck up," said Jeremy. "Maybe now the poltergeist has got here he'll like it so much he'll want to stay, kids or no kids."

"He cannot. There must be children."

There was a small clatter on an empty plate before the doctor; it was caused by the arrival of half a dozen lumps of sugar.

"There," said Jeremy. "He's trying to cheer you up. Attaboy, Doc! Don't despair yet."

The Count rose to his feet.

"Ladies and gentlemen. It was hardly possible for me to bring them down myself, but—"

"Bring what?" asked Quentin.

"Has anyone," asked the Count, "lost an umbrella? No? Strange, very strange."

He sat down again and went on with his breakfast.

"What is all this," said Jeremy, "about umbrellas? Have you got one? I get it, it's to replace—"

"Forty-eight," said the Count with his mouth full of roll.

"Forty-eight? What, 1948, six years—"

"Umbrellas," said the Count.

"Forty-eight umbrellas? Forty—"

"I don't believe it," said Mrs. Thompson crisply.

"Madame," said the Contessa, "if you will give yourself the trouble of coming to look, no doubt there will at once be fewer."

"Ladies, ladies," said Buscari, "on my knees I implore—"

A sprinkling of water, as from a watering-can with a rose nozzle, fell lightly and alternately upon the Contessa and Mrs. Thompson and ceased at once.

"This is too much," said Poppy angrily, and rose from her chair.

"Let me lend you an umbrella," said the Contessa sweetly. "My complexion will stand it but yours, I doubt not, is more delicate."

Mrs. Thompson sat down again with a bump and went on with her breakfast; no more water fell. Breakfast took its appointed and leisurely course; before it was over there came the bustle of departure from the hall and the voice of Buscari apologizing.

"If you will take my advice," said the voice of the children's father, "you will call in a priest and have the whole place energetically exorcised."

"Boo-hoo-oo!"

"Maria weeps," said the doctor, still in the dining room. "Upon my soul I feel like doing the same." He moved to the window to watch gloomily the family departure. "There, they have gone and it is all over."

He turned from the window to regard without interest the gradual emptying of the room as the guests went about their business. Mrs. Thompson got up and walked in her usual stately manner towards the door; on this occasion the effect was a little marred by the presence of four independent umbrellas who walked, two by two, behind her. A profound hush settled upon the room. Mrs. Thompson moved on unaware until she crossed a strip of polished wooden floor between two carpets; her high-heeled shoes tapped clearly half a dozen times before they were silenced upon the carpet beyond. The clear tapping was immediately mimicked by the ferrules of the four umbrellas behind and the lady turned sharply. The umbrellas stopped at once, courteously aligned their handles towards her, and waited. Poppy Thompson uttered a piercing scream and rushed out of the room, followed, at a decorous gallop, by the four umbrellas. There was a scampering up the stairs and a door slammed. The Contessa applauded.

"A-ah," said the doctor, letting out upon a note of pure bliss the breath he had been holding.

"Most peculiar," said Quentin Latimer, "most. One thing about it, a man can't be expected to marry a woman who's followed about everywhere by umbrellas. I mean what a fool he'd look."

"What did I tell you?" said Jeremy, seizing Dr. Williams by the arm. "Those kids have gone, but has the poltergeist let up? No, sir. As you said yourself, it has attached itself to the lady, and how right you were. Is this your chance, or is it? Go to it, Doctor, go to it."

He gave Dr. Williams a gentle push towards the door, and the doctor, with the fixed gaze of one who sees unimaginable visions, drifted out and could be heard plodding earnestly up the stairs. Buscari came into the room and stood staring vacantly before him.

"Buscari!" said the Contessa.

"Signora Contessa?"

"We did intend to leave this morning but we have changed our minds. We would not miss this Polichinella for any consideration."

"I thank the signora Contessa," said Buscari in a melancholy voice. "I only hope that a few more of my guests will follow her excellent example before I am completely ruined." He wrung his hands.

"Are they all leaving?" asked Quentin.

"All, signor, except the Scandinavians. They have paid their travel agency for a fortnight and, unless things become actually violent, for their fortnight they will stay. But the others, the Italians"—his eyes filled with tears—"they are all packing. They will all go home to Milan and Pavia and Verona and Turin and tell all their friends and the name of my hotel will be destroyed. *Dio mio*, it will be in the papers next." And he sobbed aloud.

The Contessa sprang to her feet and patted him kindly upon the arm. "Take courage, Buscari, it shall not happen. I myself will talk to them, every one separately. For myself I am thrilled, I am entranced. It is like a miracle play, if I may say so without intended irreverence, to behold this poltergeist acting as matrimonial agent between our good doctor and your so imposing English widow. One would say that the poltergeist is a friend of our good signor Quentin, no?" With a flash of her magnificent dark eyes she swirled out of the room, her husband trotting after her.

"A very kindhearted lady," said Buscari, cheering up.

"You know," said Jeremy thoughtfully, "I don't think that dame is as foolish as she looks, either."

"I'm sure it's very kind of the poltergeist," said Quentin Latimer vaguely. "Can't think why it should bother. Still, much obliged and all that. Sally, my dear, you're not crying?"

"Only with laughter," she said, mopping her eyes. "Oh, those solemn umbrellas!" She leaned heavily upon Jeremy. "I've got such a pain, laughing—"

Dr. Williams came back into the room. "A small glass of cognac, please, Buscari."

"Immediately, signor—"

"How is the lady?" asked Jeremy. "Still umbrella-conscious?"

"Most curious," said the doctor, frowning. "She is quite free of them so long as she remains in her room, but the moment she comes outside the door, dammit, there they are again."

"Are poltergeists," asked Quentin, "usually as delicate-minded as that?"

"Certainly not," said the doctor, "far from it. Very far, as a rule. Thank you, Buscari, I'll take it up."

"Cousin James and Cousin Charles," said Jeremy in a murmuring tone only audible to Sally, "I hand it to you on my knees. Polter-guys they may be, but always perfect gentlemen."

Chapter XX
St. Denis-sur-Aisne

THE SIGNORA Thompson's compliments," said Buscari, waylaying Jeremy and Sally Latimer in the hall just before lunch. "She begs the favor of a short interview in her room if the moment is not too grossly inconvenient."

"Wants to see us?" said Sally. "I can't believe it."

"I had an idea the lady didn't care for us," said Jeremy. "Why should she want to see us?"

"To speak precisely," said Buscari, "she does not. She wishes to see the Signor Latimer—my signor—alone and he will not. He has refused, she has said again: 'Come.' He says he is sick, that he is on a journey, that he is busy entertaining friends. She stamps her foot and says: 'Bid him come.' So he says he will go with you or not at all. I have been awaiting your return for"— he glanced at his watch— "five and thirty minutes. May I tell him you will go with?"

"Sure," said Jeremy, "Sure. Where is Dr. Williams?"

"Not in the hotel at the moment."

"Oh. What's cooking?"

"Perhaps, darling," said Sally, "if we went up we might find out."

"Well, what are we waiting for?"

They waited for a moment near the door of Poppy Thompson's room while Buscari went along the passage to summon Quentin Latimer. In a dark corner near by Sally noticed two umbrellas leaning normally against the wall; new, neatly rolled umbrellas. She laid her hand upon one of them, it was warm and friendly to the touch and quivered slightly under her fingers as the top of a piano can be felt to vibrate when chords are struck upon the keyboard.

A door closed along the passage and Quentin Latimer came with long strides.

"Well, well," he said in a tone intended for a whisper. "Good of you to come. Hope you didn't mind. I wasn't going in alone, not me." He stopped and looked at Sally. "My dear child, how well you look. Nice pink cheeks, aren't they, Jeremy? Place suits you, evidently. Well, shall we go in?"

He knocked and a voice told them to enter; he opened the door and stood back for Sally to precede him. As she turned to go in she glanced towards the corner; the umbrellas were no longer there.

Mrs. Thompson rose majestically from an armchair by the window.

"How good of you, Sally, to come," she said, "and your charming young husband, too, so attentive. I had rather hoped for a few words in private with you, Quentin, but evidently it is not to be."

"We met in the passage outside," said Sally, with strict if limited truth.

"So we just tagged along too, with Uncle Quentin," said Jeremy. "How are you feeling now, Mrs. Thompson?"

"In any case," said Quentin bluntly, "I'm sure that you can have nothing to say to me which you wouldn't wish my young relations to hear. Quite inconceivable."

"So inconceivable," said Mrs. Thompson, tapping with her toe on the parquet floor, "that I cannot imagine why you had to say it at all. Please sit down. I only wished to tell you, Quentin, that under kind Dr. Williams' advice I am going away for a few days."

"Oh, are you?" said Quentin hopefully.

"What a nice man Dr. Williams is, so kind, so understanding."

"Yes, isn't he?" said Quentin. "Well off, too. His first wife died and left him a very nice little packet indeed. No children. Good fellow, Williams."

"His first wife, you said? He has since married again, then?"

"No. Oh no, what made you think that? Dammit, he only lost her about a year ago. Give the man time."

Mrs. Thompson managed her silvery laugh. "Dear Quentin, how absurd you are! I was about to tell you that Dr. Williams advises a short absence from the scene of these ridiculous occurrences. He thinks if I do this I may be free of these—these—"

"Umbrellas?"

"Supernormal phenomena. I am going to London this afternoon and will let you know when I shall return. If I may, I should like to keep these rooms on."

"Certainly," said Quentin, "certainly. Why not? I'll tell Buscari."

"Dr. Williams," said the lady with a becoming momentary hesitation, "has kindly offered to travel to London with me. He thinks I should be attended by some experienced person in case of any recurrence of the trouble."

"Quite right," said Jeremy heartily. "Dr. Williams is a man who has fine ideas."

"Thank you so much," said Poppy acidly. "Your approval, Mr. Jeremy Latimer, was the one thing I needed."

"Sure," said Jeremy comfortably, "sure."

Sally was seized by a convulsion which emerged as a snort. She apologized, "A sneeze that went the wrong way," and retired behind her handkerchief.

"Anyone would think," said Mrs. Thompson suspiciously, "that you were amused at something."

"It tickled," said Sally, dimpling. "You know. All up my nose."

"I recommend a nasal douche," said Mrs. Thompson, rising. "And now, if you will excuse me, I have to pack."

"Good-bye, Mrs. Thompson," said Sally, shaking hands. "A very pleasant journey."

"Good-bye, Poppy," said Quentin.

"Surely," she said, "you will see me as far as the Lugano bus in the square?"

"Of course, of course. Don't know what I was thinking of. Excuse me now—a man waiting to see me—" He dived out of the door and disappeared down the stairs.

"Good-bye, Mrs. Thompson," said Jeremy. "Have a good journey and no more umbrellas."

She shut the door firmly behind him.

There was a small crowd in the Largo Cavour milling round the bus for Lugano, which connected with the fast train to Bâle. There were people intending to travel and getting agitated about their luggage, there was their luggage being handed up by hotel porters and stowed, and there were other people seeing off the people who intended to travel. Upon this disorganized group there descended a party so self-contained and dignified as to resemble the First Cruiser Squadron entering a harbor where a rather disorderly regatta is in progress; it was headed by Giuseppe's successor carrying Mrs. Thompson's luggage and the bootboy carrying Dr. Williams' luggage. Behind them there walked Mrs. Thompson and her medical attendant while Quentin Latimer, with the air of one who does his duty at all costs for the honor of Old England, stalked detachedly behind. Jeremy and Sally Latimer, skulking behind the loaded display stands in front of Rossi's shop, watched from a safe distance. The crowd round the bus parted deferentially to let the cortège through.

"No umbrellas," said Jeremy.

"Of course not," said Sally. "They'd never make Mrs. Thompson look ridiculous in public, their manners are far too good."

"Guess you're right, honey. They—oh, blazes, yes there are. Close to Poppy, look. They—she's seen them."

Mrs. Thompson sprang up the steps of the bus with the most admired agility, the doctor followed, and the crowd, who were too closely packed together to have seen four slim umbrellas in the middle of a party and would not have believed it if they had, surged in and climbed aboard. Quentin Latimer, hat in hand, disengaged himself from the crush and waited patiently for the bus to drive away. His eyes were on the lake, he plainly did not see four active umbrellas hopping frantically upon their ferrules in an attempt to slip through a crowd far too occupied to notice them. The driver started his engine, the non-traveling public withdrew, the umbrellas were lost to sight, Quentin waved his hat, and the bus drove away.

Jeremy and Sally walked across to meet him.

"Dear Uncle Quentin," said Sally, slipping her arm through his, "you look ten years younger already."

"I am. Mind you, she may come back—"

"I wouldn't," said Jeremy, "not to be hopped after by wild umbrellas, I wouldn't."

"Nor shall I ever be safe," continued Quentin, "in returning to England. Land of the free and all that. I wouldn't be."

"Never mind, Uncle Quentin—"

"I don't. I've got a few days' freedom at least and I propose to enjoy it." He looked down at the hat he still held in his hand, appeared surprised to see it and, with a carefree gesture, skimmed it into the lake. "I was wondering what you would like to do this evening. What about hiring a motorboat and having a picnic on the other side? Buscari will put us up a basket. Cold chicken and all that."

One of Menaggio's police appeared at his elbow.

"The signor Latimer no longer requires his hat?"

"What? No. No, I don't want it any more. One moment. Have I, by chance, offended against some byelaw in thus ridding myself—"

"No, no, signor—"

"I would not wish—"

"It is understood, signor. I did but wonder whether the signor had acted, as it were, inadvertently. Thinking, perhaps, that he held a cigarette end—"

"No. Nothing like that. Listen. That hat was a symbol."

"Certainly, signor."

"A symbol of servitude, of degradation. I cast off my, symbolically speaking, chains. I have no actual chains so I cast off my hat. Understood?"

"Perfectly. May I felicitate the signor?"

"You may. Good afternoon. About that picnic, Sally. Would you like it?"

"Great fun, Uncle Quentin. I wish our cousins James and Charles were back, they'd enjoy it too."

"If you will turn your eye on the third seat back," said Jeremy, "you'll see that they are. Hiya, Cousin Charles!"

"Dear me," said Quentin, "I am very pleased to see you both, but how did you arrive here at this hour? No steamer, no bus. Don't tell me you walked from Como."

"Indeed no," said James, "although when I was a young man I thought nothing of walking thirty miles in a day."

"He measures the miles with his legs," said Charles, "like a pair of compasses striding across a map. Sobbing with fatigue and humiliation, I totter miserably behind. Yes, sir, that is how it goes when James takes me for a walk."

"But we have only to mount upon horses," said James generously, "for me to appear the looby I am while Charles flies hedges and walls like a centaur."

"A sound, reliable car is good enough for me," said Quentin. "I suppose you thumbed a lift."

"Thumbed—excuse me—"

"There seems to be a certain mystery about it," said Quentin. "I suppose the car was driven by a lady, hey? I ask no more. Come indoors. Buscari has a couple of magnums on ice. I will be frank with you. We are celebrating."

"Celebrating?" said Charles innocently.

"Certainly. Excuse me a moment, there is Massimo. Massimo! Is your motorboat engaged for this afternoon?"

"Signor, if my boat had been engaged by the whole Noble Family of the Colonna they should stay ashore if the signor Latimer desired to use it."

"That means it isn't. Bring it along to my slip in an hour's time, Massimo. We're going for a picnic."

So for some days of brilliant, unclouded weather they walked and sailed and drove and made merry until Quentin Latimer became uneasy because there was no news of Poppy Thompson.

"I am afraid to go home," he said suddenly. "She may be there when we get back."

They were standing on the landing stage at Gravedona waiting for the evening steamer to take them to Menaggio.

"You have received no mail from Mrs. Thompson?" asked James.

"None. I don't understand it. I don't like it."

"But," said Sally, "you don't want to hear from her, do you, Uncle Quentin?"

"No."

"Then what's biting you?" asked Jeremy. "Let's have it."

"I want to know where she is. If she's in London at least I've got another thirty hours. She may be in the train approaching Bâle at this moment. She may be flying to Milan. She may be on tonight's steamer, she may be sitting in the lounge waiting for us to come in—"

"For Pete's sake, Uncle Quentin," said Jeremy, "she isn't a man-eating tiger!"

"Tigress, darling," said Sally.

"That's what you think," said Quentin Latimer, and showed the whites of his eyes.

James tried to encourage him while Sally turned to Charles, who, as usual, was at her elbow.

"I suppose," she said in low tones, "You couldn't do anything? I mean you can't tell what's happening, can you?"

"We have no more knowledge of what is happening at a distance than you have, Cousin Sally. I could go to London but—"

"But what?"

"I might not get back. It is a long way. Still, that does not matter greatly, if you are anxious—"

"No, no! You must not go if there is any risk—I mean if you couldn't get back here it would be too horrid."

"I might not be able to get back anywhere, Cousin Sally. Not even to where we came from, which is, as it were, the doorway to our home. But I will consult James."

"No, please don't. Cousin Charles, promise me you won't. Promise me. You won't even try—"

"Here's the steamer," said Quentin in a melancholy voice. "I suppose we must go on board."

"Oh, perk up, Cousin," said James. "If she does come back you are no worse disposed than you were before and we must try again, that is all."

"What d'you mean, 'again'?" said Quentin irritably. "You didn't do anything before. You and Charles were away in Rome when it all happened."

"Very true," said James meekly. "I only meant that we must think again. Eh, Charles, how say you?"

Quentin snorted.

Upon the following morning the four Latimer cousins were standing in the hall waiting for Quentin.

"I wonder if there'll be any news from Poppy today," said Sally.

"To speak truth," said James, "I hope so. It is the state of uncertainty in which he now lives which preys upon the spirits of our poor cousin."

There came from upstairs the sound of a caroling voice uplifted in sheer lightness of heart. " 'Come into the garden, Maud,' " it sang, " 'for the black bat, Night, has flown. Come into . . .' "

"Uncle Quentin?" said Jeremy incredulously.

"Good gracious!" said Sally.

"Gentlemen, hush!" said Charles in awed tones.

The voice drew nearer to the head of the stairs. " 'I am here by the gate alone, I am here—by the gate—alo-o-ne!' "

Quentin Latimer looked over the head of the stairs and said: "Ha!" He then flung his leg over the handrail and slid rapidly down the curving balustrade, holding a flimsy piece of paper between his fingers. "They are married," he cried, landing with a thud at the bottom. "They are married. By special license, so impetuous. Poppy and that excellent good fellow, Williams. They are irrevocably wed. I have a telegram, read it. No, let me read it again. They are married. Do you know, it's very odd, but I feel exactly as though I were drunk." He blinked owlishly at Sally. "And all I had was one glass of wine. When the telegram was brought up to me, I opened a bottle at once for, of course, I did not know what—"

He went on talking but his hearers' attention was distracted by the sight of a tiny figure sitting astride the handrail at the head of the stairs. It was Ulysses, very neat and tidy in his little red jacket and cap; his hair was smoothly brushed, since Charles had seen to his toilet that morning, and in one tiny paw he held a glass of red wine.

"I drank one glass," continued Quentin, "poured out another, and then, summoning all my courage—"

Ulysses crossed his legs casually and sipped his wine with evident enjoyment; as he was doing so he glanced down into the hall below and saw Charles looking up at him. He uttered a squeak of joy, launched himself, and came sliding down the banister rail drinking as he came. He timed it so accurately that he emptied the glass at the moment he reached the bottom.

"As soon as my eyes fell upon the message," said Quentin, "I knew I was saved, but it took a—"

Ulysses left the empty glass upon the flat end of the banister and made one leap into Charles' arms.

"When it dawned on me," said Quentin, and broke off short. "Where the dickens did that monkey come from?"

"It's mine," explained Charles, stroking the soft fur. "Yes, sir. We took a liking to each other on sight, so, now he's my monkey. Make your service to the lady, Ulysses."

Ulysses climbed up to Charles' shoulder and stood there, cap in hand, to bow deeply towards Sally with the other hand laid over his heart.

"That's a pretty trick," said Quentin approvingly. "Very pretty. Teach him that yourself, did you? Don't know what Buscari'll say, the Conte seeing monkeys and you owning one."

"Sooner than discompose the good Buscari," said Charles, "I will find—"

"The good Buscari does what I tell him," said Quentin. "I like the monkey. Good manners. Will he come to me?"

"Surely," said Charles, handing him over. "Go to the gentleman, Ulysses."

"Lunch time," said Quentin, leading the way into the dining room with Ulysses dandled like a baby in his arms. "Buscari! Serve wine to all the tables. I have a toast which I shall ask the company to honor. Be quick."

"Cousin Charles," said Sally, lingering behind to speak to him, "is that really the same Ulysses?"

"The one, the only original Ulysses, my dear little cousin. I bought him from a traveling circus in Shandon, Virginia, just before the war and he has been with me ever since. Apart from a regrettable tendency towards intemperance he has never given me a moment's anxiety. He never lies, never cheats, and is always pleased to see me. What better companion could a man require, Cousin Sally?"

"What indeed?" said Sally, looking straight before her.

"What, indeed," said Charles evenly.

James, just in front of them, glanced over his shoulder and met Charles' abstracted gaze.

"The company is served, signor," said Buscari.

"Good," said Quentin. "Ladies and gentlemen. I have just received the happy news of a romance between two people known to us all. Dr. Williams and Mrs. Thompson were married in London this morning. Long life, health, and happiness to them both!"

The toast was honored with acclamations which startled Ulysses into taking refuge under the table and a babble of excited comment which, being expressed in Italian, did not greatly interest any of the Latimers except Quentin. The other four sat at table talking among themselves.

"Cousin James and Cousin Charles, I take my hat off," said Jeremy. "When you take on a job, you do it."

"We did our poor best," said James, "with the means at our disposal. We are unfairly advantaged, as we are the first to admit."

"Yeah, I know," said Jeremy, "but it's your detail work that gets me. Those four umbrellas—"

"I notice with pleasure, my dear young cousin," said James warmly, "that our unusual attributes no longer appear to affect you adversely."

"Why, no," said Jeremy thoughtfully. "Don't know, now, why they ever did. Took some getting used to, I guess."

Quentin came back to the table and said that now all that fuss was over perhaps they might have lunch. "Where's that monkey gone?"

"Slipped off into the garden, I reckon," said Charles. "He will not go far; I can summon him when I will."

"Nice beast," said Quentin.

"Without intruding into your private affairs, Cousin Jeremy," said James, "may I ask if you purpose to stay long in this charming spot?"

"No. Sally and I should be back in England the end of this week," said Jeremy. "I have a business appointment on Monday. Why, can I do anything—"

"I thank you," said James. "If you could convey us as far upon your road as is convenient, it would be very pleasant to spend a few more days in your delightful company."

"Certainly," said Jeremy. "Where do you and Cousin Charles want to go?"

"To St. Denis-sur-Aisne."

THE END

Rue Morgue Press Titles as of July 2000

Brief Candles by Manning Coles. From Topper to Aunt Dimity, mystery readers have embraced the cozy ghost story. Four of the best were written by Manning Coles, the creator of the witty Tommy Hambledon spy novels. First published in 1954, *Brief Candles* is likely to produce more laughs than chills as a young couple vacationing in France run into two gentlemen with decidedly old-world manners. What they don't know is that James and Charles Latimer are ancestors of theirs who shuffled off this mortal coil some 80 years earlier when, emboldened by strong drink and with only a pet monkey and an aged waiter as allies, the two made a valiant, foolish and quite fatal attempt to halt a German advance during the Franco-Prussian War of 1870. Now these two ectoplasmic gentlemen and their spectral pet monkey Ulysses have been summoned from their unmarked graves because their visiting relatives are in serious trouble. But before they can solve the younger Latimers' problems, the three benevolent spirits light brief candles of insanity for a tipsy policeman, a recalcitrant banker, a convocation of English ghostbusters, and a card-playing rogue who's wanted for murder. "As felicitously foolish as a collaboration of (P.G.) Wodehouse and Thorne Smith."— Anthony Boucher. "For those who like something out of the ordinary. Lighthearted, very funny.'—*The Sunday Times.* "A gay, most readable story."—*The Daily Telegraph.*   **0-915230-24-0**   **$14.00**

The Chinese Chop by Juanita Sheridan. The postwar housing crunch finds Janice Cameron, newly arrived in New York City from Hawaii, without a place to live until she answers an ad for a roommate. It turns out the advertiser is an acquaintance from Hawaii, Lily Wu, whom critic Antony Boucher (for whom Bouchercon, the World Mystery Convention, is named) described as "the exquisitely blended product of Eastern and Western cultures" and the only female sleuth that he "was devotedly in love with," citing "that odd mixture of respect for her professional skills and delight in her personal charms." First published in 1949, this ground-breaking book was the first of four to feature Lily and be told by her Watson, Janice, a first-time novelist. No sooner do Lily and Janice move into a rooming house in Washington Square than a corpse is found in the basement. In Lily Wu, Sheridan created one of the most believable—and memorable—female sleuths of her day.   **0-915230-32-1**   **$14.00**

Death on Milestone Buttress by Glyn Carr. Abercrombie ("Filthy") Lewker was looking forward to a fortnight of climbing in Wales after a grueling season touring England with his Shakespearean company. Young Hilary Bourne thought the fresh air would be a pleasant change from her dreary job at the bank, as well as a chance to renew her acquaintance with a certain young scientist. Neither one expected this bucolic outing to turn deadly but when one of their party is killed in an apparent accident during what should have been an easy climb on the Milestone Buttress, Filthy and Hilary turn detective. Nearly every member of the climbing party had reason to hate the victim but each one also had an alibi for the time of the murder. Working as a team, Filthy and Hilary retrace the route of the fatal climb before returning to their lodgings where, in the grand tradition of Nero Wolfe, Filthy confronts the suspects and points his finger at the only person who could have committed the crime. Filled with climbing details sure to appeal to both expert climbers and armchair mountaineers alike, *Death on Milestone Buttress* was published in England in 1951, the first of fifteen detective novels in which Abercrombie Lewker outwitted murderers on peaks scattered around the globe, from Wales to Switzerland to the Himalayas.
0-915230-29-1   **$14.00**

The Black Stocking by Constance & Gwenyth Little. Irene Hastings, who can't decide which of her two fiances she should marry, is looking forward to a nice vacation, and everything would have been just fine had not her mousy friend Ann asked to be dropped off at an insane asylum so she could visit her sister. When the sister escapes, just about everyone, including a handsome young doctor, mistakes Irene for the runaway loony, and she is put up at an isolated private hospital under house arrest, pending final identification. Only there's not a bed to be had in the hospital. One of the staff is already sleeping in a tent on the grounds, so it's decided that Irene is to share a bedroom with young Dr. Ross Munster, much to the consternation of both parties. On the other hand, Irene's much-married mother Elise, an Auntie Mame type who rushes to her rescue, figures that the young doctor has son-in-law written all over him. She also figures there's plenty of room in that bedroom for herself as well. In the meantime, Irene runs into a headless nurse, a corpse that won't stay put, an empty coffin, a missing will, and a mysterious black stocking. As Elise would say, "Mong Dew!" First published in 1946.   **0-915230-30-5 $14.00**

The Black-Headed Pins by Constance & Gwenyth Little. "...a zany, fun-loving puzzler spun by the sisters Little—it's celluloid screwball comedy printed on paper. The charm of this book lies in the lively banter between characters and the breakneck pace of the story."—Diane Plumley, *Dastardly Deeds.* "For a strong example of their work, try (this) very funny and inventive 1938 novel of a dysfunctional family Christmas." Jon L. Breen, *Ellery Queen's Mystery Magazine.*   **0-915230-25-9 $14.00**

The Black Gloves by Constance & Gwenyth Little. "I'm relishing every madcap moment."—*Murder Most Cozy.* Welcome to the Vickers estate near East Orange, New Jersey, where the middle class is destroying the neighborhood, erecting their horrid little cottages, playing on the Vickers tennis court, and generally disrupting the comfortable life of Hammond Vickers no end. Why does there also have to be a corpse in the cellar? First published in 1939.   **0-915230-20-8 $14.00**

The Black Honeymoon by Constance & Gwenyth Little. Can you murder someone with feathers? If you don't believe feathers are lethal, then you probably haven't read a Little mystery. No, Uncle Richard wasn't tickled to death—though we can't make the same guarantee for readers—but the hyper-allergic rich man did manage to sneeze himself into the hereafter. First published in 1944.   **0-915230-21-6 $14.00**

Great Black Kanba by Constance & Gwenyth Little. "If you love train mysteries as much as I do, hop on the Trans-Australia Railway in *Great Black Kanba,* a fast and funny 1944 novel by the talented (Littles)."—Jon L. Breen, *Ellery Queen's Mystery Magazine.* "I have decided to add *Kanba* to my favorite mysteries of all time list!...a zany ride I'll definitely take again and again."—Diane Plumley in the Murder Ink newsletter. When a young American woman wakes up on an Australian train with a bump on her head and no memory, she suddenly finds out that she's engaged to two different men and the chief suspect in a murder case. It all adds up to some delightful mischief—call it Cornell Woolrich on laughing gas.   **0-915230-22-4 $14.00**

The Grey Mist Murders by Constance & Gwenyth Little. Who—or what—is the mysterious figure that emerges from the grey mist to strike down several passengers on the final leg of a round-the-world sea voyage? Is it the same shadowy entity that persists in leaving three matches outside Lady Marsh's cabin every morning? And why does one flimsy negligee seem to pop up at every turn? When Carla Bray first heard things go bump in the night, she hardly expected to find a corpse in the adjoining cabin. Nor did she expect to find herself the chief suspect in the murders.This 1938 effort was the Littles' first book.   **0-915230-26-7 $14.00**

Murder is a Collector's Item by Elizabeth Dean. "(It) froths over with the same effervescent humor as the best Hepburn-Grant films."—Sujata Massey. "Completely enjoyable."—*New York Times.* "Fast and funny."—*The New Yorker.* Twenty-six-year-old Emma Marsh isn't much at spelling or geography and perhaps she butchers the

odd literary quotation or two, but she's a keen judge of character and more than able to hold her own when it comes to selling antiques or solving murders. Originally published in 1939, *Murder is a Collector's Item* was the first of three books featuring Emma. Smoothly written and sparkling with dry, sophisticated humor, this milestone combines an intriguing puzzle with an entertaining portrait of a self-possessed young woman on her own in Boston toward the end of the Great Depression.
0-915230-19-4 $14.00

Murder is a Serious Business by Elizabeth Dean. It's 1940 and the Thirsty Thirties are over but you couldn't tell it by the gang at J. Graham Antiques, where clerk Emma Marsh, her would-be criminologist boyfriend Hank, and boss Jeff Graham trade barbs in between shots of scotch when they aren't bothered by the rare customer. Trouble starts when Emma and crew head for a weekend at Amos Currier's country estate to inventory the man's antiques collection. It isn't long before the bodies start falling and once again Emma is forced to turn sleuth in order to prove that her boss isn't a killer. "Judging from (this book) it's too bad she didn't write a few more."—Mary Ann Steel, *I Love a Mystery.*   **0-915230-28-3 $14.95**

Murder, Chop Chop by James Norman. "The book has the butter-wouldn't-melt-in-his-mouth cool of Rick in *Casablanca*."—*The Rocky Mountain News.* "Amuses the reader no end."—*Mystery News.* "This long out-of-print masterpiece is intricately plotted, full of eccentric characters and very humorous indeed. Highly recommended."—*Mysteries by Mail.* Meet Gimiendo Hernandez Quinto, a gigantic Mexican who once rode with Pancho Villa and who now trains *guerrilleros* for the Nationalist Chinese government when he isn't solving murders. At his side is a beautiful Eurasian known as Mountain of Virtue, a woman as dangerous to men as she is irresistible.Together they look into the murder of Abe Harrow, an ambulance driver who appears to have died at three different times. There's also a cipher or two to crack, a train with a mind of its own, and Chiang Kai-shek's false teeth, which have gone mysteriously missing. First published in 1942.   **0-915230-16-X $13.00**

Death at The Dog by Joanna Cannan. "Worthy of being discussed in the same breath with an Agatha Christie or Josephine Tey...anyone who enjoys Golden Age mysteries will surely enjoy this one."—Sally Fellows, *Mystery News.* "Skilled writing and brilliant characterization."—*Times of London.* "An excellent English rural tale."—Jacques Barzun & Wendell Hertig Taylor in *A Catalogue of Crime.* Set in late 1939 during the first anxious months of World War II, *Death at The Dog*, which was first published in 1941, is a wonderful example of the classic English detective novel that first flourished between the two World Wars. Set in a picturesque village filled with thatched-roof-cottages, eccentric villagers and genial pubs, it's as well-plotted as a Christie, with clues abundantly and fairly planted, and as deftly written as the best of the books by either Sayers or Marsh, filled with quotable lines and perceptive observations on the human condition.   **0-915230-23-2 $14.00**

They Rang Up the Police by Joanna Cannan. "Just delightful."—*Sleuth of Baker Street* Pick-of-the-Month. "A brilliantly plotted mystery...splendid character study...don't miss this one, folks. It's a keeper."—Sally Fellows, *Mystery News.* When Delia Cathcart and Major Willoughby disappear from their quiet English village one Saturday morning in July 1937, it looks like a simple case of a frustrated spinster running off for a bit of fun with a straying husband. But as the hours turn into days, Inspector Guy Northeast begins to suspect that she may have been the victim of foul play. Never published in the United States, *They Rang Up the Police* appeared in England in 1939.   **0-915230-27-5 $14.00**

Cook Up a Crime by Charlotte Murray Russell. "Perhaps the mother of today's 'cozy' mystery . . . amateur sleuth Jane has a personality guaranteed to entertain the most demanding reader."—Andy Plonka, *The Mystery Reader*. "Some wonderful old time recipes...highly recommended."—*Mysteries by Mail*. Meet Jane Amanda Edwards, a self-styled "full-fashioned" spinster who complains she hasn't looked at herself in a full-length mirror since Helen Hokinson started drawing for *The New Yorker*. But you can always count on Jane to look into other people's affairs, especially when there's a juicy murder case to investigate. In this 1951 title Jane goes searching for recipes (included between chapters) for a cookbook project and finds a body instead. And once again her lily-of-the-field brother Arthur goes looking for love, finds strong drink, and is eventually discovered clutching the murder weapon. **0-915230-18-6 $13.00**

The Man from Tibet by Clyde B. Clason. Locked inside the Tibetan Room of his Chicago luxury apartment, the rich antiquarian was overheard repeating a forbidden occult chant under the watchful eyes of Buddhist gods. When the doors were opened it appeared that he had succumbed to a heart attack. But the elderly Roman historian and sometime amateur sleuth Theocritus Lucius Westborough is convinced that Adam Merriweather's death was anything but natural and that the weapon was an eighth century Tibetan manuscript. If it's murder, who could have done it, and how? Suspects abound. There's Tsongpun Bonbo, the gentle Tibetan lama from whom the manuscript was originally stolen; Chang, Merriweather's scholarly Tibetan secretary who had fled a Himalayan monastery; Merriweather's son Vincent, who disliked his father and stood to inherit a fortune; Dr. Jed Merriweather, the dead man's brother, who came to Chicago to beg for funds to continue his archaeological digs in Asia; Dr. Walters, the dead man's physician, who guarded a secret; and Janice Shelton, his young ward, who found herself being pushed by Merriweather into marrying his son. How the murder was accomplished has earned praise from such impossible crime connoisseurs as Robert C.S. Adey, who cited Clason's "highly original and practical locked-room murder method." **0-915230-17-8 $14.00**

The Mirror by Marlys Millhiser. "Completely enjoyable."—*Library Journal*. "A great deal of fun."—*Publishers Weekly*. How could you not be intrigued, as one reviewer pointed out, by a novel in which "you find the main character marrying her own grandfather and giving birth to her own mother?" Such is the situation in Marlys Millhiser's classic novel (a Mystery Guild selection originally published by Putnam in 1978) of two women who end up living each other's lives after they look into an antique Chinese mirror. Twenty-year-old Shay Garrett is not aware that she's pregnant and is having second thoughts about marrying Marek Weir when she's suddenly transported back 78 years in time into the body of Brandy McCabe, her own grandmother, who is unwillingly about to be married off to miner Corbin Strock. Shay's in shock but she still recognizes that the picture of her grandfather that hangs in the family home doesn't resemble her husband-to-be. But marry Corbin she does and off she goes to the high mining town of Nederland, where this thoroughly modern young woman has to learn to cope with such things as wood cooking stoves and—to her—old-fashioned attitudes about sex. In the meantime, Brandy McCabe is finding it even harder to cope with life in the Boulder, Co., of 1978. **0-915230-15-1 $14.95**

About The Rue Morgue Press

The Rue Morgue Press vintage mystery line is designed to bring back into print those books that were favorites of readers between the turn of the century and the 1960s. The editors welcome suggestions for reprints. To receive our catalog or make suggestions, write The Rue Morgue Press, P.O. Box 4119, Boulder, Colorado 80306.